KING OF RIMSHIRE

DONALD HOWELL

RIMSHIRE SERIES - BOOK 1

KING OF RIMSHIRE
Copyright © 2020 by Donald Howell

ISBN: 978-1-4866-1958-0
eBook ISBN: 978-1-4866-1959-7

Word Alive Press
119 De Baets Street Winnipeg, MB R2J 3R9
www.wordalivepress.ca

WORD ALIVE
—P R E S S—

Cataloguing in Publication information can be obtained from Library and Archives Canada.

Dedicated to my wife and three children.

CONTENTS

ACKNOWLEDGEMENTS

I WOULD LIKE TO THANK MY WIFE, SHERRY, FOR HER MANY HOURS OF WORK
typing most of this book.

I'm also very grateful to my children, Jeremy, Emily, Rebecca, and my
sons-in-law, Chris and Greg, for their encouragement, advice, and support
along my writing journey. Thank you also to the Word Alive Press staff for
their brilliant work in putting all this together for me.

LOVE FOR ALL

KING SIFRUS WAS LEAVING HIS KINGDOM ON RIMSHIRE. HIS TRIP WOULD BE long, and he was missing it already. He loved his kingdom and its people, and nurturing and teaching them to love each other was his passion. He looked down one last time and saw a small group of his friends gathered and waving goodbye to him. One young woman, Kristella, was crying very hard as she tried with great difficulty to wave.

He hesitated slightly as he pressed forward on his space glider control, looking down one last time at the place he loved and waving goodbye. He knew that before long, evil men would try to take control in his absence. Had he taught them well enough to withstand the onslaught that would soon come?

He pushed the throttle forward and was instantly travelling at streak-flash speed, a phenomenon known only to his people. At such a speed, the glider elongated into a sharp, needle-like shape to reduce resistance. Constructed of special flexible material, the glider's shape could change while retaining tremendous strength.

He reflected back on a previous meeting he'd had with his producers and developers a short time ago. Troubles had been developing within their ranks, as some people had turned from just loving each other to trying to control and take the riches of the surrounding world for themselves. He was exceedingly wise and ruled his kingdom with only one rule: Love One Another. He knew that this rule would cover all evil desires. He could only hope that they would remember this most important rule when things got tough.

He recalled how it had all started when just one person decided that he should be better at growing things than his friends. The people were always equal in everything and didn't understand the concept of leading or trying to be better than each other, even when things didn't seem to work out evenly.

On that day, the rollercurb harvest had been completed, and the growers were meeting to tabulate their harvest quantities when Oris Macceroy announced that the lower fields had produced a bumper crop. The rollercurb plant was specially bred to produce heavy crops of nutrient-packed fruit with health-enhancing properties. The beautiful plant was covered with purple flowers that produced small, violet-coloured fruit when ripe. The fruit was extremely sweet with a delicate aroma that left the consumer wanting more.

"So did ours on the slope fields," said his brother, Abe Macceroy. They both smiled and looked at each other, quite pleased, while they waited to hear from Gorbow Stilk, who farmed the upper fields.

Everything was quiet and time passed as Gorbow paced back and forth, trying to gather his thoughts. He began to stutter and finally announced that he had a poor crop.

The two record keepers, Jibo and Servis, noted and averaged out the quantities from all the fields and quickly announced a small surplus. Gorbow looked at them both and quickly walked toward the door as he spoke.

"It does matter a lot to me, for I'm just as good at growing rollercurbs as you guys!"

Silence fell over the meeting, as they all were aghast at what had just transpired. They looked at each other with bewilderment in their eyes, not sure what to say or do next.

"But all is well among us, because we always average out our total yields," Jibo quickly said, with a little fear showing in his eyes.

"I need to do better!" Gorbow said loudly.

Abe Macceroy replied quickly. "We all know that you're just as good as us at growing rollercurbs, and we'd never imply anything different."

Gorbow was pacing the floor again, uncertain of what to do. Then suddenly he stormed out through the door, leaving everybody confused and uneasy. Jibo looked silently at Servis with a puzzled frown. Greatly concerned, he wondered why it had happened, for nobody had ever acted that way before. It was so different than any other meetings they'd had. Usually they celebrated with thankfulness for a great harvest.

The newest member of their committee, Monton Repa, sat quietly listening to the discussion. He'd shown some interest in getting involved with the rollercurb business, and now he smiled as he saw the divisions among the farmers. Secretly, he wanted to use the lucrative rollercurb crop proceeds to fund his plans to take control of Rimshire.

Sifrus hadn't spoken during the meeting. He needed them to learn how to deal with difficult situations that would certainly come in his absence. He also needed time to analyze what had happened and try to figure out where Gorbow's strange behaviour had come from.

"Could this be the beginning of some strange disease affecting our friend?" Jibo had asked him later.

Sifrus shook his head and glanced back at his galaxy location screen, which showed him travelling past several kingdoms that were under the control of evil leaders who wanted all power and riches for themselves. *How sad*, he thought. *Greed and the short-term desire for material wealth always lead to uncontrollable consequences and certain destruction if not dealt with. I have to figure out a way to stop this destruction of their essential life-sustaining eco-systems before it becomes irreversible for many.* He shook his head and cried. "Please help me, Father."

Sifrus longed to be home with his father on Heveris, where the rule of *Love* still prevailed. It was beautiful and peaceful there, and all the inhabitants were kind and shared with each other so that no one was ever in want. The days of his youth with his father had been a wonderful time. He loved being out in the valley, where the most beautiful fruit trees grew and he could play all day while watching his father prune the branches. As he grew, he helped him prune the vines while also working on his new space glider project. One day he asked his father if he'd had the chance to see the space glider. His eyes gleamed with excitement as he awaited the reply.

"Yes, I did. It's beautiful." He gave him a quick smile of approval and asked how could it work in such a large universe when it looked so small.

"Oh Dad, I'll make it work! It won't just fly but will travel to distant galaxies. You'll see!"

His dad was a very kind, loving father, who quickly smiled as he said, "That's great, son, but don't get your hopes up too high." He knew what the world held for him as he grew older and had to take on more responsibilities.

Just then Sifrus's friend Trifrum came to visit.

"Hi, Mr. Kraver," he said. "Is Sifrus here?"

"Hi!" Sifrus shouted from the outer room. "Come in, I want to show you my space glider I'm working on." They walked together to the outer shed, which was painted with invisible paint to hide it from anyone who might try to see his new invention.

His home keeper, Mildred, loved him and watched with amazement his abilities, kindness, and the special way he had with his friends. She had been hired by Sifrus's father some years earlier to help raise Sifrus and take care of the home. He was very busy at the Celestial Planning Centre and needed the extra help. In the absence of a mother, Mildred was very close to Sifrus and helped him through his growing up years. She wondered if, just maybe, he could bring peace to the troubled worlds around them when he grew older and wiser.

Trifrum looked through the invisible paint with special glasses and was amazed at the slender, shiny, tube-like vessel mounted on a platform. He quickly glanced inside and saw two seats with a display screen of the galaxy at the front.

"How does it work?" Trifrum asked with great excitement.

Beaming with joy, Sifrus began to explain. "My display planet searcher screen has an impulse detection system for finding any objects within detection range of several nearest stars. It can then lock onto a location you wish to travel to while avoiding all obstacles in its path."

"You're dreaming," said Trifrum. "That's impossible!"

"But it is possible," said Sifrus, rather annoyed at his friend's doubt. "If you know how to use the energy of the universe, all things are possible. My father always says, 'Have faith and believe, for there are great forces in this universe you don't understand yet, but you will learn when you're ready.'"

A shout suddenly came from Mildred. "Come in for lunch. Your friend Karmilta is here to visit."

The boys smiled at each other.

"She's awesome at air ball; I hope she's here to play," said Trifrum.

Sifrus and his friends ate a quick snack of rollercurbs and then went outside to play. The rollercurb plant was fascinating, as it had been developed by Sifrus's father to provide all the nutrients needed for a day's worth of energy. It also contained enough water and medicines to fight off any possibility of disease.

"Did you come to play air ball?" Trifrum asked, very excited to see her.

"Yes, of course," she smiled. "If you guys are interested."

Sifrus's space glider work would have to wait, as he wanted to play with his best friends. But he dreamed that some day it would fly.

Back in his glider, Sifrus smiled. *I guess it did work!* His display panel showed that he was nearing his new destination, and a voice on his receiver startled him back to his present situation.

Approaching the planet, Sifrus became uneasy. Fear of this place replaced his beautiful memories of his home. He knew that many good teachers had been sent out in the past by his father to continue to spread the message of *Love*, but regrettably, their message was always rejected by the leaders who wanted power and wealth for themselves. They had killed or imprisoned those good messengers to ensure that their message never got to the people. He was the last teacher who would be sent to give them one last chance to save themselves from destruction.

His mind went back to the several years he was the leader on Rimshire. While there, he'd chosen and trained some people to lead in his absence. They were simple, teachable folk with good hearts, and he loved them regardless of their faults and insecurities. He believed that doing good to those who hurt us is always the best way to live. To return evil with evil would only create more evil, until the evil became greater than love, creating more hurt. He'd learned these truths from his father, who was the greatest king of all time. His father had ruled wisely and lovingly for many years on Rimshire and in several other kingdoms. He was now allowing his son to be more involved with the business of running his many kingdoms. This planet of Servan he was approaching would certainly be a challenge.

Sifrus slowed his glider as he approached the landing area. He could see a dark haze for long distances in all directions. This would be a difficult mission, for the teachings of *Love* had been rejected long ago, and those who taught about *Love* had been killed, imprisoned, or forced to change their teachings.

His voice interphase radio suddenly cut in. "You are entering the territory of Servan. Please confirm your permission protocol name and number."

"I am Sifrus from Rimshire. Protocol #2200100," he quickly replied. A few seconds passed.

Sifrus was anxious, but then the voice came back.

"You have permission to land on pod #4 on Alfa terminal. Proceed with the co-ordinates transferred to you. Your arrival party will be there to meet you."

He quickly landed his glider as instructed and opened its hatch. Immediately he could see a fine filament of shiny dust in the air, and he could feel himself breathing it in. It was probably the haze he'd seen around the planet as he was approaching in his glider.

"Welcome!" A very large, rough-looking soldier-type man spoke. He was accompanied by several equally large and tough looking military creatures.

"Peace to you!" Sifrus replied. "I came as quickly as possible after I received your invitation concerning your rapidly deteriorating atmosphere. It seems worse than I had envisioned." He noticed a dust bowl forming on the edge of town, quickly intensifying until it became very dark as the sun got blocked out. "Wow! You guys really do have trouble."

"Our leader, Deman, is expecting you at his headquarters. We were sent to escort you safely to him," the soldier said without showing any emotion.

"Thank you," Sifrus said, still feeling uneasy as he studied the devastated landscape. "Your leader takes great precautions in welcoming his visitors, doesn't he?" Sifrus smiled.

The soldier looked at Sifrus sternly and said with a snarly voice, "We do whatever it takes to protect our territory. Visitors always have to be checked and escorted to our leader, no exceptions."

Ironic, Sifrus thought to himself, as he knew they were the ones responsible for the destruction of their planet's atmosphere because of their polluting, industrial endeavours to get rich. After a short walk on a dusty trail they arrived at their headquarters. Immediately he was met by Deman, a well-kept, handsome creature of medium build. His intense eyes studied Sifrus from his position above the others in the room.

"I trust you had a good trip," he stated. He then introduced himself as sole ruler, while his assistants watched very closely. "We invited you to come quickly to offer any assistance you can with our many atmosphere pollution problems. Many of our inhabitants are getting sick, and unless we correct our problem, many may die in their early age. We've been informed that your planet of Rimshire is well managed and clean under your rule, and we'd like to discuss with you the secrets of your success."

Deman instructed his servants to provide refreshments for their guest. "We make a wonderful drink from the basram plant," he said confidently. "It's a very powerful drink; in small quantities, it makes people very relaxed and happy while energizing the body and healing any disorders. Unfortunately, if over-used it can turn quiet people into mischievous, angry, and sometimes very dangerous people that could cause harm."

"No thanks," replied Sifrus, "a regular non-basram drink will be fine."

While enjoying the drink, Sifrus could sense that he was being watched closely. "Your atmosphere," he said cautiously, "is very dusty. Do you know why?"

Deman hesitated for a moment then looked sternly at his guards. "We suppose it has developed due to solar flaring of our sun, causing our atmosphere to become too dry and thus creating too much dust."

Sifrus could tell by Deman's uneasiness that he was covering the truth; besides, he'd seen this type of pollution before and knew it was only caused by over-mining and refining of the rare faldacor substance that kept the surface of the planet stable. Because it was rare, it could be sold for huge profits throughout the galaxy. It was illegal to refine due to the poisonous dust given of during the processes of refining. "Have you considered other possibilities?" Sifrus asked with great concern.

Deman turned away momentarily and took a sip of his basram drink then slowly said, "You have kept your atmosphere clean on Rimshire, so we decided to invite you here to study our atmosphere and suggest what we must do to keep it clean as well. Any advice you could offer would be appreciated."

Sifrus looked off into the distance through the large window as he cautiously replied. "I've seen many planets—some clean, some polluted, and some totally destroyed due to poor management of resources. Usually problems develop when an imbalance occurs because some type of industry or activity uses in excess of what the environment and the cleaning and purifying mechanisms can handle. Do you know of any excessive activity that could possibly cause this imbalance?"

Deman looked at him with angry eyes and began to pace the floor wildly. "Are you questioning my practices and my ability to manage this planet?" he asked with a condescending tone in his voice.

Sifrus could sense that the time for diplomacy was coming to a quick end. He lovingly and quietly said, "On Rimshire, I have taught my people to love and consider others before doing anything for their own gain; therefore, nobody has developed an industry that would hurt the support life system of our environment. Everyone must maintain that system for the benefit and existence of all creatures."

"What right do you think you have to imply that we have somehow caused this problem?" Deman shouted, as he was already losing his patience.

"I say these things only out of love for your people. I wish for them to be saved from this pollution, but I regret that you have not listened to wisdom in the past, for I am not the first to advise you of this. In fact, several good teachers came to you some time ago, encouraging you to return to the way of *Love*, but you hated them. Because of your lust for power and greed, you killed or imprisoned them and tried to cover it up. Some of their followers are in your prison to this day."

Deman screamed at him. "How do you know these things?"

"My father sent these good teachers to you," Sifrus replied.

Deman was in shock. He backed up a little, still in disbelief. "You are the son about whom we've heard rumours. Your existence has been talked about throughout the galaxy, for they say you have special powers. Is this so?"

Sifrus looked out the window again at the severe dust conditions. "I come from a place far away, where we all have abilities a little different than yours. We use these abilities to help creatures in need." Sifrus smiled at him.

Deman couldn't take any more and ordered his guards to seize and bind Sifrus and put him in prison.

"Is this how you treat your guest who has come in peace to help you?" Sifrus asked as he was being led away.

"Your teaching will only destroy my empire and bring me to ruin!" Deman shouted. He was still shaking from this revelation. *What shall I do with this Sifrus? I wish I knew, but he is different, that I'm sure of*, he thought as he looked at the dust storm outside his window and cringed.

Arriving at the prison gates, Sifrus was appalled at its condition. It was made of a see- through film of tremendous strength with an electrical current running through it. Everybody could be seen at all times, so they had little privacy. *Why do people have to be so cruel to their own species? This is a place designed for a lifetime of misery for all to see, with no hope of a better life beyond these gates.* He hung his head and whispered, "Please help, Father." *Places like this aren't needed on Rimshire*, he thought, *for love would never allow for its existence among our people. They have their privacy, dignity, and freedom, which is the way it was meant to be.*

He was taken through the security gates with many combinations of locks and check points. He passed the rooms of prisoners who had decided not to serve Deman. *Why does it have to be this way? Why all of this hatred? They were made to love and care for each other, even if they were put in this prison by an evil dictator.*

Sifrus was glad to see them, even if they weren't free. Their strength and determination under such difficult circumstances, and even possible death, was amazing. They still had the fortitude to hold on to the principals of *Love* passed down by his father, even though it had been a long time since his workers first came here to teach the people.

One of the prisoners who had spent some time on Rimshire recognized Sifrus and quietly began to spread the good news to his fellow prisoners that the king's son was among them. Their spirits were lifted, and many could be seen bowing as he passed by their cells.

The guards leading him were troubled, as they couldn't understand why the prisoners would do this. "Stop it!" they shouted. But no one would listen, for they were too filled with joy to stop.

Sifrus reached his cell and was left with the other prisoners. He quickly found a quiet corner and sat in tranquility as he began to communicate with his father through his mind control transmitting abilities. Only those who truly believed and knew the powers of *Love* and were trained could use this form of communication. He felt sad that not all would believe and have this wonderful power.

As other prisoners saw what he was doing, they remembered how they had also been taught by previous teachers of *Love* how to practise this technique. They also began to sit in quiet meditation and communicate with the source of this power. A wondrous and beautiful thing was happening. They were all absolutely quiet, which was very unusual for prisoners. The guards were in awe as they saw them smiling with their eyes closed and their lips slowly moving while a glow of bright light surrounded them.

"What are you doing?" one guard shouted.

Nobody replied. They seemed oblivious to what was going on around them. Again, he shouted at them to stop. Still no reply; beautiful silence seemed to surround them.

The guard, who was now becoming very angry at them, opened a gate to one of the cells and hit the prisoner with a full knockout stream from his laser. To his astonishment, it didn't hurt him. Increasing his laser to kill level, again he hit the prisoner, but nothing happened. Becoming very scared, the guard quickly left the prison cell and reported the event to Deman.

This is very strange, thought Deman, musing to himself as he frowned. *Very strange indeed.*

Meanwhile, Sifrus and his fellow prisoners were enjoying a beautiful experience of communication and love as their spirits were joined in the ecstasy of being one with a higher power beyond their worldly existence. While in this state of communication, Sifrus protected their physical bodies with an impenetrable cloak of bright light that couldn't be seen by the others. They were learning the true power of the greatest energy in the universe, that of *Love*. When given for the benefit of others without reservation, *Love* emits energy that can conquer any evil. It never returns void but passes through all hardness and begins to soften even the most difficult of all hearts. Sometimes this process isn't noticeable, or it may be very slow, but it does penetrate and begin to work its magic on all who receive it. A glow of light continued to surround them ever so softly and pulsated as streams of energy came from an outside source well beyond the prison cell.

Hours passed, and the guards, now accompanied by Deman, were amazed as they gazed at the most peaceful setting they'd ever witnessed in a prison.

"Why didn't you stop this?" Deman asked with great concern.

"We tried to, but nothing worked. They seem to be protected by some sort of force field stronger than any we've ever encountered. Should we try again?"

Suddenly, the loud siren sounded to signal that it was time for lunch. All of the prisoners, including Sifrus, immediately broke from their meditation and came back to a normal state. This always brought on a slight feeling of sadness as the bliss of being connected to a higher power faded. A connection that incurs such great power isn't easily broken and can lead one to want to not come back to their normal state, where life seems much more insignificant.

After they finished their meal, Sifrus was again summoned to meet with Deman. They studied each other for a while, trying to figure out their next moves. Deman began to question him about what he had witnessed in the prison cell.

"What was this quiet meditation you and the other prisoners were having?" He looked very serious, but deep inside he was worried about the unfamiliar powers Sifrus displayed.

"If I tell you, you won't believe me. You didn't believe the ones that were sent by my father to teach you and your people the secrets and power of *Love* in the past.

"In what past?" Deman asked, somewhat confused.

"There are powers in this universe beyond your sight and comprehension. They exist to keep balance and harmony in the universe; without them, there would be chaos."

"Like what?"

"Hatred, greed, power, riches, and desires for oneself," said Sifrus. "You see, the king of the universe sent inhabitants out to many beautiful planets to live and love and increase in number. They, like you, were to care for their land, to multiply and love each other in peace and harmony. All inhabitants were also supposed to love the king for what he had freely given them for their enjoyment and survival.

"While on his home planet of Heveris, the king's superior intelligence allowed him to know all the powers and secrets of the universe. Using this great knowledge and wisdom, he duplicated Heveris-like settings on other planets for his many creatures to live on."

"Are you crazy?" shouted Deman. "Are you trying to tell me that this planet, and all of us, were designed by your father and that he's the ruler of all the celestial worlds in existence?"

"Yes," said Sifrus, "but I told you that you wouldn't believe me. There's more, but it will be hard for you to hear."

"Go on then. I've listened to this much; I may as well hear the rest of your crazy tale."

"What you saw in the prison was a demonstration of a power you cannot see or understand. The ruler gives power to those who truly believe and love him so that they can be one in all essence and commune with him, no matter where they are. *Love for all* keeps my planet of Rimshire in balance, so it's still a paradise to all who live there."

Deman sat quietly for a while, not knowing what to say. He couldn't deny what he'd seen in the prison, or the reports about Rimshire, but he didn't know what to do with this Sifrus. He didn't dare consider hurting him, just in case some of what he said was true. He decided to send him on his way before he could have any effect on the others, for even in prison he was dangerous to him.

He stood and looked directly at Sifrus. "You are ordered to immediately leave my planet. Your professional advice will be considered, but you cannot stay here."

His guards quickly led Sifrus to his space glider without even giving him a chance to say goodbye to his friends.

Once in the glider, Sifrus opened his communication channel to get clearance for lift-off. He offered one last comment to Deman: "The end of my story is that the power that comes from my father to keep the planets as a paradise is also withdrawn from any planet that does not believe in him, and whose inhabitants don't love each other. That destruction is always the result of this error. Don't be blind. I've shown you the way to peace and survival. I will return when the time is right to teach you more."

Deman looked dazed for some time afterwards as he wondered about what it all meant and how to deal with any future encounter with Sifrus or his followers. He now realized that there were powers in the universe much greater than his. His quest would now entail a mission of research to try and gain these powers and knowledge for himself.

Λ PΛST ҠINGDOM

SIFRUS WAS AGAIN TRAVELLING AT STREAK-FLASH SPEED IN HIS SPACE GLIDER while mentally going over what had just happened on Servan. He suddenly recalled a story his father had told him about a kingdom he had ruled a long time ago. It had been a beautiful mini-paradise with great beauty and riches. All the creatures loved each other and helped each other with all that needed to be done. Caring when one was hurting, working together to grow food, playing and socializing, they all were in one accord. There was peace and love. All was very good. His father had loved those people. They were a small race of hairy, quiet, chubby creatures called Botkins. He showed only goodness to them and radiated with a kindness that also affected them positively.

Then one day, something bad happened. Somehow an evil germ seed entered the community and began to spread in the minds of the Botkins, causing much harm and trouble. Sifrus shuddered as he remembered his father's account of those awful days on the planet Voart.

Sifrus's next destination was that same place called Voart. His father had told him to visit it once more to try and save as many as possible from the impending disaster. But first he was to pick up a helper named Deltric on Montrov, a small supply outpost centrally located in this galaxy. There he could also pick up any supplies he needed for his long trip.

Suddenly, he felt very sad as he pondered over what may be happening on Rimshire. By now, some residents may be trying to set up their own little places of power in order to control others, likely undoing the law of *Love* he had taught them. He would give them some time before making any contact, for his people had to learn to live together in peace and harmony without him. This time of testing would be critical to their future survival. He didn't tell them how long he'd be gone, for it would be much longer than they anticipated, and he needed them to be always waiting and looking forward to his return. His heart was heavy as he thought of Kristella waving good-by to him and how his feelings for her had grown during his time on Rimshire.

He shook his head and began thinking again about his father's story of how evil desires had begun on the planet Voart. A poisonous seed of pride, causing some to want to be more important than the others, had been planted in their hearts and soon began to affect their thinking and, in time, their actions and feelings toward each other. Things continued as always, but little by little they began to compete against each other. A nasty world of evil desires and competition had begun.

Heveris, his home planet, was still very peaceful and beautiful, and all of the inhabitants still lived by the rule of *Love*. It was the essence of life itself; it was eternal, never-ending delight, in which caring and love exist. It conquered all ill and badness, for it could do no wrong. It was purity and goodness in one.

He loved his home on Heveris, where he could play all sorts of games with his best friends, Trifrum and Karmilita. He remembered when time seemed to stand still for them to be together for long hours of pure delight. Each day they would come to be with him.

"Hi, Sifrus," said Karmilita. She looked stunning with her beautiful, long, golden hair and silly little smile.

Sifrus blushed a little, as his heart raced every time he saw her. "Hi, Karmilita," he said shyly.

"Is Trifrum coming with us today?" she asked as she looked around.

"I guess so," Sifrus said as he continued to blush. "Oh, here he comes now across the golden field."

"Hi," they both said as he approached.

"What's the plan for today?" Trifrum.

"Well … I was thinking that maybe we could go play with the doscos in the forest." Sifrus looked down to hide his excitement, because he knew that the doscos would be a challenge for them at this age.

"That's a good idea," they both agreed." Karmilita smiled with excitement as she glanced at Sifrus with his mischievous look upon his face.

"Okay," said Sifrus. "Let's pack a lunch and meet at the edge of the golden field where it meets the silver forest."

A little time later as Sifrus was packing lunch at his home, his caretaker, Mildrid, entered.

"What are you guys up to with this food you're packing?" she asked with a little concern in her voice.

"Karmilita, Trifrum, and I are going into the silver forest to play with the doscos, if that's okay." He tried not to meet her eyes and show too much excitement.

"Well, you know that although they are friendly, they're extremely fast. Make sure you use your safety harness so that you aren't thrown. Be very careful so that your father won't be worried." She gave him a big hug, and he ran off to meet his friends.

A shiny bronze trail would lead them into the forest and provide an easy way back when they were ready to return. They didn't have to walk, for the moment they stood on the bronze trail, it moved swiftly through the forest. The three friends laughed with delight. In what seemed like only moments, they had travelled a long distance into a beautiful valley of shining trees and rivers of jewels. They screamed with delight all the way to this fantasy world where they would spend their day.

"What a wonderful ride," said Karmilita, who just couldn't stop smiling.

"Yes, it was," said Sifrus. "I just wish we could do it more often, but we're only permitted to come here occasionally, because the doscos are quiet creatures and shouldn't be disturbed too often."

"Look! There are some doscos by the Jewel River," Trifrum said with excitement.

There before them stood five beautiful creatures, shining like crystal with a horse-like shape and big, beautiful eyes. The doscos also saw them and came to them with lightning speed. They didn't even have to move their legs—just one push and they were there. They all greeted each other in a universal language of understanding.

"It's really nice to see you," the doscos said. "We don't see many of you two-legged kind very often, and it's always our pleasure to take your kind on a tour of the silver forest."

"It's really nice to see you too," said Sifrus. "We're not permitted to come too often, and it's a real pleasure to spend more time with your six-legged kind." He smiled and bowed to greet them.

"Come then, climb on our backs and we'll be off to show you our beautiful home."

They lowered themselves gently. Climbing onto their backs, the friends were all smiles and very excited as they clipped their safety harnesses. Suddenly, small wings came out of the doscos's sides. One of them spoke up and said that they were only used for control when moving very fast.

Karmilita looked at Sifrus and Trifrum with a little concern but still smiled as she lifted her arms, and then they were off. They screamed with delight and laughter as they whirled and streaked through fields of gold, forests of silver, and rivers of jewels. The world was shiny, sparkling with all sorts of lights, rays, and streaks of all colours to show the splendour of their beautiful home as provided by their king.

"This speed is incredible," Sifrus said as he laughed with delight.

They travelled a long distance, and then the doscos suddenly stopped at a beautiful jewel waterfall. Karmilita looked astonished and asked where they were.

The lead dosco spoke up and said, "Look! What do you see?"

The three of them gazed at the waterfall. For a short while, nothing happened.

"Do you guys see anything?" Karmilita asked.

"Look," said Sifrus. The falls were opening to show a beautiful, bronzed rest area filled with all sorts of wild flowers. They entered under the jewel falls and were greeted by several young doscos carrying wonderful treats for them to feast on.

"Do you live here?" asked Karmilita, who was excited to talk to the young doscos.

"Yes," one of the smallest said shyly. "There's a large field out back where we stay when we're small so that we can train to become guides like the larger doscos when we grow up and become strong."

They began eating their treats of delicious grumkins. They also enjoyed some singing by the doscos as a beautiful melody combined with the various sounds from the fields and falls surrounding them. "Stay and rest for a while," they coaxed their guests.

After resting for some time with the beautiful, peaceful creatures, they decided it was time to return home.

"Do you have to leave so soon?" the smallest dosco asked with a sad whisper.

"Yes," Karmilita said, "but we'll return again soon, if that's okay with you grown up doscos."

The doscos all nodded in agreement. "That would be very wonderful," said the largest dosco. "Now hop on our backs and we'll bring you back to the bronze trail for your return home."

"Thanks for such a beautiful day," they all said, hugging the doscos. They then said their goodbyes and were quickly on their way to their next adventure.

"Are we all ready?" Sifrus asked as he stepped onto the bronze trail.

Instantly they began speeding through the silver forest toward home. Screaming and laughing, they were filled with delight. Even travelling at high speeds they were always safe, because all the inhabitants of Heveris were privileged to be constantly protected by a light shield surrounding their bodies.

Suddenly they were slowing down, and the entrance to their village came into sight.

"What a trip," Karmilita screamed, trying to catch her breath from the excitement.

"Wow, what a blast," Trifrum said, smiling from ear to ear.

"This is nothing! Wait until we're old enough to fly with the malikins," Sifrus said as he swooshed his arms toward the sky. "They're so fast, you won't believe it!"

They ran as fast as they could and were soon home, to the delight of their caretakers.

"Sifrus, your father wants to see you," Mildrid said softly. "Have a quick snack then run along to the Celestial Planning Centre, where he's working."

"Thanks," Sifrus replied with a big smile on his face. He loved Mildrid, who had always cared for him and was always so patient and kind.

Reaching the Celestial Planning Centre, Sifrus entered without anybody being overly concerned by his presence. He was now old enough to learn and observe the secrets of the universe. The centre contained a fairly large, globe-shaped room that was covered all around with screens. In the centre, seated high above the screens, sat Sifrus's father, surrounded by twenty assistants studying the screens. They were in constant communication with each other, discussing and deciding on the best measures to take for varying circumstances and difficulties present on the many worlds they serviced.

"Come," his father called to Sifrus when he saw him standing there. "We'll go into the knowledge room to be alone for a while." He knew this would be a very difficult time for his son. He was growing in stature and intelligence and was eager to learn about all the civilizations within and beyond their galaxy, but he'd never encountered any evil on Heveris and would need to learn about the many dangers evil can create before he would be permitted to travel outside of his home planet.

"All those screens," Sifrus asked, "do they really show what's happening on planets throughout the galaxy?" He was astonished by what he saw on the screens while walking toward the knowledge room.

"Yes, they give us a general idea of the condition of each planet and what we should do if any help is needed. Each planet has all that is required to sustain life and provide for a wonderful existence for its inhabitants, provided that they all share equally in its resources and care for each other and their environment. Some of these areas are newly inhabited, while others have been inhabited for a long time. As you can imagine, each one has its own unique set of issues and problems." His father looked keenly at

Sifrus to see how he was reacting. "Don't worry about any of this, for you'll learn to help us as you grow."

Sifrus was growing strong and wise on his paradise home, and his father was teaching him well in the ways of *Love*. All he knew was love and peace, and it was time for him to learn of evil and contention on some other worlds.

"Come, my son, to the knowledge room displays with me," his father said. "You know only of the good in this world, but, unfortunately, there are also bad things in some places that you will need to know about."

"But Father, what does this mean, and where does it come from?" Sifrus asked.

"The knowledge room contains all the secrets of the universe, both good and evil. When I developed these places, they were meant to be places of only goodness, where all creatures would live in peace and love each other. Unfortunately, some places have been infected with an evil germ seed that enters those who have turned from the protection provided by the powers of *Love*."

"But there is only goodness here," Sifrus said, trying to sound hopeful.

"Yes, son, that's true here, but because love by its very nature has to be free for it to be truly love, it's sometimes abused and forgotten."

"I don't understand, Father," Sifrus replied.

"Well, my son, for love to be real, it has to be given by free choice, or it's not love. Love's energy only exists when it's freely given."

"I think I understand," Sifrus said. "But how does evil work?"

"When love is withheld, its energy becomes stagnant. The opposite of love is evil, where harm is given to others rather than goodness, or when we ignore others and fail to do either. All the inhabitants of Heveris, when they're grown, are given the option to know of evil and the great harm it does. In the knowledge room, they can see pictures and examples of much hurt, pain, distress, hatred, and destruction that evil causes."

"Why would we want to know this?" Sifrus asked with an ache beginning to build in his heart.

"The universe is open for all to visit and live in; there is good and evil everywhere creatures have settled. All places were meant to be like a paradise, but some inhabitants have chosen to follow evil ways. I have kept Heveris as a loving, peaceful place by casting out any who would try to practise evil here. I do love them all and would like to keep them here with us, but evil cannot co-exist with good without having a negative effect. Heveris would not be a *paradise* if we allowed evil to exist in it."

"I understand now, Father," Sifrus replied with much concern showing on his face. "But what will happen to those who remain evil?"

"Well, I have given them all a chance to change their ways by sending out good teachers on numerous occasions. Unfortunately, many still continue their evil ways and reject the teachings of *Love*. I will give them as much time as possible to change."

"Do the inhabitants who don't believe in *Love* teach others to also follow their ways?" Sifrus asked as he began to shake a little.

"Yes, they do, son, so I have limited their life span to reflect their decisions. If residents don't return to loving their fellow citizens within that time, then it won't help any civilization to allow evil to spread. Sadly, they usually become greedy for power and wealth and do things that are harmful to their world. This I can't allow to go on for ever."

"Like what?" Sifrus asked, with a little bit of trembling in his voice.

Sifrus's father hesitated; he looked at the screens again for a distraction. He didn't want to overload his son with too much negative information. "Son, look at the screens; the living worlds have balances and must be cared for. The living environment will supply all that is required for their survival and enjoyment, but some try to take more than they should due to greed. With greed comes envy, hatred, and stealing. If only the inhabitants used only what they needed for their survival, there wouldn't be any problem with supplies for all."

"My heart is breaking, Father, for all of these creatures. I find it hard to understand these concepts. Is there anything we can do?" Sifrus asked as tears began running down his cheeks.

His father reached out and took him in his arms. He knew this conversation would be very difficult. "As I've told you, for a long time I've sent out good teachers to try and turn them back to the ways of *Love*. Some have accepted their message, but many have not, and it has to be free choice if it is to be fair to all of them.

"Evil is not as strong as *Love*, but it deludes them into thinking that it's more fun, until one day it controls them, and they don't see that evil deeds are harmful to their neighbours. As well, their planets' balance and support mechanisms are at risk due to environmental pollution and the overuse of resources where evil prevails."

Sifrus slowly moved away from his father's embrace and tried to gather his thoughts. "There must be something we can do before it's too late." Smiling and nodding his head, Sifrus continued. "I know … I'll go and teach them about all the beauty and peace we have here on Heveris because of our love for each other, and then they'll turn back and want to live their lives like we do."

His father looked at his son with great pride as he considered his offer. "Yes, we must try all options. You are my son, and if they won't believe your message, they probably won't believe anyone. But this still may not be enough for some!"

His father sadly looked away for a moment and shuddered at the thought of the other option that may be required. "Run along now, son, and play with your friends. We can talk about this again some other day." His father already knew what the options were, but he wanted his son to think about his own ideas to resolve these problems.

Several months passed, and finally the day came when Sifrus's father told him of his final decision and his plan to save as many as possible on the deteriorating planets throughout the universe. Coming in from playing with his friends, Sifrus was excited to talk with his father. He smiled, held his breath, and quietly waited for his father to begin their conversation. "Is something bothering you, Father? You look a little sad."

"Son, I talked with my assistants about our plan and your offer to help. I've been very uneasy about this day coming. As I've told you, many previous messengers were hated for their teachings of *Love*. Some of them were killed, imprisoned, or forced to recant their teachings, which almost never happened, even under much torture. These evil people don't understand that once *Love* is imprinted on your heart, it's virtually impossible to remove or change. It's the most wonderful, peaceful, and powerful source of energy in the universe. The tears you see on my face are there because it seems that the best chance to help as many as possible is to send you." His father wiped his face with his sleeve and looked intently into his son's eyes.

Sifrus stood motionless, searching his father's eyes. Time passed in silence, and his father's eyes glowed with more concern than he'd ever seen. *Why so much concern?*

"Father, is there some other way?"

"I wish there was, my son, but this is the only way left to help them." He turned away to hide the pain on his face. "Some will believe your message because of who you are, but my fear is for those who do not believe." The other part of his plan would have to wait for a later time, for the fight against their major adversary would soon begin. Sifrus's innocent heart was hurting enough for now, and he didn't want him to have to deal with any extra anxiety.

Suddenly, Sifrus was jolted back to his present status. The word "Alert" was showing on his display screen. *What is this?* he thought as he studied his laser screen. A small striker vessel was closing in very quickly, but from where? There were no images of any vessels showing on his past data screen. *There must be some base on a nearby asteroid.* He decided to open a communication channel to determine any hostility and to state that he was on a peaceful mission.

A voice came on his radio with a rough, hostile tone. "You are ordered to return to Servan immediately," it demanded.

Sifrus quickly realized that he had been followed by a striker vessel from Servan. *I didn't think Deman would have the nerve to send a chaser. And why does he want me to return?*

"I do not wish to do that," Sifrus replied quickly. "I need to get to my next destination without delay." He waited for a reaction.

"That is not acceptable!" an angry voice responded. "My orders are to shoot you down if you don't comply."

Seconds passed as Sifrus considered this possibility for a moment. *I thought that Deman had learned his lesson with my display of love and power in his prison. I wonder why this change of mind and hostility? My sub-space defence mode will be needed if I'm to avoid any damage for not complying.* Sifrus's father had developed the system, known only to him and his assistants at the Celestial Planning Centre. The defence system would deflect and destroy all incoming shots, but the striker was unaware of this. He opened his communication channel again. "As I have said, I cannot comply with your order and must continue on my journey."

Suddenly, shots came at his glider at full strength. *My laser system is engaged and working, and all incoming missiles are being destroyed. This should show the advanced capabilities of my vessel and hopefully teach Deman that hostility is not always the best policy. Once again I'll get a chance to show the ways of Love, even to an enemy who wants to destroy me.*

The shooting finally ceased. When things had cleared, the striker was astonished to see that no damage had been done to Sifrus's space glider.

"This is impossible!" he shouted. Like a sitting duck he waited, expecting to be destroyed at any time by Sifrus. *Why this wait?* he thought. *I'm an easy target, and I deserve my fate.* His radio receiver suddenly sounded, startling him out of his trance of doom. Hesitating and perspiring heavily, he broke his silence and picked up his receiver. "What is your wish? I am at your mercy," he desperately whispered as he tried to control his fear.

"I left your planet in peace with the permission of your leader, Deman. Why are you following me, and why have you attacked me?" Sifrus asked with great concern in his voice.

"I was told to bring you back or shoot you down if you resisted. No other instruction was given."

Sifrus sighed, waited for a short time, and then replied. "You came with evil intent, but I will show you mercy. Return to Deman and tell him what I have done for you. I have returned peace for hatred; you do the same for others."

He pushed his throttle forward and was quickly travelling again. He changed to streak sub-light speed to ensure there would be no more followers to impede his progress to a planet that had once been a beautiful oasis for all who travelled the galaxies.

He hadn't even fired one shot at his assailant, just to demonstrate that he was indeed leaving Servan in peace. His protection was in the power his father had given him to destroy the weapons without killing the enemy, in the hope that the enemy may change and become peaceful.

RIMSHIRE

BACK ON RIMSHIRE, THINGS WERE BECOMING MORE DIFFICULT TO MANAGE. Sifrus had taught all of its inhabitants to love each other and be equal, to share and help each other in everything. A few of the more aggressive inhabitants were becoming restless and beginning to make their move to seize power in his absence. Monton Repa was especially anxious to gain control. He was so audacious, he actually claimed that he'd been given additional power by Sifrus to rule in his absence. He'd also stated at their latest committee meeting that he would take power by force if necessary.

The Maccovoy brothers looked at each other in shock. "By what authority would you assume additional power?" Abe asked.

Kristella, a new member on the committee, was studying the expression of Monton's face. He appeared uneasy and had a strange look in his eyes she'd never seen before. There was a little bit of fierce determination with a slight sign of greed in his countenance.

Monton turned quickly to look straight at them and said slyly that his desired status as leader would be for their benefit. He was lying in the hope that he could fool them into accepting him. "I want to help improve our community development and crop production to please Sifrus upon his return." He hoped that wouldn't be for a long time, as he'd avoided the real question with his answer.

Lying was not an accepted practice on Rimshire while Sifrus was leader. This pride of heart and a desire for power was now causing deception. An evil trend was germinating and increasing in this inhabitant, which could cause much harm in the future if he were to gain complete control.

Kristella looked at him again with concern as she spoke. "What good can come of this claim to power if we're no longer all equal?"

"Why am I discussing this with you?" He snapped at her and quickly turned. "You're too young to understand!"

Oris Maccovoy had been quietly listening and realized that something similar had happened at a previous meeting some time ago concerning a crop of rollercurbs. *Is something bizarre and possibly evil happening?* he wondered. A sense of anxiety began to envelop his very being.

Kristella sat motionless, cringing and a little shaken. *What did I say to deserve that kind of aggressive reaction from Monton? Is there a hidden agenda?* she wondered. She tried to replay in her mind the scene that had just unfolded. She hesitated and struggled to frame her next question, knowing that an angry reaction was certain, but knowing also that she must ask. She breathed deeply, tightened her hands, and meekly asked, "Where did you learn this philosophy of leadership and control?"

Everybody stiffened, not knowing what to expect. Monton turned slowly and looked directly at Kristella. He waited a few seconds and then unexpectedly smiled. (He knew he had overreacted earlier and didn't want to give his plan away too soon.) "I regret that you may have some concern with my suggestions; forgive me, please, but I only mean to do good for our community."

Unbeknown to them, Monton Repa had come from a corrupt planet a long time ago, where he had been defeated by another aspiring but ruthless leader. He'd been pursued after losing a long and difficult battle that his small but determined group of followers had helped him fight. Most of his group had been killed, and he had just barely escaped with his life after stealing a very fast spacecraft from his enemy's space station.

His desire for power grew each day, and he also began to influence others by promising them powerful positions if they followed him. The seed of pride and power was starting to be transformed in a person who would answer its call.

Kristella was suspicious of Monton, even though he apologized for his outburst. She continued to watch what was happening very closely and eventually decided to bring her concerns to her friend, Assednic, who was also suspicious of Monton's activities.

The following day, she went to Assednic's home to see him. She met him outside, where he was working in his back yard. "What do you think of this situation with Monton?" she asked.

Assednic liked Kristella very much and was becoming concerned with her obsession over Monton. His great desire to become their leader was a troubling fact they had to deal with seriously. He looked at Kristella, not wanting her to notice the concern in his eyes. He turned a little and decided to answer with a question. "Why are you so obsessed with trying to decipher Monton's motives?"

Taken aback and hurt by his question, Kristella became assertive. "We are peaceful people who never try to lord ourselves over anybody else. We are equal in all aspects of society, as we were taught to be by Sifrus, our king. How can we not be concerned when someone tries to make himself leader of us all in the absence of our beloved leader and teacher?"

Assednic, now on the defensive, looked for a way to calm the situation. He reached out and held her shaking hand while looking calmly into her beautiful blue eyes. Staring quietly for what seemed like forever, he spoke gently and calmed her. "Maybe you're overreacting a little."

"Maybe, but I'm still going to keep an eye on him," she firmly said with gritted teeth.

Kristella was young and very pretty; she loved her home and people and would do anything to protect them. Somehow, she could sense evil motives from within people who no longer believed in *Love* as the supreme rule. This sense would serve her well, but she needed to control her emotions and not reveal her secrets!

Sifrus suddenly felt very uneasy and restless. He knew that he had some special powers to enable him to sense feelings from long distances away. He felt that something was wrong, maybe even evil, on his beloved planet of Rimshire. His heart ached for a way to be with them, but he knew he would have to wait for now, for he must fulfill his assignment. He whispered a request to his father to protect them while he was away. He knew his father had many special powers he could use to help his many creatures on many worlds. He even had many powerful creatures in his service that could be sent in an emergency situation to intercede on their behalf, if necessary.

He also knew that they weren't permitted to interfere with the ongoing affairs of the planets, but only help influence an outcome through mind signals of *Love*. All the inhabited planets were like a paradise and given all the resources necessary to live and prosper, as long they shared with and loved each other.

Sifrus's followers decided that they would follow no other king, even if it meant slavery, prison, or death. Monton may be able to claim physical control of their lives, but he would never control their inner beings, where true love resided.

Kristella opened her eyes to a beautiful sunrise and found she was somewhat rested but still uneasy about what was transpiring with Monton and his friends.

"Good morning!" a voice called, startling her for a moment. She recognized the speaker as Gorbow Stilk. *What could possibly be on his mind this early?* she thought to herself.

"Hi," she said. "What brings you out so early?" She began to wash her face and stroke her hair out. *What a mess*, she thought as she examined herself in the mirror. *I wish people wouldn't surprise me so early*, she sighed to herself.

"Sorry for bothering you so early," he said, "but I needed to talk to someone I could trust. I've been thinking about our meeting yesterday, and how things got a little testy between you and Monton."

"I didn't realize you'd noticed," she said, coming out to the deck to meet him. He was very tired looking, unshaven, and poorly dressed. Maybe he hadn't had much sleep either.

"I did watch your little skirmish with him, but I didn't say anything to expose myself." He looked from side to side uneasily, as if trying to see if somebody was watching him.

"Expose yourself! As what?" she asked, squinting her eyes and looking directly at him.

He met her stare and looked around cautiously. He began to speak very quietly, as if he was scared somebody would hear him. "I met with Monton at his home last week to go over some details for this year's rollercurb crop. He asked me to join his group, which is growing in number daily."

"But how is he getting others to join?" she asked with great concern.

"Well, here's the deal. He's offering power and riches to all who join him, along with protection from the punishment levied on those who don't join him."

"Why tell me?" she asked with a little shake in her voice. She was beginning to realize that she would become Monton's target if he thought she stood against him.

"Don't you see?" he said with dread in his eyes.

"See what?" She was at a loss and squeezed her eyes to show her confusion.

He rubbed his arm uneasily. "You stood up to him! That means you've been chosen for this time!" He smiled at her and raised his arms to the sky.

"I've been chosen for what?" she asked blankly, again looking straight at him with a little unsettled feeling beginning to churn in her belly.

He dropped his arms and reached out and took her hands in his. "Whenever there's a possibility for evil or other threats to enter our paradise planet, someone is chosen and empowered to confront the evil. I believe you are that person," he said with confidence.

"Oh no—that's crazy! I'm too young for this kind of responsibility." She was stunned by the statement and fell back on a seat beside her. She breathed deeply for a few seconds, as she felt almost nauseated. Her stomach churned as the gravity of the situation sank in. "I'm only eighteen."

"It doesn't matter what you think, for as in the past, the powers of the universe will select the best candidate for this job. It is you, I am sure. Good day, Kristella. I'll be around if you need to talk." He then turned and went on his way, leaving Kristella to ponder his strange revelation.

As the days passed, Monton gathered more followers and became more powerful, as they had all feared. Kristella and her friends tried to distance themselves from him as much as possible, and they always did their work as required by their positions in the community. They obeyed all the laws and remained peaceful to ensure that he had no excuse to confront those who remained loyal to Sifrus.

Kristella decided to visit with Spectrum, Sifrus's best friend on Rimshire. She needed to find out if he was also concerned and suspicious of Monton's growing power. She desperately wanted to discover where the evil desire for personal power had come from and what could result if it continued to grow stronger.

The hike to Spectrum's home was spectacular. As she rounded the last turn, she could see his house overlooking a beautiful, sparkling lake surrounded by centuries-old forest.

"Kristella, it's so good to see you." He put out his hand in greeting but suddenly changed his mind and hugged her tenderly. "Come, walk with me through my garden. There are many types of beautiful flowers to see and smell this time of year. I sense something weighing heavily on your mind. What's bothering you to come this far?"

She hesitated and looked away from him for a moment. "Is it possible that an evil germ seed has entered our peaceful home planet of Rimshire?"

He seemed shocked at her question. Spectrum turned and looked straight into her beautiful eyes, searching for clues. "What is this worry of yours?" he gently asked with a concern that only one with very strong feelings for another could understand.

She was unable to speak as she studied the fear in his eyes. "Forget it, maybe I'm mistaken." She quickly dropped her head and looked at the ground by her feet.

There was silence for a while as they both studied the beautiful rows of flowers around them.

"I fear this too," he said abruptly, "for I observed something strange happening at our farmers' meeting several weeks ago when Gorbow Stilk became upset about not producing as many rollercurbs as the other farmers."

"Do you think it has already begun to spread?" Kristella asked with a tremble in her voice.

"What have you observed different?" he asked gently.

"I believe that Monton is infected or is a carrier. He openly became angry at a recent meeting and stated that he deserved to be leader in Sifrus's absence." She grimaced at the thought.

"That's absurd! Sifrus made it clear that we were all to remain equal in his absence. Sifrus didn't detect this while he was here. It must have been dormant in someone's heart."

"How can this be?" she asked with great concern, knowing that the situation could be dangerous to their whole system of equality and even their very existence.

"As you know, I've spent a lot of time with Sifrus, and with great patience he has told me many stories of other civilizations where this has also happened, leaving many problems for the inhabitants to deal with. Oh my," Spectrum sighed.

"Kristella!" he screamed as he looked directly at her. "In most cases where this couldn't be suppressed, destruction came to those civilizations in one form or another. All creatures died from causes brought on by the abuse and misuse of their natural resources for personal gain. It caused fights and all sorts of conflicts, which also caused imbalances in their environmental support systems, and many other maladies."

"But how can we stop this?" she asked with more concern than she really wanted to show. She turned a little sideways to hide the fear in her eyes. A tear slowly trickled down her warm cheeks as her stomach began to churn.

"It's almost impossible, once the evil germ seed in deeply planted in the heart of anyone who allows themselves to turn from the ways of *Love*. We need to be careful not to fall into Monton's proposed trap of power and greed." He said this while looking skyward, as if trying to see something.

"We've been taught the ways of peace and love," she exclaimed. Kristella turned pale as tears pooled in her eyes. "How can our people deal with this evil if they don't even know what it means?"

Suddenly the door opened, and standing in front of them was Assednic. He was shaking and his face displayed concern. His breathing was laboured, for he'd run all the way from the city square.

"What is it?" Kristella quickly asked, trying not to show the fear building in her stomach.

"I fear we are in deep trouble," Assednic said, looking outside at a beautiful sunset, which seemed so ironic at that moment. "Our greatest fear has come true. Monton just publicly declared himself Governor of Rimshire. He has a large number of followers, and I doubt anybody will oppose him."

Shock overtook them all. Kristella fell into a chair, trembling. Time passed as her mind filled with horrible visions of an evil leader forcing his rules and sadistic ways upon a peaceful people. Nobody could speak for a long time as the gravity of the situation sank in. Kristella silently cried out to Sifrus for help, even though she knew he was far away, unaware of what was happening to them. Still, she knew she had to try something, and this could be all they had in the end.

Sifrus was far away but was suddenly aware of much pain coming from Rimshire. *How can I feel this?* he thought. He was aching to be with his beloved people, but no matter what was happening, it would have to wait until his current mission was complete. He closed his eyes and quietly said, "Please help them, Father."

"Come quickly," Spectrum said while still trying to get his emotions under control. "New rules will likely be posted on the city square screens and throughout the city for all citizens to see and to solidify Monton's control over the people."

Coming back to reality, Kristella staggered to her feet. They followed Spectrum and approached the city square very cautiously, not knowing what to expect. Assednic was holding Kristella's hand tightly, obviously going into protection mode. They were well aware that they had opposed Monton's plan to be leader and that there could be consequences.

"He may want our allegiance," Kristella said, "or ... I can't ... think of it,"

Crowds of people pushed forward to a desk where several armed soldiers were stationed. They weren't very pleasant looking as they passed out leaflets as quickly as possible.

"You two stay here behind this barrier," said Spectrum. "I'll go alone and get a copy, just in case they're looking for you."

Returning a short time later, he opened the flyer with great hesitation. It read: "To all the citizens of Rimshire: I, Monton Repa, having all authority in the absence of Sifrus, your king, will hereby immediately take on all duties as your interim leader and governor. I expect full allegiance and will tolerate no dissenters. Those not wishing to obey laws enacted by me will be punished and could lose all rights and freedoms."

"Already this man's pride and desire for power are leading to intolerance," said Spectrum as he hung his head in disbelief.

A cold chill ran up Kristella's spine. "Where will all of this end?" she asked as she shook her head in disbelief. "Chosen, chosen," she mused. "How can I be?"

Assednic squeezed her hand tightly as he looked at her with a feeling of fear. He tried to show tenderness in his eyes as he studied her. They had met only several months ago while at a musical concert for disabled children. It wasn't love at first sight, but they both seemed to be drawn together and enjoyed their long conversations about celestial places and other worlds. They both had dreams of travelling to far off, exotic places some day.

Kristella had never considered herself pretty and was a little overweight, so he'd surprised her when he approached her and requested a dance. Being a little shy, she blushed and nodded her head. Their dance wasn't anything special, but they talked for a while afterwards and had promised to keep in touch. Before saying goodnight, he'd held her close and looked deep into her pretty eyes. In his eyes, she looked very beautiful. At that moment, he knew she was someone special.

They'd now been dating for a month, and she sadly figured that this could be a short romance if she were really chosen. She'd been told that a "higher power" would be summoning her in some way to confront this impending evil, or whatever it may turn out to be.

Sifrus was quickly approaching Montrov and was still feeling shaken by his impressions of doom concerning Rimshire. He had to concentrate again on his present situation, even if his mind was distracted by concerns for his friends left behind on Rimshire.

A very good friend of his father was waiting for him on this outpost for exiled travellers. Deltric had been commissioned to help ensure that the inhabitants of Voart remained loyal to the teachings of *Love*, which his father had taught them while visiting there some years ago. Deltric had been pleased with the peace and love on his beautiful home planet created by these teachings, until one day a stranger came into town and decided to change things. Deltric and many others opposed him, but he gradually garnered a group of followers and grew in power, until in time he exiled any who stood against him. Deltric had left his home and family and travelled to Montrov, while others went in various directions rather than stay and suffer possible death, exile, or prison.

Sifrus signalled his request to land and quickly put down near the town's border—not that anybody cared about someone who would come to this desolate place for any reason, anyway. A short, chubby, furry creature came toward him, moving quickly for its size on all four legs. Stepping in front of Sifrus, he stayed silent, looking intently at him, studying every detail of his being. In a squeaky voice, he said excitedly, "There it is!"

He startled Sifrus. "There what is?" Sifrus asked, somewhat confused.

"Don't you know?" the furry creature squeaked out again. "Your father leaves a part of himself with all of his true followers who love him. He said to look intently into their eyes; if love is there, you'll see them glow. It's only visible to true believers, of course."

"And did you see it?" Sifrus asked as he held out his hand.

"The brightest and most beautiful I have ever seen," he said excitedly.

"You are as my father described—a beautiful creature with a beautiful heart." Sifrus held his hand out as a friendly gesture.

The little creature looked away and giggled as he held out his furry little hand while standing on his back legs. He sensed a great feeling of warmth, almost like love, emitting from his whole being as Sifrus held his hand gently.

"You are Deltric, I assume. I'm pleased to meet you," Sifrus said as his second hand was held out to cover his other.

"Likewise, your honour." He giggled and shied away.

"My father told me I would find you here with many other exiled creatures. What's your story? Do you still have family on Voart?" Sifrus could see the pain showing in Deltric's beautiful little face. He lost his original excited look as he struggled with his words. A strange look of turmoil covered his expression as he tried to explain his story.

"Your father, who was also my king, left me and all our creatures a beautiful home planet to live on. Love and peace were our ultimate desires, as he instructed and showed us from his own example while with us. I fear now, to our shame, that we have turned our beautiful home into a despot of evil, hate, and greed. Our environment is totally out of balance and contaminated, to the point of being barely liveable. We were hoping that as the king's son, you would know a way to save our planet." He frowned with a desperate look of anticipation, waiting for some nugget of wisdom.

"I've spent my last three years as king on Rimshire, a beautiful, peaceful planet as you just described yours as once being. I've only been gone for a short time, and already I sense something evil beginning to take place in my absence. The evil germ seed that travels the universe looking for a place to grow is very strong. It can only be repelled by the stronger power of *Love*." Sifrus hesitated briefly, not sure if his new friend could handle the answer. *What if all hope is gone, and things can't be changed back to the way they were before this evil entered?* he thought. *I've been taught by my father and teach Love for all creatures.* He looked deep into Deltric's frightened eyes and allowed him to see inside his own eyes to understand the true look of *Love*. He kept staring intently at him until he could see his expression calming.

Finally, Deltric smiled. "I can see where love comes from; it is within you, as it was in your father." He slowly closed his eyes to capture the image being imprinted deep in his memory.

"We all have it; it's deep within us, but it does no good if we don't give it away to others, for that is where its real strength lies." Sifrus smiled and held Deltric's hand. "Come with me, and we will find a way to help your people." He put on his bravest face to conceal the great fear invading his whole being. "It's time we get moving, as we have a long trip ahead of us to your home planet of Voart." He gently smiled as they walked toward his space glider.

"How did you find me?" Deltric suddenly asked.

Sifrus hesitated, wondering how much he should share about the communication powers he had with the Celestial Planning Centre, where his father's intelligence and abilities are beyond explanation. He smiled and said, "It's a special communication thing my father and I have. He told me where to find you. Of course, he's extremely worried about your situation, so he sent me as his representative as quickly as possible. Come quickly to my vessel so we can get out of here and be on our way to help your people."

Arriving at his vessel, Sifrus held open the door for Deltric. He smiled with a little pride in his design abilities and asked, "What do you think of my space glider?"

Deltric began studying the space glider all over with amazement. He touched the shiny outer shell, which seemed to be made of some special material unknown to him. "This is fascinating; it's the most beautiful work of art I've ever seen. Who built it?"

Caught off guard and a little surprised, Sifrus turned slightly red as he said, "I did all the work myself."

Deltric looked shocked. "But how could you do this all by yourself?" Suddenly, he began to comprehend the depth of Sifrus's abilities. His eyes opened wide. "Awesome!" he shouted. "You really do have your father's abilities in you!" He seemed a little more hopeful for the future with such a brilliant person helping him.

THINGS GET BAD

BACK ON RIMSHIRE, MONTON REPA AND HIS FOLLOWERS WERE GROWING strong and defiant. He was determined to make his own rules. He was no longer satisfied with just being leader; he wanted to be king, which was only possible for members of the royal family, namely Sifrus and his father. "How can I get the people to accept me as king?" he asked his most loyal followers.

They all looked at each other, but none of them would dare to speak negatively, for fear of his determination to destroy anyone who stood in his way. How could they reply to a question with no safe answer? The authority to be king could only come from a higher power and passed down from the royal family.

Reading their thoughts, he looked at them directly in the eyes and asked what they were afraid of. "I will claim the title by force!" He scowled at them. (Peace would now give way to the evil desire for power!) "How do we accomplish this task if I declare myself king?" he again asked them, with much irritation in his voice.

His first officer stepped forward and slowly bowed his head, wondering if he should even reply. "King Monton! You are King Monton for now and always," he exclaimed as he repeated the statement several more times.

The others followed, shouting, "King Monton! King Monton!"

Looking up, his first officer said, "We will force all inhabitants to do as we have just done in obedience to you as our new king."

"Well done," Monton said with a look of great satisfaction on his face. "And what shall we do if anybody refuses to acknowledge me as king?"

Again his first officer raised his hand to indicate that he had the answer. He spoke very cautiously. "A decree will be issued by you, advising all citizens that refusal to acknowledge you as their king will result in slavery—working in the faldacore mines—or death, for those unable to work."

"Very well," said Monton. "Have the decrees written and posted in the city square as previously done for my leadership announcement to ensure all my new followers will see and humble themselves before me."

People came from all over to the city square to read the decrees. All the citizens were in shock as fear moved quickly through the crowd. Many rushed to their homes, farms, and small villages to advise all they knew that something very bad was happening to their peaceful home on Rimshire.

"Spectrum!" Kristella called as she looked across the city square. "Let's go see what new information is posted on the bulletin board and screens. It seems to be causing such commotion in the city square."

"You better stay here, Kristella," he said, looking at her with great concern in his eyes.

She gave him her fearless look, although her stomach felt a little sick. "I can't hide forever, but I will stay until you return and we figure out what we're dealing with this time."

Spectrum moved quickly through the crowds to where the decrees were posted. As he began to read, his knees became weak, and then he fell to the ground in total disbelief. He couldn't move, for it seemed like a mountain had been placed on his shoulders, crushing him to many pieces.

Assednic came in through the door and saw the concern on Kristella's face. He quickly put his arms around her for comfort. "What's wrong?" he quietly asked.

Kristella spoke quietly as she pointed across the city square at the gathering crowds. "Whatever is posted on the city bulletin board is upsetting the crowds."

"Where did Spectrum go? I saw him leave a few moments ago." Assednic looked out through the front window toward the square. "Is he gone to the city square to see what's new on the board? I hope he's safe; I don't trust anything that's happening with Monton Repa at this time." A cold chill went down his back as he squeezed Kristella's hand a little tighter than usual and noticed she was shaking a lot.

A woman screamed as she read the decree, startling Spectrum back to his senses. Getting to his feet, he quickly ran back to Kristella and his friends. Out of breath and shaking violently, he tried to tell them what was written.

"Slow down and sit for a moment," said Kristella, realizing he was badly shaken and very pale.

He lay there for a few moments catching his breath, and then said with great difficulty: "Monton wants all residents to acknowledge him as king. Those who resist will be enslaved or killed."

"This can't happen!" Kristella screamed. "We are peaceful, loving people who acknowledge only Sifrus as our king. We cherish his teaching of *Love* and need no other king. What shall we do?"

No one spoke for a long time, as all of them were deep in thought, contemplating various options and dangers, depending on the direction they decided to go.

The silence was broken by a loud knock on the door. All their faces went white as panic filled them with the magnitude of their situation. No one dared to move. Another knock, then another.

"Kristella, are you there?" came a familiar voice. "It's Chlorise. Let me in."

A great sigh of relief came over each one of them as they gradually calmed a little. "Be right there," said Kristella as she went to open the door.

Opening the door, she could see many people with concerned, doomed looking faces going to and from the area of the city square. She stared up at a beautiful sunny sky. *How ironic for such a gloomy day*, she thought. "Hi, Chlorise. Are you okay?" she asked, seeing much fear in the girl's eyes.

"Things are crazy out here; people are crying, shouting, and running to and fro, not knowing what to do with themselves. We never had to face such dire circumstances before, and I guess the residents are very confused and scared." Chlorise looked around at her friends' faces and saw that they also looked concerned.

Spectrum put his arm around her shoulder to try to calm her shaking body as he led her into the warm den. They sat for a while in silence until she was ready to talk. Tears filled her eyes as, stuttering and trembling, she managed to ask a very difficult question: "Why is this happening to such a peaceful and loving place as Rimshire?"

Holding her hand, which was wet and clammy, he tried to hide his fear by looking down at his hands while he attempted to come up with an appropriate answer. "I'm not sure," was all he could say.

Kristella, who was watching them, came over, knelt down, and placed her hands on both of theirs. She spoke softly a word of comfort to assure them that all was not lost. "Don't worry. Remember what Sifrus taught us: *Love* is the most powerful force in the universe. We will overcome this evil somehow with love and not with violence or retaliation."

Their spirits were lifted a little as they tried to smile at her, but they knew that real danger lurked outside their doors, and that many difficult times were likely ahead of them.

Monton Repa enforced his rules and wouldn't tolerate dissension. Many people were taken by his followers to his headquarters to swear allegiance to him. Those who feared for their freedom and life obeyed, but the few who loved Sifrus above all would not capitulate. They were immediately and with much disdain taken away to prison to await their fate.

Kristella shrieked when she saw them through her window. Six of Monton's guards were coming toward her home, which was located near the city square. She'd known that this moment would come, as it already had for many of the others who were loyal to Sifrus, but she couldn't shake the fear that enveloped her. "We have to do something; they're coming!" she screamed.

Panic overcame them as Spectrum, who had been reading a copy of the new laws in the adjacent room, moved quickly to a trap door below a seat that led to the abandoned subway tunnels below.

"Kristella, Chlorise, Assednic … quick," he shouted. "We have to get out of here!"

"We can't run!" Kristella shouted. "That will acknowledge defeat and imply that we're criminals with something to hide."

"Kristella, you opposed him directly. You are his biggest threat right now. You can't stay here, and you're no good to anybody if you're dead or imprisoned." Spectrum cringed as he looked at her with beckoning eyes.

"I … I … am chosen to resist this." She was shaking her head in disbelief.

"Kristella, if you've really been chosen, we need you to live until we figure out how to deal with this evil," Assednic said as he crossed the floor to take her hand. "Grab your hiking packs quickly, for they have food, extra clothing, and other survival equipment we may need."

"Lock the door," shouted Spectrum. "Run to the opening I've uncovered in the floor. Hopefully this passage will help us get away for now."

They began to climb down the rough stairs to an abandoned subway tunnel below the city of Lystrus. They could hear shouts and banging on the door above them when the guards reached her house. They closed the hatch and moved the chain lock back in place, just before the front door came crashing down and dust filled the room above.

"We're now dissenters on the run, and there's no turning back if we care for our lives," Spectrum gasped. "Run … run! Just keep running. I'm not sure if we're being followed or if the trap door has them fooled for a little while.

"We need to take a rest … I can't breathe," Chlorise cried after running for some time. "This awful smell and clammy air are hard to run in."

"Okay, but just for a minute," said Spectrum, who was also gasping for air. "We don't know if they've followed us or how close they are."

They were very tired and dirty after running for what seemed like hours when, finally, they came to the end of the tunnel. It emptied into a pristine valley near a beautiful forest.

"Wow, this is beautiful," said Spectrum as he lay on the ground, gasping.

Monton Repa was very upset when he saw the guards return empty-handed. "Where are they?" he shouted as he marched across the field and stood looking into their faces.

"We searched Kristella's home, but it was empty," the leader said with a shaky voice. "It seemed very warm in her house, as if someone had been there recently."

"Have someone watch the dwelling and advise me as soon as she returns with her friends. I want her under my control. She may be a problem to my leadership!" Monton shouted as he looked off toward the mountains in the distance.

"Where are we?" Chlorise asked, feeling totally out of breath and lying on the forest floor.

"I'm not sure," Assednic replied, "but assuming we travelled west for several hours or more, we should be at the edge of the Magic Mountains." In the distance, he could see several groups of people heading for the mountains and carrying bags of supplies. "I guess those people are also on the run."

"If we're to survive and keep the teachings of *Love* alive among our people, we must go to the mountains for refuge, as these others must be doing. I don't believe we have any other choice for now." As she spoke, Kristella could feel a power growing deep inside, like someone calling her to not give in to this evil but to believe in a higher calling of peace and *Love*. She knew that a time would come for her to stand against it, but she just hoped she was strong enough when that time came. *Me—chosen. Me, me ... but how can this be?*

Δ DESOLΔTE PLΔCE

SIFRUS AND DELTRIC WERE ENJOYING EACH OTHER'S COMPANY WHILE travelling to the planet of Voart. Deltric looked at Sifrus with a tear in his eye. "All was peaceful and well while your father was with us as our king. He spent a short season on our planet and taught us the principles of *Love*." He closed his eyes and reminisced of happier times with his family and friends, when love and peace were so natural. Sharing, giving, and helping each other were ideals and part of their lives until … he couldn't continue as he shook his head at the thought.

Sifrus could feel Deltric's pain. "You're in much turmoil," he whispered. "How do you deal with not knowing the situation of your family still on Voart?"

Keeping his eyes closed, Deltric concentrated deeply. Then his lips slowly opened. "Hope for the future keeps us believing that there will be a better tomorrow. Faith and love help us believe that your father can correct the damage evil has brought to our society—hope in you!" He looked at Sifrus with a sparkle in his eyes.

"You are correct in all of these, but don't forget the great sacrifices we have to pay for having a loving and just way of life." Sifrus smiled, hoping to raise Deltric's spirits a little.

"Our planet was so beautiful, and all our residents were so happy." Deltric lowered his head to conceal his pain. "Then ... then some Botkins got greedy for riches and power, no longer willing to share, and now it's all ruined!"

Sifrus's heart was breaking. He wanted to say all was well for this planet, but he knew that greed comes from an evil spirit and, once infected, it's nearly impossible to change. This would be a rescue mission for those who still had pure hearts and had hung on to the teaching of *Love*. Sifrus smiled again at Deltric. "Don't worry, we'll get your family safely out of there."

Much time had passed since his father had been at Deltric's home planet as their king, leader, and teacher. He had taught them everything he could for them to prosper and be happy. Unfortunately, things no longer were good and sustainable, as their environmental balances were totally out of sequence and their planet was on a deadly course with their sun.

"We're going to get them out of there?" In shock, Deltric looked at Sifrus with a questioning stare of great concern. "I thought the plan would be to try and save the planet."

Sifrus stood frozen in deep thought. *How can I make this as painless as possible yet be truthful?* He looked out his window at a beautiful sun shining across the galaxy near a frozen planet. "Look out there," he pointed. "That planet can't support life, and it's possible that Voart may suffer the same fate. We'll do our best," he said, controlling his emotions. "Re-establishing essential life-giving balances becomes extremely difficult, and sometimes impossible, if too much damage has been done. I want you to be ready for all possibilities."

Deltric sighed and dropped his head into his hands; a tear ran down his cheek. "I ... I never considered the possibility of having to say a final farewell to my home planet."

"I know it's very difficult to comprehend, but destruction eventually comes to all who turn from the ways of *Love* and embrace evil as a normal way of life. Societies will come and go, but only those who embrace *Love* will survive forever."

"There it is!" Deltric shouted, looking anxiously at the display screen. "We'll soon be within visual range to make contact with my family again."

As they approached the planet, a sudden shock of despair enveloped Sifrus's whole being. Voart seemed to be covered with very dense smog, and much of the planet seemed void of the green, vegetated areas needed for normal existence.

"Has it been like this for long?" Sifrus asked with genuine concern.

"It has been pretty bad for a while, but it seems to have accelerated since I left. That's not a good sign, is it?" Deltric asked with fear and resignation in his voice.

"Let's wait and see. It's hard to tell how bad things are on the surface through this thick covering." Sifrus could see an abnormal tilt as the planet moved on its axis.

"What caused such a severe smog problem?" Sifrus asked as he cut the throttle of his space glider for their final approach to the planet.

"It was greed," sighed Deltric with clenched teeth. "Once some Botkins wanted more for themselves, we lost control. Some Botkins started many industries and produced more than was needed, just for extra profit. This process continued until competition became so great, hatred for others increased to a point of deceit and even murder. The excessive processing of precious minerals created much smoke and dangerous chemicals, resulting in tremendous smog clouds that blocked our sun."

"That is very sad," Sifrus whispered. "Shouldn't we be expecting some contact from Voart for permission to land by now? I'm not detecting any signal from the surface at all."

As they broke through the smog cloud, it became obvious why they weren't getting any signal, for everywhere there was evidence of devastation. Neither of them spoke as they took in the scenes before them. Deltric was in shock, for his deep concern for his family and their safety was now much intensified.

Sifrus could see the look of fear on his face. "Where should we go to find your village?" he asked with a tone of optimism, which was definitely needed. He could now see that this planet was nearly finished. The evil that had been embraced by many of the inhabitants had taken its toll, and now sure destruction would come, as the environmental balances would no longer support life.

Deltric pointed. "My village is in a small forested area just outside the city, west of where we are now." Fear was written all over his face, and his hands were trembling as he spoke.

Trying to distract him, Sifrus said, "You didn't finish your story of what happened after the greedy developers started excessive mining and processing of your precious minerals for extra profit."

Deltric looked at Sifrus rather confused, while at the same time trying to look away from the scenes of destruction before his eyes. "Yes! It was greed; they all wanted to get rich. We formed committees to try and halt the developers from their aggressive pursuit of wealth. We knew that the speed of this development could be dangerous to the healthy balances of our natural systems and our life-giving essential resources."

"Did they listen to your logic?" Sifrus asked, still trying to process the magnitude of what was happening.

"Yes, at first, but as they grew stronger in number and more powerful, something strange and foreign to their normal nature seemed to take over. They became more aggressive and greedier, no matter how rich they became. It seemed like they had a new nature; a spirit of evil seemed to control them. Our teaching of *Love* suddenly seemed meaningless to them."

Interesting, thought Sifrus, reflecting back on the anxious feelings he had about his own planet of Rimshire. The evil germ seed was spreading to various civilizations much faster than he expected. He wondered if it could have reached his planet in his absence. He tried to shake off the horrible feeling and not show his concern to Deltric. "What happened then?" he asked.

"They exiled anybody who took the lead and tried to defy them, including me. The remainder of our loyal followers were enslaved and used to run their operations. They were abused physically and mentally by being forced to work on something they knew to be harmful. They were immediately taken away, never to be heard from again. We were told they were taken to another work site, but rumour spread that they were killed." Deltric stopped; he was in tears and could not stop shaking. "How did this evil enter into our home planet?" He cried and looked at Sifrus with tears streaming down his face. "How can we stop this?" He again sobbed uncontrollably.

Sifrus was also shaking; his heart was breaking for Deltric and his cuddly, beautiful, little race of people. "It seems that it may be too late to stop it. We can only try to get as many of our followers out of here as quickly as possible before things get worse." He looked again at all the devastation and cringed as he quietly sighed in final resignation. "This can't be fixed," he said gently.

How sad, he thought. *How could a peaceful, loving race of sweet creatures become like savage beasts just for wealth and power? How could they turn from loving each other to hating the very ones they once adored?* He shed a tear for them all. "What is the population of your planet?" he asked Deltric, who was now weeping with his head in his hands.

He raised his head and glanced at Sifrus with blurred eyes. "Well, we only have one main town remaining, and some outsiders living in small groups. There were millions in good times, but since our atmosphere became polluted with toxic smog, the numbers have fallen to just a few thousand. We live in one town to preserve our remaining resources of food, water, and power."

"That's very sad," Sifrus sighed. "We'll have to approach your home from the back of the forest if we don't want to be detected. I'll put on my cloaking device to make our space glider invisible. There still may be some powerful leaders who would try to do us harm."

Sifrus turned on his special detector designed to pick up positive emotions emitted by people who truly love others. *Love* emits a very strong impulse that his Father gave to all creatures. Use it and it grows strong; don't use it and it dies and is replaced by many other desires, many of which are not good.

Only seven blips were showing on his emotion screen; they were coming from one location at the edge of town. He knew this would be Deltric's family, whom his father had sent him to locate and bring back home with him to Heveris.

Landing wasn't a problem, and they didn't seem to be detected. "Come quickly," said Sifrus, "we better use breathing masks because of the high concentration of toxic smog particles in the air."

Exiting the glider, they entered into very cold conditions, well beyond what they had expected. Sifrus sighed, for he knew that the same situation was playing out on the planet of Servan, where he had recently been greeted with hostility.

On Servan, Deman had not forgotten his incredible encounter with Sifrus. He couldn't help but wonder if things may have been much better had he followed Sifrus's teachings of *Love* for all inhabitants. *Time is passing quickly*, he thought, *and the environment continues to deteriorate. Many people are getting sick, and some are dying. Many who wanted riches may now only wish they had their health back.*

A loud knock sounded on his door and startled Deman back from his daydreaming. "Who is it?" he asked with a commanding voice.

"It is Rickter," a man replied with great reservation. He knew Deman was not a pleasant person to deal with at the best of times, and now with all these problems surrounding him, nobody wanted to approach him with any additional bad news.

"Enter!" Deman replied with a stern voice from inside the solid and very secure room. Many latches and locks began to open as Deman allowed Rickter to enter into his presence. Since Deman had seen the special powers demonstrated by Sifrus, he had become uneasy for his own safety and was now securing himself within his control office as much as possible.

Entering, Rickter noticed it was dark, with most of the shades still partially covering the windows, although it was midday. *Curious*, he thought as he moved toward a desk in the middle of the room.

"You bring good news, I hope," Deman said while staring at a picture in the far corner. The picture was that of a joyous king parading through the streets lined with crowds of followers, beautiful trees, flowers, and sunshine. It was his father, who had also been leader at the height of his power. He thought it was such a contrast to the present situation under his present leadership.

Hesitating and a little shaky, Rickter began to sit on a chair. "May I?"

Deman waved his hand toward the chair as said, "Of course, relax, you look a little uneasy."

"Well, I just returned from our environmental assessment centre, and I regret to report that the news is bad ... really bad. For some unknown reason, we can no longer control the faldacore dust levels. Our atmosphere is officially slightly toxic and will become much worse if we can't get a handle on the cause."

No reply came from Deman, who kept staring at the picture in the corner.

Rickter knew what he was probably thinking about. He and his father could only keep control of their followers by paying them good salaries derived from the sale of illegal quantities of the precious faldacore mineral that was mined from their planet's surface material.

Deman turned to finally face Rickter. "A tricky dilemma, don't you think? All of this— my power, riches, killings, slaves, prisoners—gone to dust! Ha! Ha!" He sighed. "Dust that will have the final power." He laughed with a strange groan. "How ironic this is! The dust that gave us everything will now take it all away." He hesitated, again looking at Rickter. "What did the scientist say? Is there any way out? Can we survive this?"

Stroking his beard slowly and meditating on the question, Rickter knew he would have to answer very carefully or maybe pay with his life. "The scientist said that there are no guarantees, but there is one possibility. Mining would have to cease completely and a massive re-vegetation project over all the damaged surface areas would be needed."

"You're crazy!" shouted Deman with fire in his eyes. "It's out of the question! There has to be a better solution. Get out now, and don't return until you have some better suggestions on how to fix this awful mess we're in."

Rickter hung his head and left the room quietly without whispering another word. Deman turned, fuming at the picture in the corner. His mind wandered unexpectedly to what Sifrus had said about Love's power to heal. But to even consider that would be a show of weakness. He needed to maintain total, unbending control of his people, and Love just didn't fit into that picture.

Returning home from work, he was surprised at the concentration of dust in the air. His mate met him in the doorway of their cave home. (Underground was the safest place to live below the dust storm on the surface.) She didn't look or feel very well and was coughing continuously as he greeted her. He smiled and held her hand softly as he hugged her, trying to avoid showing the fear he felt inside.

"How was your day?" she asked with a little sigh of concern in her voice.

"It was pretty much the same as always," he replied, not wanting to alarm her about what was really happening to their planet.

"You look like you're really concerned about something." She looked directly at him and noticed a tear building in the corner of his eye.

He quickly wiped his eyes and turned to walk to the window overlooking his town of Quantin. He studied the skyline for a moment as far as he could see. *Very dusty*, he thought. *And now toxic. What have I done?* He glanced over at his mate. "Seles," he said quietly, to not alarm her. "What do you think is happening to our planet?"

Seles moved slowly toward him, cautiously considering the question, for she knew her answer would directly affect his mood. (He was very loving with her but dealt ruthlessly with those who defied him.) Touching his arm gently, she looked out the window with him. "What do you see?" she asked softly, hoping he would answer his own question.

He looked away from her and glanced across the city. The two suns were getting low in their orbit, and their rays were making the toxic dust more visible and brighter than usual. He choked a little. "A great city is what I see."

All was silent for a short time as they stood side by side, looking out over a very dusty city. Seles looked at him with a small, questioning smile on her face. His eyes dropped; he couldn't match her stare, and he choked again. "But it's dying, isn't it?" He reached out and hugged her tightly, tears again filled his eyes. *I'm killing the ones I love*, he thought. "Things will be okay." He tried to assure her, but he knew deep inside that they were in serious trouble.

"Let's just go to bed; you're very tired, and we can talk some more in the morning." She tried to offer a genuine smile but struggled, as it didn't seem to reach her frightened eyes.

The morning came quickly. Deman immediately checked the conditions outside. He hesitated as he gazed out his window and double checked his time. He again looked to see that it was still very dark outside. "This is not good," he said out loud in shock. The dust concentration was completely blocking the light from the two suns.

"What is it?" Seles asked as she entered the room.

He looked away from her and toward the window to hide his fear. "It's just still very dark and much more severe than usual." He silently kept looking out the window, contemplating his answer for the next difficult question.

"Is there anything you want to tell me?" she asked with great reservation in her voice.

"I had hoped a solution to our problem would be found before I had to inform the people that we have a major problem on our hands."

"How serious is this?" she asked, clenching her hands and bracing herself for the worst news.

He took her hands in his and squeezed them gently. They were now trembling, and obviously fear had gripped her, as shown by the pale colour in her face.

"Sit here with me," he said with as much control as he could muster. He was feeling a little stomach sick as he looked directly into her eyes. "Our atmosphere has become too toxic for our long-term survival."

She began to cry. "What will we do? What will be the result of all of this?" she asked.

He hesitated, finding the words hard to say. "I created this environmental problem; it's my fault. My greed, my lust for power, has brought us to this point, and I must figure out a way to fix it."

"No, no!" Seles stopped him. "It's my fault too, and the fault of all of our rich friends. We all wanted to reap the rewards of exploitation, even knowing the risks involved."

"Where did we go wrong, my love? We had all we needed when we were young." He smiled warmly at her and held her close as he noticed the cute little dimple in her cheek.

Even as a hardened leader, he loved her smile; not many did that for him. It softened him a little, made him feel good about life. She was special, a little delicate flower in an otherwise destructive place. He tried to laugh a little, showing his lighter side but not letting his guard down too much. "We still have a chance to change our dire situation back to something beautiful and peaceful, but it may be a long shot."

She looked deep into his eyes, searching for the glimmer of hope that would be there if he was serious. There was a brightness in his eyes that she hadn't seen before … or a least in a long time. As his eyes suddenly met hers, she seemed to be transfixed on them for some unknown reason. "What are you focused on at this moment, and what is that light?" she asked, barely able to break away from the wonderful, warm glow of light that emanated from his eyes.

"What light?" he asked. He could see that she was obviously startled by something.

She pulled back a little as they touched, for his hands seemed very hot.

"Are you okay?" she asked, a little perplexed as she studied the beautiful, warm smile that had appeared on his face. *This is strange, for he hardly ever smiles*, she thought.

"I'm feeling great! I haven't felt this happy in a long time. We can fix this; I'm sure we can. I was thinking of a solution to our problem, and my mind went to a meeting I had some time ago with Sifrus, the leader of a beautiful place called Rimshire. I hated him at the time, because he tried to blame my leadership for our problems. I later saw him in prison with some others, and he seemed to be a peaceful man with some special powers and a glow of light that surrounded him."

"Is that what I saw in your eyes? Is it possible that when you think of this man, some of his light enters you?" She was amazed and stood staring at him in wonderment.

"Incredible! All I ever thought about was riches and power, and now all I can think about is how to fix this mess we're in. I hope it's not too late to help our people recover and maybe even prosper in a new, cleaner world."

A loud knock came on his front door and startled him and Seles.

"Who could that be so early in the day?" He grumbled as he went slowly to the door. Opening it, he couldn't see anybody. "There's nobody here, Seles. That's very strange!"

Suddenly, a laser dart struck him in the chest, slamming him back against a wall.

"Seles! Seles!" he cried out. "I'm in extreme pain; there's something in my chest."

She stood there in shock, unable to move. "What's happening?" she shrieked as she dropped to her knees next to him. She could see the hole the dart had made, and blood flowing profusely from the area surrounding it.

"The pain is too great," he cried, gasping for breath. He tried to remove the dart, but it only increased the intensity of the pain. "It's anchored in with barbs going in all directions," he screamed as poison slowly moved from the dart into his system.

"Hold on! I'll try to pull it out with my two hands," Seles cried.

She pulled hard, but it wouldn't move. She only caused more pain and activated the tip to emit more venom.

"I can't hold on much longer," he said through clenched teeth. "Cut it out! Get a knife and cut it out now … please!"

He felt himself slipping into a dark hole as the pain eased, slowly dropping—deeper, deeper, and deeper into a murky pool of confusion. A distant voice seemed to be calling to him from somewhere. It was a very soothing voice and calmed his confusion somewhat.

"Who are you?" he asked.

"Come over here; we can help you."

"Where are you?" he whispered with a weak voice.

"Over here. Can't you see the light?"

"It's dark here in this hole; I can't see any light at all. No, wait, there's a small pinhole of light off in the distance. I can see it, but how do I get there?"

"Hold on to the light," the voice softly said.

I must be dreaming, he thought, trying to understand what was happening. He reached out his hand. *I can't hold on to the light. This is totally crazy.*

Λ WINTER STRIKE

WINTER WAS COMING FAST, AS SIFRUS'S FOLLOWERS WHO HAD FLED TO THE mountains were beginning to realize. It was cold, and not much food was available except for the few snacks they had managed to grab with their hiking packs containing survival supplies before they'd had to flee. The small plastic canopy they managed to build from a tarp they had taken with them would keep out the snow for a short time, but eventually they would have to find better accommodations if they were to survive the cold winter. Their solar cloaks, which were in their hiking bags, would retain their body heat by capturing and retaining heat from the sun. Their hearts were warm with love for each other as always, but that could only sustain them for so long.

"Kristella, are you cold?" Assednic asked as he reached out to gently touch her hand, which was shaking.

"I'm okay, but I could use an extra solar cloak, if we have an extra one available." Her lips were trembling as she spoke.

Assednic was worried about her condition. He quickly fetched his extra solar cloak without letting her see where he had gotten it from. He returned and wrapped it around her to ensure her body heat would be retained.

"Here, my love, this will help," he said as he cuddled into her for extra warmth.

Spectrum came in from his watch outside on a peak overlooking the valley. They had found a small valley that led them up the mountain to a small peak where they could see if they were being followed. "There doesn't seem to be any sign of Monton's army anywhere down in the valley or along the mountain ridges," he said with a sigh of contentment.

"They'll come when he knows we're weakened by the winter cold and our supplies begin to run out. Kristella is a threat to his leadership, and I don't believe he will ever give up until he has her under his control," Assednic said as he tightened his grip around Kristella.

She looked at him and smiled, but great fear showed in her eyes. She slowly glanced toward Chlorise, who she could see also seemed to show much fear. She looked down to hide her eyes, as they would certainly give her feelings away.

Monton Repa was furious that his followers had allowed Kristella and her friends to slip through their fingers. They had followed Kristella's trail through the subway tunnel after discovering their secret escape hole in the floor of her house. Through the forest they followed until the trail ended in a strange swamp at the base of the mountains. The men pursued them into the swamp as quickly as possible, with the hope of gaining some distance on their fugitives. Suddenly, they realized that some of their members were beginning to disappear into sink holes that swallowed them up completely. Each time a scream came for help, it scared the remainder of the search party so much, they retreated back to safe ground near the forest entrance. They held their position there for two days to see if their fugitives would return if they got scared in the swamp. The pursuers eventually returned to their base when it seemed that they couldn't safely go any further.

"What just happened back there?" the captain of the group asked as he shook his head in disbelief.

"I don't know, boss," spoke a very frightened soldier. "But whatever that place is, it certainly doesn't want us to pass."

"But how did they get through? How do I explain this to Monton without losing my head?"

"Well, boss, whatever we do, we'll have to find another route to the mountain base before we can follow them up the slopes, if they're hiding in the caves at the top. He looked up at the snow-covered peaks towering above them and shook his head.

Kristella remembered that a very bright, shining light had appeared across the swamp when they'd gotten to that dangerous place that night. The lighted trail had guided them safely through the swamp to the other side and to the edge of the high, rugged mountains.

"What are you thinking, Kristella?" Spectrum asked as he looked up the steep slopes.

She glanced away for a moment and then looked back at him. "The light in the swamp… what was it, and where did it come from?"

Spectrum looked at her with a puzzled frown. "What light? I didn't see any light; I just followed you, as all the others did."

Chlorise also looked puzzled as she listened and shivered in the corner. "I never saw any light either!"

"But … but there was a light that shone a narrow path for my feet through the swamp. It was clear … bright … shimmering. How could you not see it?"

"Well, we're safe, and that's what's important!" Chlorise said, glancing at Assednic as he got up to begin his next watch outside their shelter.

"What are you guys talking about?" Assednic asked while putting on an extra cloak to fight the cold outside.

Chlorise also grabbed an extra cloak to try and stop her shivering as she repeated what Kristella had said about the light in the swamp.

Assednic, sensing that Kristella was getting a little tense, came quickly to her defence. "Well, it's amazing that she safely led us through a swamp in the dark that was filled with sinkholes. She's got something working for her, that's for sure."

They silently looked at each other.

"Then it's my turn to keep us safe," said Assednic. He slipped out the entrance, touching Kristella's hand as he quietly said, "Thanks, my love."

The stars were shining brightly, and it was calm while the snow sparkled beautifully from the reflection. Little fires twinkled along the mountain ledges as groups of Sifrus's followers watched the many valleys below for signs of Monton's army. Assednic pulled some dry wood from a small pile under a tarp to fuel a fire Spectrum had burning to keep him warm during his three-hour watch.

Spectrum had just finished a three-hour shift and had witnessed an unusual quietness in the valley. "It's too quiet—just a little too quiet for my liking," he said softly to Assednic as he approached. "I suspect that Monton's followers won't want to return without us and will likely continue their pursuit at daybreak. I'll go get a few hours' sleep. Don't forget to call me if you see anything happening down below."

Kristella came out carrying a warm drink for Assednic. "You look worried. Are you thinking about Sifrus up there somewhere in his space glider?" she asked as she sat beside him near the fire.

"Thanks," he said, taking the drink from her. "I always think about him. In my heart, I can feel him and his wonderful teachings of *Love* for all of us wherever her travels."

Kristella's eyes sparkled in the glow of the fire. "I think and worry about him also, but I know he's safe, for something inside me tells me so."

Assednic studied the sparkle in her eyes that always fascinated him. She looked absolutely beautiful in her winter-tanned skin. She seemed to have a little glow of light around her face as she studied the star-filled skies. *There is something special—different, maybe*, he thought as he studied her at length.

Closing her eyes, she could almost see Sifrus travelling in his glider to distant places, bringing his message of *Love*. Her heart was instantly filled with love for him; she tingled all over, like little needles gently touching her in a million places. A warm sense of peace filled her whole being, making her wish she could stay in this intense feeling forever.

"Kristella, is your mind wandering again, chasing after Sifrus?" He was intrigued by how often her mind seemed to wander whenever Sifrus was mentioned.

Slowly opening her eyes, she saw Assednic looking at her with a puzzled expression on his face. "Are you okay?" he asked.

"Yes, of course, why do you ask?"

"You were staring off into space for such a long time and — well, Kristella, you were glowing like you were being filled with a light from somewhere beyond here. It was so bright and beautiful to behold!"

Puzzled, she studied his eyes, knowing he wouldn't lie. "Glowing?" she mused with delight. She grabbed his hand excitedly. "Assednic, I think I know what this means."

Totally confused, and thinking maybe the cold was affecting her sanity, he stared at her.

"Listen," she said with great excitement. "Remember what Gorbow Stilk said about me? He said I had been *chosen* and am filled with the desire to confront evil and defend Sifrus's teachings of *Love*."

"Yes," Assednic said, still puzzled. "But what has that got to do with this situation?"

"It's Sifrus," she said as she squeezed his hand. "The greatest power in the universe comes from *Love*! He teaches *Love* everywhere he goes. He is filled with *Love*; he is *Love*.

Therefore, he is filled with the greatest power in the universe. Don't you see?"

"I get it ... I think," shouted Assednic. "Sifrus was taught the secrets of the power of *Love* by his father, so he has the ability to transfer that love to others who love him ... right?"

"It seems that our love for Sifrus and his for us connects us in some mystical and powerful way and also empowers us. He must have the ability to transfer his father's love to us as well," Kristella said ecstatically.

"This is wonderful. Maybe we're not so far from King Sifrus as we thought." Assednic contemplated the meaning of this new revelation as he studied the stars shining above.

"Our escape from the swamp and the glowing light ... it seems we were being helped all along," she whispered as she snuggled into his shoulder and joined him in studying the stars in amazement. The night was quiet and peaceful, and beautiful lights danced in the sky over the sparkling mountains.

A sudden noise from far off in the valley below startled them from their star gazing. They looked at each other with worry in their eyes. "Kristella, did you hear that noise?" Assednic asked very quietly.

"Yes," she replied as she looked through the small scope she'd pulled from her pocket. "I can see some movement along the lower edge of the forest just beyond the swamp." *If I have been chosen to defend my friends, who are also followers of Sifrus, I will have to be strong and show no fear*, she thought. But seeing a large number of creatures emerging from the forest edge certainly caused her great fear deep inside. "I'm the one they want the most, and if I have to surrender to keep them safe, so be it," she said softly without any hesitation.

"Do you remember what Monton said?" she asked. "That he wouldn't tolerate any dissent and would hunt down all who refused to pledge allegiance to him. Do you think they've come all this way just to capture or kill us? He could leave us here in these mountains and allow us to die slowly over time as our food supply ran out. No, I fear that he wants much more than just our deaths. He would gain a lot more by using us as examples for others who may attempt to defy his rule. We'll probably be put on public display, and possibly even tortured over time to maximize his display of absolute control."

"It's winter, so the swamp has probably frozen over during the night. He'll most likely send his strongest warriors to ensure they don't return without us. Who knows what will happen when they find us," Assednic said, trying to keep a brave face. He didn't want to scare her too much and have her lose the little bit of confidence she'd shown a short time ago.

"What shall we do?" Kristella cried.

Chlorise heard the commotion and came out to investigate. "What's all the noise?"

Kristella looked at her, trying to hide her fear. "There's movement in the valley below."

Rushing to the lookout, Chlorise could see a large number of creatures moving in the dim light. "What's our next move? Can they climb these steep cliffs?" She put her hands to her face and let out a low squeal of anguish.

"The entrances to the mountain caves above are sealed and hidden, to the best of my knowledge. If we can get to them before they get up there, we may have a chance of surviving this winter." Assednic looked at each of his friends. "We're safe for now, but they'll probably bring toelions with them to scale the mountains. These creatures live most of their lives in the mountains and are tremendous climbers with their six legs and deep claws to grip the rugged edges."

Chlorise was shaking. "I'll go inside and awaken Spectrum to advise him of the situation. Spectrum," she called as she entered, "we have trouble. We need you outside as quickly as possible."

Coming out to have a look, Spectrum knew immediately the danger they were in. "We can't fight those creatures or the army Monton has sent to capture us. I know the capabilities of these animals; they're fast and ferocious and will stop at nothing to get their prey. Our only hope is to move to the snow caves at the summit and hope the weather up there will be too severe for them to find us."

"We must move quickly," said Assednic. "A scout party of toelions and riders will likely come up quickly as soon as they reach the mountain base."

They began the ascent through the ice tunnels, snow bluffs, and dangerous ledges. The going was very difficult, but they pushed on as fast as they could.

Chlorise lost her footing on a narrow ledge and screamed when she almost fell over the edge. She screamed again as she tried to hold on to a tiny tree branch. Spectrum quickly reached out and grabbed her hand and, with great effort, pulled her to safety. She hugged him tightly, trying to get her breath. "Thank you for saving me," she whispered. She could feel the pounding of her heart against his chest.

He knew she would have surely died on the long drop to the bottom of the ravine had he not reached her in time. That puzzled him a little, because he wasn't as close as Assednic, but he'd gotten to her instantly when she'd screamed. He couldn't even remember moving to grab her, as it all had happened so fast. *Strange*, he thought to himself.

Suddenly a toelion went past them, searching the peaks and crevices. "Come quickly!" Spectrum whispered. "There's a safe place to hide in this ice tunnel behind the snow drift."

"Chlorise, are you hurt?" Assednic asked with great concern.

"Just a few scratches and bruises from hitting the ledge, but I'll be okay. That toelion creature came very close to seeing us, though, and it may come back this way if it doesn't find any sign of us elsewhere."

"Yes, it did," said Assednic as he looked at Kristella, who was sitting on her pack with her eyes closed, concentrating very hard. "We better move fast as soon as things look clear and try to reach the peak snow caves, or we'll be easier to see and track in the light of day. Kristella, come. We must move. Kristella! Kristella!" She never responded, so he had to give her a small shake. "Are you listening?"

Breaking from her meditation, she was instantly aware of what was happening around them. "Yes, I'm listening; I was just trying to contact Sifrus to let him know of our situation." She jumped up, grabbed her sack, and said, "Let's go!"

Assednic looked at her strangely and whispered as she went by. "Trying to make contact with Sifrus here on this distant mountain? Are you sure you're okay?"

As she turned to move, she smiled back at him. A small, beautiful glow surrounded her, and no fear showed on her face. *Intriguing*, he thought. He'd always thought she was pretty, but this extra glow made her different, beautiful—but somehow deeper, like from inside her being. She was definitely changing.

They began travelling with much difficulty through snowy paths for several hours until they came upon a family of four people in a small shack in a tiny village. They looked fairly poor and certainly a little hungry. The dad was trying to hunt for food among the scattered bunches of brush surrounding the shack. The travellers had taken some food with them when they'd escaped from town, but it had run out several days ago and they weren't sure how much longer they could last.

"Have you any food?" asked the mom desperately.

"We have some," replied Kristella as she took her pack off her back. "Here's some bread, crackers, and water for you." She quietly handed them the small snacks.

They ate very quickly, as if they were starving. They soon finished and were curious to know their company. "Where are you going in such winter weather?" the mom asked Kristella.

"We're being followed by Monton's men coming up the valley. They also have some scouts searching on toelions. One almost saw us a little way back near the ledge."

"You will never outrun them in this snow without some help," she said with a sheepish smile, as if she were hiding something. "We've heard of his plans to become king and that he will not leave any with freedom who oppose him. We're also running from them and will go with you if that is okay."

Assednic cut in with some urgency in his voice. "But if we travel together, we'll be easier to see. We're lucky that the blowing snow is covering our tracks as it is."

She smiled again, and no fear showed in her expression. "Come out back; follow this way. My name is Soris. I lived in a small town near these mountains, until Monton's men came to town and forced all to swear allegiance to him. We escaped before they started taking away those who wouldn't comply with his orders."

"What's out here?" Chlorise asked, looking a little impatient.

Soris showed the way out back, and she smiled as she opened the door to a shed.

"Wow! Wow!" Chlorise screamed with excitement when she saw several beautiful, white, furry creatures the size of two men standing and looking toward them.

"They have large paws to travel over snow, and sharp claws to grip the sharp rocks and ledges," said Soris as she pointed at them with excitement.

"Oh my!" Assednic shouted as he turned the corner and saw the creatures. "Are they fast?" he asked with much anticipation in his voice.

"Fast, very fast," came a deep voice from behind him. "They are also very strong and smart. They can outrun almost anything in these mountains."

"My husband, Jiltu," said Soris. "He uses them to hunt on the high mountain ledges."

"What are they?" asked Chlorise, who was transfixed on the most beautiful animals she'd ever seen.

"They are mountain zells—very rare and obviously very special. They can only be ridden by someone of good heart who is truthful, honest, brave, and trustworthy. They can sense any tension, anger, or aggressive vibes when approached by anyone they don't know."

Kristella, who was now entering, suddenly stopped as she saw the largest zell; she couldn't take her eyes off him. He was also watching her with a deep sense of curiosity. *Why this fascination with each other?* she wondered. Their eyes were locked together by some force neither could understand.

Jiltu walked between them, interrupting the moment. He was able to sense when any of his zells took a liking to others and might attach to someone.

Kristella broke her stare, a little dazed and confused. *What was that?* she thought. *It's only an animal, but something … something very different just happened.*

"It's too stormy to continue," said Spectrum, coming in from checking to see if they were followed. "We're safe for the moment, but it won't take long for the toelions to find us once it clears."

Soris looked at Jiltu with great concern in her eyes. "They'll find us here too if we stay. It's not safe in our mountain valley anymore. We've hidden here long enough; we must think of the children's safety."

Jiltu knew the urgency; he was a mountain man. He had hunted all his life on the ledges and valleys and was physically strong and very wise. He could survive, but what about the others? He had met Soris in the town many years ago while getting supplies. They had dated, fallen in love, and gotten married. They lived in town and were raising their two children, but he continued to come to the mountains to hunt whenever he could. He gently closed his eyes and then turned to them all. "We have to move very fast while hidden by the snow storm!"

"But how will we see where we're going?" Assednic looked concerned as he asked.

Kristella looked again at the large zell and smiled. "They can see in the snow." She could sense the zell telling her this. It seemed to smile back at her in understanding.

"You're right," said Jiltu, "they can travel in all conditions with their senses and knowledge of this terrain." He studied their faces for affirmation.

Lights and noises could be heard slowly coming up the mountain passes. Assednic held Kristella close to his side for warmth and a sense of safety. "Don't worry, we'll figure something out, my love."

"I feel we'll be safe riding these creatures," she said, squeezing his hand gently as she gave him a smile of satisfaction.

Spectrum, who was out on guard, came running in. "We've got to get moving," he said. "A group of armed creatures with the toelions in the lead are getting close."

"We must get to the mountain snow caves as quickly as possible," said Jiltu, with great concern in his voice. "The toelions don't move as well in deep snow as on the solid ledges, so they won't come inside. If we travel the interior passages, we may stay undetected for a while, but the passages always lead to the outside."

Soris ran inside to get the children while Jiltu moved to ready the mountain zells. The zells, already sensing the danger, were anxious to leave and race up the mountain. The largest zell quickly came up to Kristella and nudged her hand in acceptance. She smiled at him. "Okay, you can be mine."

"Only take some food and warm clothing so that we travel light," said Jiltu. "They're strong, but the lighter the load, the faster they'll travel."

"Look!" Chlorise screamed. Two toelions with riders were charging at them.

LAST STAGES

"THIS WAR IS DESTROYING EVERYTHING," CRIED DELTRIC.

"It's very cold," said Sifrus, passing Deltric a blanket in which to wrap himself. "There are no sun rays penetrating this heavy smog. Cold—very cold," he shivered.

"Come this way," said Deltric. "My home is just over on the far side." He smiled at Sifrus, showing his pleasure at being home. *Thanks to Sifrus,* he thought.

"Wait a moment until I engage the invisible cloaking device for our vessel and mark our location on my scanner; we may have to leave quickly. It's too quiet, too quiet indeed," Sifrus whispered.

"Look out!" shouted Deltric as a strange flying creature came straight at them, just missing Sifrus as he ducked his head.

"What was that?" Sifrus asked with great concern.

"We're being tracked. That was a locator bird trained to find strangers. We better move fast; the ones who sent this bird will soon know we're here. Follow me," signalled Deltric as he quickly ran toward his home area.

"Wait," said Sifrus, "let's use my streak travel; it will be safer and faster. Hold my hand and concentrate on where you want to go and just say your home location, please."

Deltric pulled back for a second, a little confused, but when he looked in Sifrus's eyes, he knew it was safe to trust him. At the moment he held his hand and said the location, they were outside his home. "What a rush," said Deltric, shaking and a little pale. "How did you do that?"

"My father gives me special powers for when I'm in need or danger. I only have to think of him, and the best solution comes to my mind." He glanced at Deltric. "We're very close, my father and I. There are powers you don't know about—that's for later, you'll see." He winked at Deltric with much confidence in his eyes to strengthen him for what may lie ahead.

"Wow!" Deltric said, shaking his head in amazement. "I wish I could do that."

"You will someday, when you're ready. But come, we must try and get your family from this place before it's too late."

They were panting and out of breath as they ran toward the door of his house. A little flash of fear crossed Deltric's face, and he quickly turned to hide it. Suddenly, several disfigured creatures came out of the shadows and headed toward them. Deltric looked at Sifrus with fear in his eyes. Nobody moved.

"Can we help you?" Sifrus asked, breaking the silence. He continued to watch them, but nobody answered. One of them, the largest male, with scars all over his face and tattered clothing, suddenly lunged at them. They both moved quickly and he missed them, stumbling to the ground. He tried desperately to get back up but kept falling, too weak to attack them anymore. The other two strangers moved back into the shadows and vanished from sight.

"Poor soul," said Sifrus. "He's too weak to even hit us."

"Food became very scarce, even while I was here. He's probably weak from hunger," said Deltric. "Besides, just look at the scanty rags he wears to protect himself from this cold. His face is scarred and disfigured; he's probably hurt from trying to provide food and protection for his family."

"Let's see if we can help him," said Sifrus as he slowly moved toward him with a piece of food in his hand. Sifrus touched him on the shoulder to roll him over, and the Botkin swung at him suddenly with his clenched fist, grazing him on the cheek. The blow was so weak, Sifrus barely felt it. The man looked intently at Sifrus, who gently smiled back at him. He studied his bright blue eyes, which were surrounded by a very dirty and disfigured face.

The Botkin watched Sifrus and knew that a kind, gentle person was looking back at him. He began to relax and fell back to the ground as Sifrus studied him and then gently caught him in his arms. Lying there, the stranger seemed to feel a wonderful, strange, warm current flow through his body that seemed to strengthen him. He basked in the wonderment of the beautiful, peaceful feeling of indescribable bliss. His mind went back to a time before all of the destruction, to his beautiful home and family. Physically, he was also healing, and the many scars and cuts on his face began to vanish, allowing for his clear features to appear.

Suddenly, Deltric came running and gasped as he stood there in amazement. "It can't be," he stuttered. Looking intently at the Botkin, he shouted, "Jarock, is that you?" His heart was pounding as he bent forward to look closer. He began to smile.

The Botkin looked up at Deltric with warm, inquisitive eyes. Nobody spoke as they studied each other. Sifrus was also studying them both with great interest.

"That is you, Jarock, isn't it?" Deltric shouted again in amazement.

Jarock, who was a little confused, again closed his eyes and thought to himself that maybe it was a dream. His mind flashed back again to a peaceful time of good friends and family before all the madness started. He dreamed of good times with his favourite cousin, Deltric, before he was exiled.

A voice again called to him. "Jarock, is that you?" He slowly opened his eyes and saw two friendly faces staring back at him.

"I am Jarock," he said slowly, "but who are you?"

"Don't you remember me? I'm your cousin Deltric."

"Deltric … Deltric," he said slowly. "No! Deltric is dead. He was sent away many years ago; they all died."

"It's really me—Deltric. I didn't die; we stopped to refuel at a small outpost called Montrov. I escaped there when our ship was taken over by some local criminals."

Jarock began to cry. Reaching up, he embraced Deltric with his furry little arms. "You came back," he cried.

"My family," Deltric whispered, "are they okay?"

Looking cautiously in all directions, Jarock whispered back, "They are, but they're constantly being watched in case you try to return to rescue them. The heavy smog has gotten much worse since you were taken away, and its toxicity continues to increase. I'm afraid we can't survive on our home planet much longer." Jarock released a deep sigh. "The bombs were infused with toxic chemicals," I fear.

"Bombs! They used bombs?" Sifrus looked at Deltric with great concern.

Deltric was also feeling anguished for them all. He knew that his friend was correct in thinking that bombs would eventually be used by the cruel factions of the civil war to gain complete control. Their planet was dying and had gone beyond the point of rehabilitation. Sifrus could easily sense this and had suspected it was the case from the amount of destruction he'd seen as they approached the planet. He listened silently and felt their pain as they discussed their perilous situation.

"What have we done?" Jarock cried. "Our desire for wealth, power, and pleasure has destroyed our beautiful home. How destructive have been our ways! Oh, our beautiful home! What have we done?" He looked at Sifrus with tear-filled eyes, his heart breaking. "Can it be saved?" His eyes and heart pleaded for any hope Sifrus could offer.

Sifrus was in deep thought. He slowly looked around and then sighed and shook his head. "It's gone too far, my friend. Your atmosphere is so heavily polluted, purification is no longer possible." He hung his head in silence. "We must save your family before it's too late!" He hesitated before looking up and quietly saying, "There was a time when it could have been saved, when helpers like me were sent to teach the message of *Love* for your neighbours and your planet. They were hated and killed by your leaders, and this is the result of their error."

Deltric looked surprised at this statement. "What do you mean when you say helpers were sent here? We have no records of such helpers."

"That's the beauty of teachers of *Love*. They're seen as regular citizens among you trying to do good for all citizens. They risk their lives for this cause each day, for there are leaders who want full control of all the inhabitants and who oppose their teachings and feel challenged by them. Many have died for this cause."

They were all silent for a moment and hung their heads in respect for those who had died trying to do good in the past.

Suddenly, four armed creatures came running and shouting at them from around the corner of a building. "Who are you?" they shouted.

Deltric, sensing the danger, said, "We are fellow citizens of Voart!"

The creatures stopped and studied them suspiciously for a moment. "You look like a citizen, as does that one on the ground, but you are not a citizen." He pointed at Sifrus. "Who are you, and where do you come from?"

"I have come from far away; my father was here once a long time ago. He has sent me to bring home my friends."

They looked at him, puzzled. "Who is your father?"

"He was a ruler here a long time ago when the settlers were first being taught to live in peace with one another. He helped them develop the required skills to care for all the living systems that were put in place for survival and enjoyment.

"He also dropped off some good teachers a long time ago before returning to Heveris to rule. They were to help keep your planet running in good order in his absence. They were loved for a long time when they helped clean up your planet's essential survival systems. Regretfully, your leaders grew to hate these workers, because they didn't agree with the excessive use of processing plants, which caused terrible air pollution, for extra profit. They were killed or imprisoned for trying to curb the pollution caused by the numerous processors. These conditions will kill all of you in time."

Shocked, they all pointed their weapons at Sifrus. "Kill us? You will kill us!"

"No! Not me," sighed Sifrus, "but this terminally toxic smog will. You have killed yourselves by allowing these things to happen!"

They looked at each other in disbelief. "No! We don't believe you. We will take you to our leader, and he will decide on what to do with you."

Sifrus smiled at them, but then he stared straight into their eyes and said, "I'm sorry, I can't do that. I must find my friend's family and leave here before it's too late." (Already the winds were increasing as the planet was spinning out of balance, its rotation increasing beyond sustainable levels.) "Come," he said to Deltric and Jarock, "let us go and find them."

They began walking around the corner without the guards saying another word. Deltric looked back at one of the guards just standing there, watching them leave.

"This way," said Jarock, "they're at my home for safety. I couldn't leave them at your home, Deltric, because you were exiled and … well … they would be deemed to be suspects."

Deltric looked at Sifrus with a puzzled expression and asked, "What just happened back there?"

"Oh, it was just a little mind game trick I use when I need to convince people that all is well. They just imagined that we were safe to let go on our way."" He offered a light chuckle and turned to look at him. "Maybe I'll show you some day."

Arriving at his door, Jarock grabbed Deltric's arm. "Wait, you should know before you enter that they look pretty bad! The lack of food, the pollution, and the fight to survive has taken a toll. But they're alive, and that's what's most important."

"Thanks," said Deltric, "you're a good friend for taking care of them and keeping them safe."

As they opened the door, they saw some figures move back into the shadows of the dark room. A low, sweet voice asked, "Is that you, Jarock?"

"Yes," said Jarock, "don't be scared. I have some friends with me. You can come out now; it's safe."

Cautiously, they came into the open. Jarock said, "This is my wife, Seili." He pointed to the first figure. "And these are my two girls, Shalei and Selda. In the corner are my cousin's wife, Creathe, and her son and daughter, Fris and Fatemee. These are my friends," he said, pointing to Sifrus in the doorway, "and just outside is Deltric."

Nobody moved as a low cry came from the corner. "Deltric? Not my Deltric?" Jarock nodded his head in response. "It can't be!" Creathe screamed. "He's dead! Nobody ever comes back."

Suddenly, she came flying across the room. Deltric entered and caught her in mid-air. They crushed each other in an embrace and fell to the floor, kissing, clutching, holding, squeezing, and rolling on each other as the two children joined in. Everyone watched and smiled. Jarock hugged his own family and gently said how lucky they were to all be together once again.

Sifrus was very pleased to see them together again, for he knew the love of being with his father and also the pain of being separated for long periods of time. Eventually he got Deltric's attention. "Quickly," he said, "we must go before we're noticed again. That mind trick won't last much longer."

"Go where?" Deltric's wife asked with a surprised look upon her face. She studied Sifrus's eyes as she awaited his reply. There was something very exceptional in his eyes; the warmth and love in them was intense. She couldn't break away, as there seemed to be a glow about him. She felt a sweet sense of safety, as if he were saying, "Trust me! I will save you."

Sifrus quickly looked away to Jarock. "Get your family ready; we must go quickly. This place is becoming very unsafe. Follow me!"

They walked out into the alley. The smog had thickened, and the winds were blowing. It was difficult to walk, as they were losing their balance. A strange, screaming noise was coming from above the winds somewhere, as if the planet was screaming for survival.

"We must get to my ship quickly while we can still fly out of this. Hold on to each other," Sifrus shouted.

Stumbling and struggling to breathe, they managed to follow Sifrus to his space glider.

"It's too small for all of us," Jarock said as he looked at the glider.

"Don't worry," said Sifrus, "it's designed to hold as many who believe in my teachings of *Love* and my father's rule over all the worlds. It will expand to accommodate as many as needed."

"I don't understand," said Jarock. "Do you come from our teacher's home planet, where the power to balance all things comes from?"

"Yes, I do indeed," smiled Sifrus. "I am his son, the last teacher of *Love*, sent to return you to him because of your loyalty and love for each other and his teaching."

They all listened in awe, looking at each other and not knowing what to say. They realized they were in the presence of one of the humblest yet most powerful beings in the universe. Jarock, who was struggling for the right words, looked at his family members around him. They were so scared, dirty, and wretched looking. "You came all this way to save us, who are so unworthy! Why? Why us?" He looked down, too ashamed to even look at Sifrus.

Sifrus sighed as he looked at each of them with a warm smile. "Do not be ashamed of your outward appearance, when inside you are warm and loving. You are all great servants and loved very much by my father. You have always loved each other and tried, through much opposition and difficulty, to teach the ways of true *Love* to your fellow citizens—*Love* that knows no limits or barriers, for these are the greatest powers in the universe, and you have them within you."

At that moment, several guards came running toward them, shouting for them to stop and fall to the ground, or they would kill them with their fireballs.

"Quickly," Sifrus said, "stay behind me and get into the space glider." As they ran inside, the glider expanded to accommodate them all, with room to spare. The guards started firing and were still running toward them, shouting for them to stop.

Sifrus pulled up his cloak, exposing his glow shield and deflecting the fireballs with it. He entered the glider and closed the door as the guards fired again and again. Fireballs kept coming at the glider, but again they did no harm, as they were deflected from the hull. Suddenly, a large, fire-breathing machine hurled a massive stream of fire at them, engulfing the whole glider in a very hot flame. Deltric, Jarock, and their families were very scared in this inferno and figured it was the end for them all.

Screaming at the top of her lungs, Creathe shouted, "What will we do to survive this?"

"Trust in Sifrus," said Deltric, "for I have witnessed his power. He wouldn't travel such a long distance just to let us die. This space glider must be very special to make it this far, and I doubt that it will fail now."

Sifrus sensed their despair and quickly spoke softly to calm them down. "Don't be scared. I designed this glider, with the advice of my father, to withstand anything that can be thrown at it. Already the sensors in the hull have signalled the release of a cooling substance, nullifying any heat damage. Hold on tightly, as we're about to exit this place very quickly."

Instantly, they were forced back into their seats as they sped away from the planet's surface at an extreme speed.

Astonished, the guards fell to the ground in disbelief. "What kind of material was that glider made of?" one of them asked. "How could it withstand such intense heat? I've never seen anything like that!" They were choking in the toxic smog and wishing they could also leave and follow them to a better life on some distant, clean planet.

"Our flying machines can't fly in all this smog and wind. Besides, the force created in the atmosphere by the unequal spin of the planet would cause them to lose control. We're doomed to stay here and die on this forsaken planet," they grumbled to each other.

"Hold on tight! This excessive pull on the glider will be a problem as we try to slingshot away. I'll have to engage the additional engine thrusters I installed for emergencies like this." Sifrus felt a little concerned but didn't show it.

They were all feeling panicked, but they knew Sifrus could be trusted to get them out safely, and they had no other choice, anyway. The noise from the engines made it seem like the glider was going to be ripped apart. The extra boost from the thrusters was doing its job as they strained against the suction created by the planet's excessive spin. Finally, they broke free. They were all delighted, knowing that they were lucky to be on board. They shouted and hugged each other and thanked Sifrus for saving them.

Sifrus slowed the glider as they entered calm space outside the planet's effects. They all looked back with troubled and heavy hearts, knowing they couldn't help the remaining inhabitants of their home.

"How sad," Jarock sighed. "If only they'd listened."

"We all tried," said Deltric, "but greed and the lust for power changed their hearts and turned them from the ways of *Love*."

"Oh Deltric," said Seili, "our friends, our home—it's all finished. Couldn't Sifrus with his special powers make them see the bad effects of their decisions?"

He looked at her with deep pain in his eyes. "Yes, I believe he probably could, but that would go against the whole concept of *Love*, which has to be freely chosen or rejected. Forced love is never true love; it has to be given without conditions attached. Sifrus teaches the goodness and pure truths of *Love*, but he cannot force anyone to live by its principles." Looking back toward their planet, Deltric cried. "Look at the intense amount of smog covering the planet completely as the winds continue to strengthen to try and clean the atmosphere to no avail. The natural environmental balances are trying to compensate for the damage done by its inhabitants, but there's just too much damage. The end of a planet, the home of many, is difficult to believe and watch, but there's nothing else we can do."

Sifrus, sensing the anguish, interrupted their discussion with a story of his recent home on Rimshire. "When I left my present home planet, things were going very well. Unlike many planets that have become engulfed with much evil, Rimshire remained loyal to the teachings of *Love* and is peaceful and clean both environmentally and socially. All inhabitants there love each other and share all resources in common. Nobody would ever consider doing anything that would hurt their neighbour or their planet. They have learned and accepted that *Love* is the greatest power in the universe, and that its strength and message is eternal while all else will eventually fail and be destroyed. Hold on," he suddenly said as he pushed on his streak propulsion lever. They were instantly out of sight of their planet.

Sifrus sighed and was sad that only eight were saved out of a population of thousands. He knew that the planet would soon spin out of its orbit and burn up as it moved toward its sun. *How sad*, he thought. *What a waste of life when things could be so much better!* He turned and said to his friends, "Sleep now, and try to get rested for your journey to Heveris, where you'll meet my father and many loving inhabitants who have come from throughout the universe."

WINTER ATTACK

WINTER WAS NOW UPON SIFRUS'S FOLLOWERS UP IN THE MOUNTAINS ON Rimshire. It was a narrow escape, as they'd encountered Monton's soldiers riding on toelions. At one moment they had seen them charge toward them, then a severe snow squall covered them. When it cleared, they were gone. *Strange*, they thought as they looked around, waiting to be attacked.

"Did anybody see where they went?" Assednic asked, with much stress in his voice.

Kristella, looking very puzzled, asked, "How could this possibly happen?"

Assednic put his arm around her to reassure her that it was okay. "I'm not sure, but it will help us if they're not around until we get to the hidden caves at the summit."

"I was shaking so much. I thought we were about to be killed. I closed my eyes for the attack and then cried out to Sifrus to help us. I could almost feel and see him as I imagined him travelling to a distant land to help others. I could see his hand reaching out for me to come. Then he was gone. When I opened my eyes, our attackers were also gone, taken by the snow squall. I could sense a strange charge of power pulsing through my body. It was a warm, loving feeling of desire to protect my friends, and I knew it was coming from Sifrus."

Kristella looked around to see if they believed her. They all looked at her with questioning expressions in their eyes, but their hearts were telling them that what she was saying, although very strange, was true. They knew that Sifrus had taught them about the great and wonderful powers in the universe that they didn't yet understand, but if they remained loyal to him and his father, and the teachings of *Love*, one day they would. With pure hearts they could call out to him, and no matter where he was, he would sense if they were in trouble and would help them in some mysterious way.

Sifrus had been leaving Voart when he'd sensed a cry from Rimshire. Not knowing exactly what was happening, he cried out to his father to help them across the universe with his great power and communication abilities.

"Kristella," Assednic shouted, "we have to go quickly before some other attacker comes and finds us."

"Okay," screamed Kristella, "let's ride out of here as fast as we can."

Mounting their zells, they were quickly galloping through the deep snow. In the darkness, the zells constantly communicated with each other to ensure none of them went astray.

"Can you see anything up there in the lead, Jiltu?" shouted Spectrum.

"No, not a thing," he shouted back. "We have to trust the zells; they know their way around these mountains."

"Are we all here?" shouted Kristella.

"I can see four zells," Assednic yelled back to her.

"I see two," answered Kristella. "That should be everybody."

Suddenly, two more creatures were pursuing them at an angle from the two ledges on either side.

"Look!" Chlorise screamed, "We're being followed by those horrible creatures."

"Kristella," Jiltu shouted, "we have the fastest zells. Turn back and head toward our pursuers, and then draw them in different directions away from the group. This will give the others, especially the children, a chance to get a good lead toward the summit."

Instantly, they turned and were heading straight at the two toelions with their dismayed riders. They were temporarily confused and halted when the zells almost hit them at full speed, sending a blanket of snow over each of them. Turning in opposite directions, the zells flew quickly through the deep, soft snow with their large, furry paws.

The toelions came in pursuit, at first gaining on the zells because of their greater speed, but as they sank deeper into the snow because of the smaller padding on their paws, they grew exhausted and slowed to a crawl. Kristella and Jiltu soon pulled away from them and quickly turned to pick up their friends' trails headed for the mountain caves near the summit. Soon they caught up with them and were relieved to see that they were all safe and unhurt.

Unexpectedly, a toelion came flying out of a crevice and hit the zell on which Spectrum was riding, sending them both tumbling over an embankment and onto a ledge overlooking a deep ravine below. Spectrum, dazed and bleeding, managed to climb back on his zell, which was also limping. The toelion was coming at them again with his mouth wide open, revealing his sharp fangs.

"Go! Go!" Spectrum shouted as they navigated the narrow ledges as quickly as possible.

The toelion now had the advantage with its long claws and rubbery, padded feet. It soon sped around rocks and ledges, catching the zell by the back leg, ripping through its muscles, and sending him over a high ledge toward the valley below and certain death. Spectrum closed his eyes as he grabbed at the long fur of his zell, hoping by some miracle to hold on to the ledge.

The group above had been watching in horror as all this unfolded so quickly. The other two toelions and riders were again gaining ground while the group had been distracted, and they knew they were still vulnerable. They had to move quickly and couldn't stop to assist Spectrum and his zell. Their only hope was that they would hold on to the ledge and survive so that the zell could follow their scent and meet them at a later time.

"We can't leave him," cried Kristella.

"We can't help him now," said Jiltu softly. "If they survive the fall, the zell will know where to find us."

Assednic came over to Kristella and put his arms around her for comfort. "Remember what Sifrus said," he whispered. They both closed their eyes and whispered a cry for help.

"We have to move now!" Jiltu shouted. "Those creatures and riders are getting too close."

They quickly turned toward the narrow trail and moved up the mountain in very deep snow. Even for the zells it was slow-going. There would be no toelions up this far in the deep snow, so they were safe for now.

"How much farther do we have to go to get to the caves?" Chlorise asked as she gasped for a breath of air. "The children are getting tired, and I'm not sure if they can last much longer in these conditions."

"It's hard to tell in this storm, but it can't be too much further. The air is getting very thin, and it's more difficult to breath." Jiltu hid his concern and tried to study the rock formations for clues as to where they were. He knew most of the landmarks from the many hunting trips he had made up these mountains.

"The children will soon need rest. Let's find a sheltered spot and try to dig a snow cave to keep them warm."

"Over there!" Jiltu pointed at a large crevice in the mountain. "Quickly, follow me to that sheltered spot."

Dismounting their zells, they were exhausted and collapsed into the soft snow. Assednic, seeing how tired they were, said that he and Jiltu would get the snow cave ready while they rested. The zells had already found a quiet, protected corner under an overhang and were all snuggled together to stay warm as they moaned over the loss of one of their members.

Removing the snow scoops from their packs, Assednic and Jiltu began digging. In a short time, they had made a comfortable snow cave for them all to rest in.

"Come!" Jiltu said. "Bring your blankets and supplies for a small meal before we sleep for the night. We won't need a guard tonight this far up in the dark, and besides, the zells will alert us if anything approaches."

They were all quiet as they ate their meal. Their thoughts were on Spectrum and their hopes for his survival. They held hands and whispered a request for Sifrus to keep him safe somehow.

Kristella's mind drifted to the distant space above them, searching somehow for Sifrus. "Wherever you are, hear my thoughts; help Spectrum be safe! Help us reach the summit of this mountain and the safe caves out of the reach of our enemies. We love you and want to serve you by teaching the message of *Love* to others. We miss you so much and wish you could return to keep our people safe," she whispered before drifting into a deep sleep.

Morning came too quickly, and they were all awakened by the zells groaning at the entrance, ready to go.

Soris awakened the children and gave them a little snack to fill their stomachs. "Where are we going, Mommy?" they asked with big yawns.

"We're going to the mountaintop caves where it will be safe. Our friends will meet us there. Don't worry, we'll be fine," she said with a smile.

"But when can we go home again, Mommy?"

Soris looked at them both with a big, glowing smile. "When it's safe, we will go home, okay?" She reached out and hugged them both.

Outside, as they exited the snow cave, the sun was shining gloriously. The snow sparkled like a billion glistening diamonds, and as the peaks met the sun's rays, they exploded with light. They were close to the summit and could now see how far they'd come. Many miles below, their enemy lurked in the forest. They were haters of the *Love* message and all who tried to teach it.

Their pursuers would be coming up after them very soon, now that the snow storm was ended and the visibility was good again. Soris felt a shiver go up her spine and knew her focus must be on protecting her children at all costs, even with her own life if necessary.

The zells lay down in the snow to allow easy access to their backs for their riders.

"Climb on," said Jiltu, "we must move quickly for this final flight to the top."

Within minutes, they were quickly moving through valleys and over steep ledges. They were totally dependent on the beautiful and quiet creatures they rode on. The zells were their lifeline and were carrying them to safety where no other creatures could follow, if they could just get that little bit further to the safety of the caves.

"It's getting very cold and becoming more difficult to breathe," said Chlorise as she looked toward the children with great concern.

Jiltu looked at her and then at the children. "It's not very far now. Just hold on a little longer; we'll be fine." He tried to smile a little, knowing that she could see his concern in his eyes.

The zell carrying the children sensed their concern and arched his back to get his thick fur to move up and around them to keep them extra warm. The older zell acknowledged his move with a snort and a bow of his head and did the same with his riders.

"Kristella, you're very quiet. Is everything okay?" Assednic asked. He studied her beautiful face as she rode her large zell with confidence. It seemed very comfortable with her on his back. He tried again to break the silence. "We're going to make it, Kristella. If it's Spectrum, we can go ..."

She spoke before he could finish. "No, it's not that, but I see a vision of us having to leave here for a while until Sifrus returns."

"Leave here! But how can that be?" he said with great reservation. "Look where we are— only sky above us and our enemy below!" He looked away quickly to hide his concern. "Have hope! Things are never as hopeless as they seem. Remember what Sifrus said to us? There are great and marvellous powers in the universe for those who believe in him, his great abilities, and *Love* for all creatures."

Kristella's voice was firm yet loving as she smiled at him with confidence. "We'll see him again, for I can feel it in my heart."

What is it with her lately? he wondered. *She's wonderfully irresistible to be around, yet she seems very distant at the same time. How strange!*

"The zells!" shouted Jiltu. "They're slowing. They're almost exhausted; this deep snow is taking its toll on them, and we must stop for them to rest."

"Okay," said Assednic. Dismounting, they left the thick fur and heat of the zells' backs and almost instantly felt the bitter cold of the high mountain air burn their exposed skin.

"The children won't survive this cold," said Soris through her chattering teeth. "We must find shelter very soon, or ..." she stopped.

"We must get to the summit caves," ordered Kristella. "Let's try to walk for a bit to stay warm. Wrap yourselves with whatever you can find extra for insulation."

"But we can't walk," said Chlorise. "The air is too thin! We can't make it; it's too hard."

"Here, take this," said Kristella as she pulled several little leaves from her pack.

"What are they?" Chlorise asked, with much confusion showing in her eyes.

"They're mountain chews. I've worked on them in my lab for some time. They absorb extra oxygen from the atmosphere each time your mouth opens as you chew, and release it into your lungs each time you contract and close your mouth."

"But why did you think we'd need them?" she asked.

"I've been having visions for some time now of us having to escape to the mountaintops and the trouble of breathing up there, so I worked in my spare time on these." She glowed with delight as each one took some. "I just hope they work okay," she said as she put up her thumb for approval.

RETURN HOME

SIFRUS WAS TRAVELLING AT FULL SPEED NOW TOWARD HEVERIS WITH HIS friends from Voart. They were very tired and were sleeping, even though they were distraught about leaving their home. Sifrus was also struggling with his emotions as he tried to keep his mind off what was happening. Soon Voart's deteriorating orbit would bring it too close to its sun, and all remaining living creatures would be burned up quickly with intense heat. He was glad that at least his friends were safe and wouldn't have to witness the destruction.

How sad, he thought. *If only they had continued in the ways of Love for each other and their home planet.*

He suddenly had a strong sense of pain that he knew to be from Rimshire. *No*, he thought, *not Rimshire too*. He quickly cried out to his father. "This evil must be stopped. But how, Father? Please help! I can't bear to see my beloved Rimshire destroyed."

Deltric awakened and saw the anguish on Sifrus's face as he mumbled some words to someone unseen. "Are you okay?" he asked, startling Sifrus a little.

Sifrus hesitated for a moment and then looked at Deltric with tear-filled eyes. "Are the others still asleep?"

"Yes," said Deltric, with a little sign of worry in his voice as he studied Sifrus.

"As you can see, I'm quite sad," said Sifrus. "I have bad news to tell you concerning your home, which I did not tell you while we were making our escape."

"What is it?" he asked with a tremble in his voice.

"Your home planet of Voart and all of the evil its inhabitants have developed is being incinerated as we speak. I'm sorry I couldn't do more, but your people chose evil rather than *Love* and now will suffer the consequences of their bad decisions. He wiped tears from his eyes with his sleeve.

Deltric's head fell into his arms as he began to weep. "All those people," he cried. "All gone! All gone! It can't be."

He cried for a long time as he shook his head and moaned with grief. Sifrus remained silent and allowed him to weep without interruption. Regaining his composure after some time, he looked at Sifrus with sympathetic eyes. "What shall we do for a home?"

"For now, I'm going to bring you to my father's home on Heveris. There you will enjoy love at its maximum fulfilment and the company of the finest creatures in the universe. I must try to get back to my kingdom on Rimshire, for I fear some evil has entered my peaceful home as well."

Deltric looked warmly at Sifrus. "Teach me the powers of *Love* as you love your father and others. It is powerful and special in you, and I want to be even a little bit like you."

Sifrus looked at him intently, studying his eyes, looking for the real Deltric deep inside—not the one that lived in this world and fought for survival each day, but the real spirit of the one who was above it all.

"Do you truly love your family and friends?" he asked without taking his eyes off Deltric.

Deltric glanced at his family and then, looking at Sifrus, said, "Of course I do! I'd do anything for them."

"Would you die for them? Would you die for a stranger?" Sifrus asked as he glanced back at all of his family and friends.

Deltric thought for a while, rubbing his hands to calm his anxiety. (He always got anxious when things became too personal.) He stuttered a little. "I … I think I would die for them, but for a stranger—I'm not sure." He looked down and rubbed his hands again.

Sifrus let some time pass so that Deltric could reflect on his answer. *It's so difficult for them to understand the true meaning of Love*, he thought. "Look at me and tell me what you see," he said lovingly. "Am I family, or a stranger?" Sifrus knew that Deltric believed in *Love*. Now he just had to get him to believe in it at a much higher level.

Deltric slowly raised his head and looked at Sifrus. He intently studied his eyes, the warmth in them. "You are my special friend, the one who has shown us much love and kindness, and who saved our lives. You are equal to family and more, much more."

Sifrus smiled at him. "You are learning, my friend, but there is still much more for you to learn. There is more power in *Love* than you can imagine. On Voart, you loved your family as part of a biological attachment to each other and your need to help each other survive as a group. On Heveris, all of us are family. There is no biological attachment or groups of any distinction, for there is every type of being from all parts of the universe loving as one."

Deltric was totally absorbed in the conversation and couldn't take his eyes off Sifrus. "Please tell me more," he said, for he knew somehow this all must be true.

Sifrus continued. "We are all given free choice to love or not to love. Regrettably, many go through life not choosing either. They live in a neutral state, just living from day to day to provide for themselves and their family. This is good, but there's a greater level of living when you can choose to rise above this and love and help your neighbour regardless of circumstances. On Heveris, all the inhabitants have risen above to attain this much higher level of existence. They all love each other as family, without distinction, to the benefit of all."

Looking amazed, Deltric asked, "But how can this be with creatures who sometimes hate each other? On Voart we were taught *Love* by some travelling teachers, and we've tried to live that way, but there was always some who didn't believe in this and disliked others who did. Why couldn't we get this type of love to work for us?"

Looking at his face, Sifrus could see his pain. "As I've said, we're all given the ability to choose not to love. This decision sends them on a path of self-evaluation, and then a path of self-destruction begins. The power and benefits that come with *Love* are withdrawn, and their ability to rise to a higher level is nullified."

A voice came from behind them. "Whose level of living is nullified?" asked Creathe as she awakened from her deep sleep, somewhat confused.

"It's okay, my dear," replied Deltric. "Nobody's nullified; Sifrus was just explaining the true concept of *Love* to me." He looked back at her and smiled; he could see her concern. "Don't worry, it really is okay."

She smiled back and said, "If Sifrus is with us, I'm sure it's okay."

They continued in silence, streaking through the universe toward Heveris with love in their hearts for each other and especially Sifrus.

SERVAN

THE STRIKER PILOT WAS NOW LANDING ON SERVAN. WHAT WILL I SAY? he thought. *If I tell the truth about my encounter with Sifrus and his impenetrable space glider, will he believe me? Or will Deman order my death immediately?*

He held his breath as he walked into the control office. Looking around with worried eyes, he didn't see Deman at his station. "Where's Deman?" he asked the controller, who was busy studying the many screens.

"He hasn't come in today or called in to advise us why," said the controller without any sense of concern.

"Well, that's strange, isn't it? There must be something big going on; he always comes in for work. If he's not here soon, I'll travel over on my flier and check things out at his home."

"I can't reach the light," Deman cried desperately, reaching out with all his might.

"Try harder!" came a voice beyond the light. "You are a leader; you must be stronger than your servants."

"Who are you? Your voice sounds familiar; I've heard it somewhere before, but where?" Deman asked in desperation as his head spun with confusion.

"I work with Sifrus. Do you remember him?" the voice softly said.

He tried to clear his mind and think for a moment. "Sifrus!" He now remembered the good visitor who had come to help them some time ago. "Yes! I do remember him, but what does that have to do with this tiny light?"

Sifrus is the light who shows people the way out of their darkness. When he visits people and shows them his great love, he leaves a little of his light for them to follow."

"I don't understand," said Deman. "He didn't touch me or leave any light for me to follow!"

"But he did. It's in you. Haven't you been reconsidering the direction you're going, the harm that you've caused your people and your environment? This change didn't come from you. Do you think you could change so quickly without power from outside yourself?"

"All right, let's say I've been enlightened by my encounter with Sifrus. How can that help me now?" Deman asked with a little hope in his voice.

"You are in a place of decision, a time of reflection, and have a chance to gain the power and light of the universe. You're only being given this chance because you were willing to change and embrace the light given to you by Sifrus."

Deman took a moment to reflect back on his life, his cruelty, and his desire for power and riches. He slowly asked, "How does someone as evil as I've been change their ways and rectify things? What should I do?"

"Reach out and grab the light; then you can come here where I am."

"No … sorry, I'm not ready. I have to make things right here, where I am. The light is fading, my chest—the pain is unbearable! I guess this is the end."

"Deman! Deman!" a voice cried out.

"I know that voice, but how do I get back to it? I'm stuck here, wherever here is. The pain in my body, the dart, it must be poison … burning through my veins. Someone wants me dead. Ha! Maybe many people want me dead. Well, that should be no surprise, considering all the lives I've destroyed, and now the damage of this toxic mining dust. The end must be near for my planet and all its people, and I won't be here to do anything about it. The pain is unbearable—my chest—ouch! Somebody's at my chest. A knife! Someone is cutting me! Stop! Please stop! Why can't they hear me?"

"Pull gently on the dart," said the physician. "I'll try to cut the barbs anchoring it."

There's too much pain. I can't feel any part of my body, and the poison must be doing its job. I must be dying, and the light is too far to get to now. I must go back somehow. I can't be dead yet; I must fight this pain. I must! I have to correct the harm I've done. Fight … fight! I can do this. Help me, Sifrus, help me. Please help!

"How's he doing?" Seles asked between her crying sessions.

Jabis, the physician, looked at her with bewilderment in his eyes. "I was getting ready to tell you that we'd lost him, but now, unexplainably, there seems to be some life back in him. This is very strange. I thought he was gone."

Seles stopped crying for a moment. "Will he be okay?"

"He's still very weak, but his heart is beating much stronger than it was a few moments ago. This is astounding. His case is very unique, and that poison should have killed him," Jabis mused as he scratched his head.

Deman's mind was clearing. *I can hear them speaking. Seles is crying. The pain is lessening; I must be on my way back. I can see a dull light in the distance, not bright like the other light where I heard the voice of Sifrus's friend, but at least it's not dark as death would have it.*

"Seles, look at his eyes and the colour of his face. He's regaining his normal colour at an astonishing rate," said Jabis, looking in awe at what he was witnessing.

A door! It's opening for me to go back. I can see the way now. Deman began to cry, something he seldom did.

"Look," cried Seles, "his eyes are opening, and he's alive!"

The door is open! The light … Seles, Seles, I can see you. I'm back; I'm back to my life on Servan.

"Are you okay?" she asked with tear-filled eyes as she hugged and kissed him. "I thought I'd lost you forever, but you're here, you're alive. Thank you, Jabis." She smiled at the physician, who was still bewildered.

"You're welcome," he said cautiously. He was still studying Deman's eyes, as if waiting for him to regress and go quickly back into a coma.

Deman tried to speak, but no sound came. *What is this? I'm alive, but I can't speak.* He pointed at his throat, waved his hand, and then shook his head from side to side.

"That's okay," said Seles, "just give it some time."

She looked at Jabis with questioning eyes. Shaking his head a little, Jabis pointed to the door.

"I'll be back shortly, honey," she said as she turned toward the door.

Jabis followed her outside, shaking his head a little.

"Why can't he speak?" she asked as the door closed behind them.

"Well, the poison, assuming it was poison, may have done some nerve damage and affected his vocal cords. In a short time, he may be fine." Looking away from her, he thought for a moment. "I'll have a sample tested for confirmation of the poison. He's very lucky to be alive, and I don't know how he survived."

"Thank you again," said Seles as she opened the door and entered Deman's room. She sensed that this wasn't the end of this story.

Deman was awake and watched her cross the room toward him. She moved gracefully, and although she was middle-aged, she looked very young and pretty to him.

Lying there with nothing else to do, he could finally spend some quality time with his love mate, who, regrettably, he'd been too busy to be alone with for much of his recent years. Strangely, he had to almost die to realize his need to be close to her.

She sat next to him, smiling and looking deeply into his eyes. "How are you feeling?" A little hint of worry hung on her question.

He reached out, squeezed her hand, and nodded his head. *I'm back where I belong with the one I love*, he silently mused, looking off into space as if trying to see someone.

VOART

THE SITUATION ON VOART WAS BECOMING CRITICAL. THE GUARDS WHO HAD watched Sifrus and his passengers depart so quickly in his space glider were forced to go inside to breathe.

"The speed and power of that glider was out of this world," one guard said to another as he removed his breathing mask.

"Yes," the other guard said in surprise. "We can't even fly in these high winds and smog conditions, but he moved so easily."

"Could he be the one who had been promised to return to save them? It was foretold in their stories that a great teacher of *Love* would come."

"You don't believe those silly stories, do you?" Narob shouted at him.

"I suppose not, but you have to admit that something very strange just happened here," Torab said as he walked to a small window and tried to look up through the smog. "Very strange things are happening." He shook his head from side to side.

"It's very dark out there, and it's midday. This isn't normal. I don't know, Narob, what the end will be, but I think it's getting very close. It seems that they left just in the nick of time; nobody else will be leaving this place by the look of things."

Narob looked at him with fear in his eyes. "Those winds are extreme."

Screams could be heard in various places, causing tense feelings all around as both Narob and Torab tried to see where they were coming from. Things were flying everywhere. All the inhabitants were now going into their shelter places and caves, which had been dug from solid rock to protect them from a planet now falling apart.

"What's happening to us?" A voice from down a small lane cried out as many other lost souls began to shout and scream with panic.

Narob looked at Torab and spoke with much fear in his voice. "Our beautiful environment is now out of balance and control, and we have no technology or weapons to fight such a powerful menace. It seems that the time has passed to save our planet. The teachers in the past, who were ignored, shared their message of *Love* and were killed for trying to help. They were trying to warn our ancestors of this horrible end if things didn't change and their message not accepted."

Torab shook his head and cried out with a loud voice. "Too much industry without controls! Too much greed! Too much pollution! The environmental balances have been unable to clean its living environmental systems for some time now. My detector screen shows that we're now spinning much too fast to sustain life on this planet much longer."

Losing its orbit, the planet quickly spun toward their sun. The winds screamed as they spun at excessive speeds, and the heat from the sun was becoming unbearable. Within minutes, the extreme heat from the sun incinerated all living creatures and laid waste the entire surface, leaving only solid, bare rock, scorched as a reddish, smouldering testimony to their existence. Smoke was rising from what was once a beautiful home planet for those who lived there in the early days of peace and love.

Sifrus shook his head and cried as he sensed the final cries from Voart. "What else could I have done to save more of them?"

"Are you okay?" Deltric asked with great concern, somehow feeling some of Sifrus's pain.

"I'm … I'm … in great anguish from the loss of so many … so many poor souls." Sifrus cried and smashed his hand against the side of his space glider.

"They're all gone, aren't they?" asked Deltric, hoping that what he felt deep inside was not so.

"We tried so hard, and many teachers were sent. They pleaded with the people to return to the teachings of *Love*, but to no avail. All those poor souls, and only a few remained loyal—you, Deltric, and your families were all I was able to find who kept these teachings in your heart and gave to each other," cried Sifrus. He turned and looked at Deltric with so much love in his eyes, he was momentarily spellbound with a feeling beyond himself.

Trying to control his emotions, Deltric was experiencing mixed feelings. He was glad that he and his family were saved, but he was also extremely sad for the loss of his fellow inhabitants. "We all tried," he mumbled with a broken voice. "We all tried so hard! In the end, we who continued to hold true to these teachings of *Love* and taught them were killed or sent into exile. What else could we do? Did we fail?"

"No—no, you did what you could and more. Under much pressure you survived, and that's a miracle. It's a great accomplishment that deserves a great reward." Sifrus smiled at him once again and glanced back at his family, who would be soon welcomed to a most beautiful home beyond their wildest dreams.

"Reward!" Deltric exclaimed as he looked at Sifrus, puzzled. "But we don't …"

Sifrus spoke before he could finish. "Soon you will see and understand all things."

ATTACK ON RIMSHIRE

"IT'S GETTING DARK," SAID KRISTELLA AS SHE TOOK HER LITTLE SACK FROM her friendly zell. "We better get moving before we freeze." Touching the zell gently, she thanked him and told him to rest. He struggled to follow, but being totally exhausted, he lay down and watched her move up through the deep snow.

"Are we all here?" cried Assednic.

"I'm here," Kristella said. "Here with Chlorise."

"Jiltu, Soris, kids! We're all here," shouted Jiltu.

"Stay together; it's very poor visibility, and I don't want to lose anybody," he said with a deep sound of fear trailing on his voice.

Suddenly, streaks of fire came toward them from the valley below, and loud sounds echoed from snow crashing down as the ledges just above them were hit.

"No!" cried Kristella. "The zells! The zells!"

Piles of snow completely covered the zells, who were too exhausted to try and escape.

"We must have been seen," shouted Jiltu, "or how else would they know where to target their shots?"

"Luckily, they were a little off on their shots and probably thought we were still with the zells under the ledge. Fortunately, we moved higher when we did, or we would also be buried with snow," said Assednic in a quiet voice, sensing Kristella's feelings for the zells.

"Don't worry," said Jiltu as he lifted the children to his shoulders and put them in his carrying pouches. "Zells are used to snow avalanches; they'll be fine."

Underneath the snow, the zells had buried their heads in their deep fur, which contained many air sacks. Slowing their breathing, they would rest for several hours before digging out to surprise any attackers.

Chlorise's teeth were chattering. "Let's go," she mumbled as she held Kristella's hand and pushed again against the deep snow.

"We'll take turns leading," said Jiltu as he reached out to pull Soris along with him.

Spectrum awakened in much pain, trying to figure out where he was. Beside him for warmth was a zell, with his long fur pushed over him to block the cold winds. He tried to remember what had happened, but his head was fuzzy. *I was being chased by a toelion creature... the ledge ... falling ... bang ... hitting something hard, then blackness*, he thought, as best as he could remember.

Turning to look away from the zell, he saw only the sky—no rock or trees. Slowly moving his arm to feel on his left side, he realized with great horror that the zell was holding him in its legs on the edge of a ledge overhanging a very long drop to the valley below.

The zell was breathing very shallowly, and its eyes were closed. It was using all its energy, although severely hurt itself, to hold him. One small slip and the zell would lose its hold, and he would surely fall to his death.

This beautiful animal was giving up its own life to save him. *What to do?* he thought, as he couldn't feel his right arm but only sharp jabs of pain going through it. Maybe it was broken. He wasn't sure how much ledge was available for the zell if he moved.

Unable to move and in much pain, he went in and out of consciousness. He focused on his teacher and friend, Sifrus. *What would he do?* he thought as he tried to figure out how to get out of the extremely dangerous mess. *Sifrus taught us about Love, the powers of the universe, and helping each other. How could he help me now in this impossible situation?*

Closing his eyes and concentrating on Sifrus, he said, "I'm in big trouble. I can't move, and I'm hurting so much. If you can hear me, I desperately need help. I believe in your powers, although I don't know how they work. Thanks, my friend and my king."

Exhausted and not able to move, time passed slowly as he tried to stay awake. He wasn't sure how much time he'd spent on the ledge. The zell's breathing had almost stopped, and he was making short gasps for air. "Oh no, he's going to die, and his legs may release me over the edge," gasped Spectrum.

He tried to move, but it was too late. The zell gave his last desperate gasp for air and then went limp, releasing his grip on Spectrum. "No!" he screamed as he rolled over the edge and started falling, falling faster toward the ground and certain death. Closing his eyes to not see what was happening, he made one last cry to Sifrus, and then—*thump, thump.* "I'm dead!"

A loud scream startled him as his eyes opened. Confused by his surroundings and soft landing, he opened his eyes to see that he had landed on a very soft, downy substance. It looked like very large feathers surrounding him. He tried standing but it was hard to keep his balance. *It's moving*, he thought. *But how? What is this?*

A low-pitched voice cried out from nearby. "Are you okay?"

Startled and shaken, he managed to reply. "Yes! I'm not sure where I am."

A small, shiny creature came into view from just behind a bunch of soft feathers. It was beautiful, with golden eyes and sparkling silver all over its body. It stood at only half his height. A pure white robe hung to its feet. Its voice was soft and sweet and seemed to linger in his ears, affecting his feelings. The voice was so warm it was intoxicating, like a feeling of love and trust penetrating his whole being.

"Who are you?" Spectrum was trying to focus, but he was absorbed in the intoxication while studying this most beautiful creature.

"I am Starid," came the sweet voice. The creature lifted a shiny, little wing to touch him. "You are hurt; hold my wing and let me help."

Spectrum hesitated, not sure if he should trust this creature, but his feelings were warm, loving. *I must trust*, he thought as he reached out his hand and touched the wing tip.

Instantly, a surge of warmth went through his whole body, taking away all of his pain. His mind exploded in euphoric love for this creature that was now healing him. He felt fully alive inside, like never before in his life. He couldn't describe this new feeling filling his whole body. His physical body was exhausted as he fell to his knees.

Drifting off into another plane of existence, he seemed to travel through his past in a flash. For some reason, his mind quickly changed and began looking forward to a future time of bliss. Time seemed to stand still. *There's nothing else in this world I want but to stay in this feeling of intense love and warmth forever.*

"Are you sure you're okay?" came the soft, sweet voice again, breaking his moment of bliss.

Trying to concentrate on where he was, he opened his eyes. *It's not a dream*, he thought as a beautiful, shiny little creature came into focus.

"I'm feeling great!" Spectrum said, still touching a little wing so delicately. "What are you, and where do you get such power to heal like this?"

Starid glowed even more as he smiled at Spectrum. "You are healed, yes, but not by any power I have in myself. My master who sent me has the powers of the universe."

"Who is your master?" Spectrum asked with a hesitant heart, thinking the answer would be Monton or his followers. His heart raced as he awaited the answer.

"I received a message from my master to come to Rimshire immediately, for his followers were in great danger. My master is Sifrus, son of our great king on Heveris." He shone even brighter as his wings fluttered with excitement.

Spectrum was astonished as his mind whirled. "But how? Sifrus, our leader, left on a trip a long time ago. I cried out to him for help. But how?"

Smiling with delight, Starid touched Spectrum again with his shiny, little wing. "Hold my wing," he said. "There are powers you don't fully understand, so I will reveal some to your mind. Close your eyes and hold tight."

Spectrum closed his eyes and held the glowing wing of his new friend. "I'm ready," he said cautiously.

Suddenly, his mind was filled with the light of many civilizations coming at him with visions of good, loving creatures living in harmony and love on what seemed like paradises on beautifully vegetated, clean, well-maintained environments. He also saw visions of creatures in much conflict living in dark, dirty, dusty, polluted environments. The light from a far-off world was extremely bright, penetrating to the surface of the good environments, but it couldn't penetrate through the atmosphere of the polluted environments. He was confused by all these visions.

"I don't understand."

"You can only receive light when things are clean and not polluted," said Starid. "While you're ready to receive knowledge and power, you'll need to clear your mind. Empty your mind of all evil thoughts and concentrate on pure light coming from Sifrus. The pure light you see is from the power of *Love,* which is given to us when we're willing to love in return. *Love* allows us to always do what is good for our fellow creatures and living worlds."

Spectrum's mind was spinning as he tried to understand what these revelations meant. "You're telling me that *Love*, light, and Sifrus are all connected and signify secret powers of the entire universe in some way?" He shook his head to show his uncertainty.

"Yes, of course they are, and they all come from the ultimate source of power and love on Heveris." Starid pointed upward toward the many shiny lights in the heavens. "Can't you see?" he asked with the most beautiful smile Spectrum had ever seen.

Starid was glistening all over. "*Love* and its infinite power comes from your king, Sifrus, and his father."

"Wow!" Spectrum was now wide-eyed, contemplating the meaning of Starid's words. Suddenly, they were moving at an extreme speed beyond his comprehension. "What are we on that is moving so fast?" he asked with great concern.

"I'm here to also help your friends, who are in great danger on the mountaintop. Come up to see where we're going. Follow me, quickly!"

A narrow trail led through a forest of gigantic feathers. Up above he could hear the wind howl as they sped through the sky, but it was calm and warm around them. No light was needed to follow, because Starid shone the way through the feathers with his glow as he moved effortlessly without moving his wings.

They soon came to an opening in the feathers, where another small, shining creature who looked much like Starid was standing behind a clear shield. He was looking straight ahead and speaking in a strange language to some other creature Spectrum couldn't see. He turned when they approached and, shining brightly and smiling at Spectrum, said, "You are alive, I see. We weren't too late, but it came very close, though. Come up front and see where we're going."

"You're so bright and beautiful and glowing all over … I've never seen anything like you creatures before in my whole life. What are you called?" Spectrum asked in astonishment.

"You already met Starid. I am Tarus of Heveris. We are galaxy zeracks at your service."

"Galaxy zeracks, you say? Pleased to meet you, and thanks for the rescue."

As Spectrum looked out, he could see the heads of a gigantic, bird-like creature swinging from side to side, with fire-red eyes looking in all directions and assessing all that was going on around it.

"Are we on this creature?" Spectrum asked with much fear in his voice.

"Do not fear," said Starid with his sweet, calming voice. "We're quite safe and do this work all the time. Whenever a rescue is needed, we go and are always successful. We never fail!" He opened his wings wide, showing his pure, white, shiny body—not a flaw, no stains, no damage. Just perfection.

Spectrum was dazzled. *This sure is like a crazy dream*, he thought. *Shiny, little creatures, monster-sized, bird-like creature with two heads. Wow!* "What is this creature we're on?" he asked, still a little shaken in his voice and thinking the whole situation was possibly a dream.

"This is our friend who takes us where we need to go throughout the galaxy. He's very friendly to those who are loving, but not so nice to those who harbour evil in their hearts. Look! The mountaintop is in view; hold on tight for some extra manoeuvrings. He is known on Heveris as a great perad. He's very wise and can see everything going on for long distances. His only desire is to help those who love his master and bring honour to him. He will help you and your friends."

Monton's army positioned themselves at the base of the mountains for their final attack. The toelions were restless as their riders mounted them with all the supplies they needed to finish the job. Weapons with extra shooting range were pointed at all strategic passes to ensure none could escape this time. Climbers with great cleats and stone grabbers were readied. The order was to not take prisoners except for Kristella, who would be used to display what would happen to anyone who defied Monton.

At the crest of the mountain, Sifrus's followers moved toward the safety of the caves "I can see the camps," said Assednic, who had taken the lead and was breaking through the snow. No reply came from his group. Quickly turning, he could see Kristella face down in the snow. Diving toward her, he quickly rolled her over to check her breathing. *Shallow, but still alive*, he thought. Placing his mouth on hers, he blew warm oxygen into her lungs. Wrapping himself around her to keep her warm, he continued to breathe warm air into her. "I can't lose you now," he said as she gasped to breathe on her own.

She had come to mean everything remaining of his life. His love for her kept growing more and more each day, especially since they'd decided to defy Monton and hold to their allegiance to their king, Sifrus.

"Are you there?" came a weak voice, startling him.

"You're okay! You're okay!" shouted Assednic as he gently kissed her on the cheek.

"I'm so tired! I can't go any further; you take the others and continue without me." Kristella closed her eyes again.

Lying there unable to move, she thought she heard Sifrus call to her: "Kristella, don't give up. You are chosen to lead my people with your wisdom and a pure belief in my teachings of *Love*. Get up now; summon your strength, for help is on the way."

Kristella could feel a sense of something warm going through her body, a tingling sensation from her head to her toes. She began to feel much better; she had a reason to live, to continue on with strength beyond her own.

"Kristella, Kristella, wake up! Don't go to sleep; come on, you can do it." Assednic was now shaking her.

Jiltu, Soris, and the children were now next to them, watching with great concern for Kristella.

"Is she okay?" Soris asked as she reached into her bag for her special healing herbs.

"Time to awaken now, Kristella. You are strong; I have sent my power into you." The voice seemed so real, she thought that maybe Sifrus was right next to her. "Open your eyes." She forced her eyes open with renewed zest for life. She saw Sifrus, as if he were standing beside her.

"Look!" said the little girl. "Her eyes are shining, and they're opening. Look! Look! Mommy, they're so bright."

"What are all you looking at?" Kristella whispered as she saw them looking at her with tears forming in their eyes.

"You're back," cried Assednic. He embraced her so tightly, she was almost smothered in his heavy coat.

"Okay, okay," Kristella choked, trying to focus on their situation. "What's that noise?" She asked with a weak voice.

"What noise?" Jiltu asked while removing his head cover to listen more clearly. "Is that heavy snorting coming toward us the toelions that pursued us earlier? Quickly, cover yourselves with snow," he shouted.

The noise quickly came upon them, and then suddenly it was quiet. Something stopped right above them, sniffing the snow. *We're doomed! We're caught!* They thought for sure this was the end of their attempted escape.

Kristella's senses told her that whatever was upon them wasn't dangerous. She dug a small peep hole up through the snow to see what it was that was sniffing directly above them. Suddenly, a warm, fuzzy nose met her hand as it broke through the snow.

"No, it can't be," she cried. "The zells! The zells!"

They uncovered themselves quickly and saw, to their astonishment, the mountain zells they had left behind for dead under the avalanche of snow. They were all standing there, excited to see them and full of energy to carry them again toward the mountain caves.

"But how can this be?" Assednic asked, looking totally puzzled. He knew that only a few hours before, they were totally exhausted and buried with deep snow.

Jiltu was rubbing down his zell with great pride. "They have the ability to rebuild their energy levels very quickly. Being underneath the snow piles, totally inactive, accelerated the process even more than normal. I told you they were good, didn't I?"

"Well … yes!" said Kristella excitedly. "Perfect timing! We're totally exhausted, and we could really use a ride. Come, let's get out of here before those horrible toelions find us."

The zells dropped quickly to the snow again, allowing the riders to get on easily. Within seconds they were racing over the snowdrifts toward the summit. "Yo-ho-ho," came a cry of delight from the excited riders.

At the base of the mountain, Monton's army was in the final stages of preparing their attack. The toelions were getting edgy, snapping at the rock grabbers who were tearing at the ground, ready to ascend.

"Can we see our prey with the long-range viewers?" asked the army leader, becoming impatient. He knew their time to get their prey before the winter snows closed the mountain completely was getting short, and Monton would not take kindly to them failing again.

Suddenly, a strange scream and a gust of wind came from the sky, startling the whole group and unsettling them for a moment.

"What was that?" their leader cried as he beat on his chest of armour.

They all looked to the sky but couldn't see anything.

"I don't know, boss," shrugged his captain, "but I'm sure I heard what sounded like many wings beating. Strange, though …"

"Boss! Come look," called his spotter. "Look in the viewer; they're moving toward the summit and are riding strange, furry creatures. *They're moving very fast*, he thought, puzzled. *They should be very tired by now. How can this be?*

"Get the grogs ready. We'll need them to locate the snow caves once we get to the top. They can't go much further. They won't get away this time. Monton will have my head if they do escape." He felt the back of his neck with his hand as a shiver went up his spine.

"There it is, the summit," shouted Assednic, who was leading them now. "Look, several other people are standing outside a snow cave. We're not alone!" He cracked a little smile of hope as he glanced back at his friends.

It was a beautiful sight to behold—the loving, furry creatures carrying the last of Sifrus's loving people, flying through deep snow with powder flying in all directions. There was a breathtaking view of pristine mountains, snow-covered peaks with golden rays of sun reflecting off every prism sending rays of coloured light in all directions.

Kristella looked at Assednic in shock as he suddenly came to a stop and was no longer smiling. He was looking straight ahead at four toelions with riders mounted and weapons drawn. In an instant that seemed like time was standing still, their hopes for escape, which a moment ago seemed so certain, were now at an end.

Kristella was in a trance of mixed feelings. *Why this? After just surviving tiredness, an avalanche, and a swamp, why would we have gotten this far for it to now end like this?* She steeled her eyes on the enemy and their creatures. Jiltu looked at her but did not move, for fear of the weapons pointed at him.

"Kristella," came a voice inside, a quiet voice she recognized from previous times when they were in peril.

Sifrus! Is that you? she thought. *Help! Help us!* She called silently in desperation for their lives.

"They're going to shoot your friends and capture you if you don't trust me. Don't stop—you were chosen for this. Go straight at them, and I will protect you."

This is crazy, she thought. *I'm going to die!* But believing fully in Sifrus's power, she leaned into her zell and pushed him full speed ahead. The zell streaked through the snow zig-zag-zig-zag as shots started blasting all around her.

"No!" screamed Assednic when he realized what she was doing, but to his horror it was too late. "Drop to the snow," he shouted to the others. "Hide under the zells!"

The riders on the toelions were startled when, unexpectedly, Kristella came at them at an unbelievable speed. They shot erratically, missing with every shot.

Kristella was now on top of them, spraying snow over them everywhere as she prepared to smash into all of them as she lunged into a sideways sweep. Her heart was pounding in her chest, and her mind swirled with mixed emotions, knowing it was crazy and most likely suicide. But still she could feel the ever-soft voice of Sifrus pushing her on.

Time stood still for what seemed like minutes, but only seconds had passed. Flying snow had blinded everybody, including her. All eyes were frozen on where Kristella had last been seen. A loud sound had been heard, startling them to flee backward as much as possible. Falling back, waiting in terror … knowing their lives were in Kristella's hands now.

Assednic was sick to his stomach. He loved Kristella, and he didn't want to live without her. He knew she was a little different and compulsive, not to mention she seemed to always be thinking of their king, Sifrus, but this was a bit insane. He just hoped for a miracle.

Kristella had fallen off her zell as she'd swept to the side and was buried in the snow completely. She was almost in a daze. Her mind was wandering back to a beautiful, peaceful Rimshire before this. *A wonderland place—we never hurt anyone—all we do is teach Love for each other. What a strange world. We receive hatred in return for love—strange –very strange. Our beautiful home, and now no one knows where they stand or what to believe anymore with these evil rulers!*

Jiltu rolled over to see the area finally clear, but he couldn't see anybody. He stared at Soris with a blank face, trying to control his emotions before looking toward Assednic. Assednic was transfixed on where he last saw Kristella. "Where are the toelions? Where is she?" he anguished, slowly moving forward. He ached with every step. "Kristella … Kristella!" he called with pain in his voice.

Kristella's head was clearing, and she heard his voice. *I'm still alive*, she thought in disbelief as she felt something warm lick her hand. "My zell, my zell, you're still with me. Thank you, Sifrus," she whispered. She was unsure of her pursuers' situation, but she was glad to still be alive.

Kristella and the zell suddenly burst from the mound of snow, shocking her friends and causing Assednic to scream with delight as he raced toward her with arms outstretched. As they embraced with love and passion, they radiated pure love to the others standing nearby and watching with great happiness.

"But where did our pursuers go?" Kristella asked as she looked in all directions with disbelief clearly showing in her eyes. "I figured I would surely die," she whispered as she kissed Assednic.

"The force of the enormous snow spray you created when you turned and fell back forced them over the edge, and they tumbled down the ravine," Jiltu smiled as he announced to her. "You're our crazy hero!"

Looking up above, she quietly said, "Thanks, Sifrus!

"Did you hear that sound above us?" Kristella kept looking to the sky, seemingly expecting to see something.

Soris looked puzzled as she turned to Jiltu, who was looking at Assednic in bewilderment. "What's happening here?" she asked Jiltu with confusion and a shaky voice.

Jiltu looked at Soris then back at Kristella, who was still looking to the sky, trying to understand something bigger than them. "Well … well," he stuttered, "there is a greater power surrounding Kristella than we can understand at this time. Her strong belief in Sifrus's ability to help us seems to be empowering her in some strange yet real way."

"The wings fluttering around us — can't you hear them?" Kristella cried. Then they were suddenly gone.

"Let's get out of here," Jiltu shouted, "just in case there are more of them coming soon with flying creatures of some sort."

Climbing onto the zells, they were quickly dashing through the soft snow on their final leg to their temporary homes of safety on the peaks of the mountains where in times past miners had dug deep caves under the snow and into the rock in search of precious minerals.

HOPE BEGINS ON SERVAN

TWO DAYS HAD PASSED, AND DEMAN WAS STILL UNABLE TO SPEAK. HIS dreams were haunting him to the point of leaving him sleep deprived and very cranky. His experience with near death and the light, the voice in the light … well, either he was dreaming or imagining things, or there was really someone out there waiting for him to die.

That man, he thought, *Sifrus I believe was his name. There's something different about him—a power about him! The brightness around him and his loving ways! Why is he so different?*

"Seles! Seles!" He tried to shout, but only a mumble came, a little louder than before.

Seles came in. "What is it?" she asked, looking at him with great concern.

He took out his note pad and began writing with what seemed to be an urgent message.

"I need you to contact my office and have my chief information officer dig up as much information as possible on Sifrus, King of Rimshire." He looked up at her and smiled a very unusual, warm smile.

He wrote on his pad with great concern: "I have done much harm to my people and the environment of our planet. Please help me get strong again and try to help make things better." A smile again met her stare.

She gave him a very warm hug of acknowledgement and understanding, knowing he was changing for the better. "I will help you always, if I can," she said as she gently kissed his cheek.

The phone rang at the control centre. "Rickter speaking," came a strong voice.

"This is Seles," came a soft voice across the line. "Deman told me to call and inform you that he isn't feeling well and won't be in today. He wants the chief information officer to get as much information on Sifrus of Rimshire as possible, and quickly. He will be out for a few days and will call when he is ready to return."

"I hope he gets well soon," Rickter said and hung up. He waved to the officer to get his attention. "Here, get on this immediately; leave no stone unturned," he said as he passed the note.

Deman was seated comfortably in a large plush chair, staring out at a severe dust storm. The pain in his chest from the dart injury was eclipsed only by the pain in his heart from what was happening outside. Seles came in with a warm drink to help calm him, knowing that he was very tense from all the difficult things going on in their lives.

Deman knew he was struggling with many mixed emotions: guilt, helplessness, and a strong desire to not meet the voice in the light again until he'd fixed the many problems he had created. He was mumbling to himself as she quietly approached A little startled, he quickly went for a small dagger he kept concealed under his robe. She froze in place only a few centimetres from his weapon.

Shaken a little, she looked into his eyes. "Are you sure you're feeling okay?" she asked, not moving. She could see great fear in his eyes. In the past, he never allowed any fear to show. The events were obviously taking a toll on her once-strong mate and would have to be resolved before he could go back to ruling their planet.

He slowly shook his head and closed his eyes with embarrassment as his dagger dropped to the floor with a loud bang. "What is happening to me, Seles?" he pleaded with his now-watery eyes.

Wrapping her arms around him in a comforting embrace, she could feel him tremble as they remained intertwined in silence.

Several hours later, the information officer at the control centre returned carrying a small galaxy map with some charts and a library log. Passing the material to Rickter, he began briefing him with a somewhat perplexed look on his face.

"I checked the memo Deman sent several months ago to Rimshire for a meeting with their chief environmentalist at that time. The reply we received from them indicated that their king, Sifrus, would be best suited to visit, as he understood the perplexity of the many systems in each location throughout the district."

"Hold!" said Rickter, shaking his head. "Wasn't he the one we put in prison only a short time ago. But then Deman released him after some strange encounter with the inmates in our prison?"

"Yes, the same person," he said, passing him the charts. "Look at the records of his departure."

"That's weird! Deman secretly sent out a destroyer to bring him back or be destroyed after he'd been released. He must have changed his mind and decided he was a danger to his rule or something." Rickter shook his head.

"Look at the results," shouted the officer.

Rickter was silent for a moment. "This can't be!" he exclaimed.

"Yes! Astonishing, isn't it? Our most powerful destroyer with the most advanced weapons couldn't penetrate his shields, and this Sifrus didn't attempt to destroy him or even fire one shot in defence. This file is coded Top Secret, so only Deman knows what happened out there. I cannot decode the access filter to learn any more."

Rickter was puzzled. "Then why does he want to find this Sifrus again?"

"I sent out a distress signal chaser locked onto the last known vessel to leave our territory. We'll have to wait some time to see if our chaser can even lock on and locate this strange vessel Sifrus is travelling in. Its technologies may be well beyond our own."

"I hope this works, or we may have to pay with our heads. Deman does not appreciate failure." He hesitated for a moment as he felt the hairs on his neck rise.

His officer looked at Rickter with fear on his face. He then passed Rickter a report showing the toxicity in the latest air quality test. "We may not have much longer to save our heads if we don't soon figure out how to reverse and stabilize our environmental problems."

Rickter studied the report, sighing occasionally, and then exhaled. "I assume Deman is aware of this report and must be planning to take immediate action. He stared off toward the sky, thinking that it may be connected to the search for Sifrus. *I wonder...*

Deman had fallen asleep in his large chair, so Seles released him and went back to her chores. She could see his eyes flicking wildly, as if something was bothering him. He was dreaming of a beautiful field of flowers; the sun was shining through beautiful, clean air. He saw a waterfall with pristine, clear water, and no dust storms or other pollution were visible. He was trying to get to the waterfall where he saw a man holding a very bright light. "Come over," he called, "it's nice over here!"

He tried to move toward the light, but his legs wouldn't move. They were too heavy from all the riches he possessed. "I can't move," Deman called back.

The voice called again. "Come over, it's peaceful here. Drop the possessions; you don't need them here."

Deman looked at the bags filled with gold, gems, precious diamonds, and other valuable items. *Maybe if I leave a few, I can get to the other side*, he thought. Leaving one bag, he began to walk a little lighter, but soon he began to sink in some mud. "I can't make it," he called.

He suddenly awoke, sweating profusely and shaking. Looking around, he realized he was home and began to calm down while he wondered about the meaning of his strange dream.

It seems that if I'm to get to the peaceful voice holding the light near the waterfall, I'll have to travel very light and leave all my possessions behind. This will be very difficult, because I've accumulated so many possessions as leader of this place. What could I do with it all? But I must see this beautiful, peaceful place, or I will never be happy. But how? He felt great frustration as he looked out at the severe dust storm.

Just then, Seles came back to check on him. "You're awake, I see. Do you need anything?"

He again tried to speak. A small, squeaky "yes" came out. They were both surprised and delighted to hear a little noise, even if squeaky.

Seles hugged him. "Your voice is coming back, and that's wonderful! Hopefully soon we can talk together like we did in the past."

She sensed there was much he needed to tell her. She knew there was probably many secrets yet to be revealed about this new road they would be travelling together. She closed her eyes and remembered back to when they were young and the beautiful places they would travel to together. They would hold hands as they visited beautiful forests, clear water streams, and fields of beautiful flowers. They were in love, and the days seemed to last forever. He'd been so loving, but his personality changed when he became leader. Oh, how she missed those wonderful times and ached for them to come again. Glancing toward her window, she could see only darkness and dust blowing all around outside their home. *Where did the beauty go?* she thought with a heavy heart.

As the days passed, Seles spent all of her time caring for Deman. He grew stronger each day and was able to speak short sentences in a very low voice. Over several weeks, he recovered substantially and felt he could soon get back to his job as leader.

The storm had slowed somewhat, and Deman was ready to get back to his office, even if he wasn't feeling his best. Things would be different now, for Deman was not the same man he'd been a few weeks earlier. He now saw things more clearly. His near-death experience and encounter with a voice in a beautiful light had changed him. He now knew that he must use his power and insight to try to restore some balance and beauty to their homeland. He would start with his home city of Quartin and gradually expand his efforts outward until all the inhabitants had been helped to make their homes liveable. But he knew deep inside that his wisdom and insight would have to come from beyond himself if he were to get this to work properly.

There is a much greater power out there, if only I understood it. Maybe it's connected to this King Sifrus, and perhaps all the ultimate powers in the universe come from his great knowledge and abilities. I must find him and determine if I could have access to these powers. Maybe if I were to believe in his teachings …

HEVERIS

SIFRUS WAS TRAVELLING NOW AT A MAXIMUM SPEED AND WOULD BE BACK on his father's home of Heveris within the hour with the precious cargo he'd picked up at Voart. He knew there would be a celebration planned for their arrival—there always was when good people who followed the teachings of *Love* came home. He also felt a sense of urgency coming from his own kingdom of Rimshire, and some kind of change was happening on Servan. His time with his father on Heveris would be short before he'd have to go and help others.

Sifrus looked at Deltric, who was awakening from his deep sleep. "You look a little more rested," he said with a smile. "Are you ready for some more stories about your planet of Voart?"

Deltric looked at Sifrus and then closed his eyes to hide his pain. He looked away for a moment at the silver streaks of planets and stars going by. "I guess," he said with apprehension.

Sifrus could feel his pain. "You shouldn't blame yourself; there were many evil things you were unaware of that were going on to undermine your work."

"What things?" Deltric asked, now more awake and inquisitive than a few moments ago.

"Well, for many years on the other side of Voart there were tensions between two groups of inhabitants. They both wanted to own a beautiful area where it was thought a special plant grew that contained the secrets of living a long life." Sifrus passed him a small purple flower.

"What's this?" Deltric asked, looking at and feeling the beautiful flower in his hands.

Sifrus smiled. "It's called the everlasting flower. They believed that if they dried these flowers and ate them, they would become strong and wise and live forever."

"That's crazy! Isn't it?" he asked with a sense of bewilderment.

"Not to the people who believed the story. People who once loved each other were now fighting and killing each other to get control over this area. Many had eaten the flowers but were no wiser for their efforts, so they assumed that it must take many years for the flower to mature."

"But," said Deltric, "they must have realized that if they continued in this manner, they would eventually destroy one another."

"Exactly!" Sifrus exclaimed. "One group was technologically advanced and had decided to end the fight once and for all. They developed a powerful laser that would completely evaporate their enemies' bodies so that no evidence could be found to prove they had destroyed their neighbours."

"Could neighbours hate each other enough to do this?" Deltric frowned as he tried to control his ragged emotions.

Reaching over, Sifrus gently took his hand. "I know it's hard to believe, but once any creatures turn from loving each other, hate controls them and grows until they're capable of unbelievable acts. Some of them became so radical, they began to hate anything or anybody good."

"Did they use it—the super laser?" Deltric asked with astonishment.

"Do you remember some years back when a great blast was heard, and the ground was shaken? Many assumed there was a great planet quake."

"Yes! A great planet quake was reported, after which we began experiencing solar flaring of our sun," cried Deltric, now beginning to get the picture. "You mean ..."

Sifrus shook his head. "They killed more than their enemies, for they inadvertently killed your planet. That laser cut a deep hole in the crust of your planet, igniting a large pocket of volatile gases and causing a huge explosion. This shifted the balances and the path of the planet in relation to your sun."

Deltric was now wide-eyed. "So that's why our environmental systems became so strange and uncontrollable! We had too much heat at times, dust storms, long periods of darkness and cold, and crop failures.

"You see, it's not your fault! The things that were happening at Regus were bad and causing much smog, but only minor compared to what was happening on the other side of your planet. Ironically, the blast killed both groups and destroyed the beautiful and only area where the purple flowers grew." Sifrus shook his head. "How sad."

Deltric looked at the flower in his hand and slowly back at Sifrus. "But where did you get this?" he asked as he lifted the flower.

"The story of strength, wisdom, and longevity of life had some truth. A very old teacher had lived in the valley of purple flowers. He had been wise and travelled for many years teaching *Love* to all who would listen. When tired, he would return to this valley to rest and was occasionally seen by many generations of people."

Deltric again looked at the flower. "So did the people think that maybe he had a secret of immortality right here in their midst?"

Sifrus smiled. "I knew this teacher!"

He looked at Sifrus in astonishment but said no more, knowing deep inside that he was in the presence of somebody who was very old yet who looked very young.

Sifrus was suddenly alerted by a beeping noise coming from his control panel. "We have a chaser following us. It's used to locate vessels that have been engaged in battle within striking distance of a known planet. This one must have been deployed when I engaged the destroyer while leaving Servan." *But why track me?* Sifrus mulled over the question in his mind. He knew he had felt that something was happening that was changing Deman.

"What will you do about this chaser?" asked Deltric, trying to figure out what was happening to them.

"Not to worry," said Sifrus softly to calm his anxiety. "The chaser will follow us until we shut down our propulsion system. Then it will send out its location signal and deactivate itself. It's harmless and will fulfill the purpose of its mission."

"But why is it trying to locate you?" Deltric was intrigued.

"I'm not sure, but it seems they don't want to wait until I return to Rimshire. My encounter with them was interesting to them for sure, so I suspect they need to know more about my destination before making contact again. Heveris is far out at the outer edge of the galaxy; even if their chaser can emit a signal strong enough to show its location, they'll have no record of Heveris on their systems maps.

"There it is!" shouted Sifrus. Like a schoolboy coming home from a long trip, he awakened everybody who had been sleeping in the back. Before their eyes was a beautiful world of pristine light, shining like a jewel. The brightness of the light was greater than that of their sun back on Voart, but it seemed purer, and it didn't hurt their eyes to look upon it.

They continued on their approach to Heveris in silence as they all looked in every direction at the unbelievable beauty surrounding them. Sifrus was becoming excited, for soon he would see his father, friends, and especially Karmilita and Trifrum. How he longed to see them again! He had been away from home for an extended period of time and was anxious to get back. His time on Rimshire was served first as a teacher and then as their king for the past few years.

He glanced at Deltric, who was absorbed in his surroundings, his eyes dancing from place to place, trying to see as much as he could. "What do you think?" asked Sifrus quietly, still studying the amazement on his face.

Deltric kept looking around at the unbelievable visions exploding before him; he choked and then finally reached out to grab Sifrus's hand. "Tell me I'm not dreaming and that this is all real. Squeeze my hand if I'm awake … please!"

A voice came from behind them. "What is this beautiful, shining place?" Jarock asked with great excitement, trying to contain himself.

Screams of excitement came from the children, who were now wide awake and anxious for some play time.

"Jarock! My friend," said Sifrus with a sound of glee in his voice, "this is my home, where I grew up. My father and his helpers work here to keep the universe as safe and stable as possible. This is Heveris, the centre and power source of our galaxy!"

"Wow!" shouted Creathe, unable to contain her excitement. "Do we get to stay here?"

"Yes, you do, all of you," exclaimed Sifrus. "This is your reward for staying true to the teachings of *Love*. You see, love originates from here and eventually returns in the people who retain it."

Seili was still quiet and transfixed on their beautiful new home. She was still hurting from the traumatic experience of having to leave their old home on Voart. She hesitantly asked: "What if someone turns from *Love*? Will they have to leave?"

Sifrus hesitated while he considered her question; he could feel the pain in her voice. He knew how much they were all hurting from having to watch what evil did to their people and home. With a very quiet voice, he answered: "This place is different than any other; we all love and care for each other. The power of true love is very great here. Once taken into your heart, it fills you to overflowing, and you'll never want to turn from it. Evil cannot exist here, because it's destroyed by the pure light of *Love*."

They were now getting close to their landing area and would soon be in the presence of the most beautiful and loving creatures in existence. They had passed by what looked like fields of gold, forests of silver, hills of bronze, and streams of jewels that seemed to be everywhere. They saw strange shining creatures flying around all over the place without having to use any of their wings. They all seemed very happy, singing and playing games.

Approaching them was what seemed to be a very bright city with many mansions strung along what looked like streams flowing gently, filled with shiny jewels of many types and colours. They were surrounded by crystal trees with brilliant fruit of many types and colours to feed them and keep all the inhabitants healthy.

"What are these shiny flying creatures? They seem so happy and so beautiful. So out of this world!" Deltric questioned without even breaking his gaze from the scene before him. He was beginning to feel much different on the inside—they all were as they got closer to their new home. This place of pure love was permeating from everywhere and enveloping them into a mystical and undefinable deep feeling for their fellow beings around them.

"Those are galaxy zeracks and live here to serve our great, loving civilization," Sifrus said as he smiled and pointed across the vast area of pristine beauty. "They live here and are sent out to help creatures on other worlds when my father needs them to help with rescues."

"Other worlds to help?" Deltric asked with a hint of surprise in his voice. "But they're so small! I'm sure they're not able to do much."

"Small they may be, but very fast and powerful," sighed Sifrus as he told Deltric to look at one streaking over a small forest in the distance. "Never judge strength by size, but always remember that all creatures possess special strengths we may not be aware of."

Suddenly, they landed in a most exquisite area with many shining zeracks standing all around and singing welcome to them in the most beautiful sounds. Coming toward them, Deltric could see a larger group of shining beings moving over the surface of clear, smooth material that seemed to carry them forward without moving. Streaks of light filled the sky, with the many creatures flying in every direction.

"Welcome home! Welcome!" shouted the largest of them. "My son! My son! It's so good to see you back." They embraced with such tenderness that all those standing around could feel it. They both glowed and radiated their love for each other.

"You have brought some friends, I see. Welcome to you all. Come to my house for rest and refreshments. A great celebration is planned for you all. We must wait for a little while, as we are expecting two of my zeracks and a great perad to return from Rimshire with a friend of yours, Sifrus."

Sifrus was a little surprised at the news, but he had felt a call come from Rimshire for help, which he'd passed on to his father.

"Thanks for your rescue of my friend on Rimshire. I felt it was Spectrum who needed it, but it also seemed like Kristella and all her friends were in trouble."

"Come," said his father, "I'll explain all that's been happening since you left Rimshire. For now, let's get you all settled into your new homes after you are refreshed. I must return to the Celestial Planning Centre to deal with an emergency for a short while, but I'll return as soon as they arrive." He hugged Sifrus tightly.

RIMSHIRE—NEXT BATTLE

"THERE THEY ARE!" ASSEDNIC CRIED OUT AS HE POINTED TO THE CAVE entrance just ahead. "We've made it, we've made it," he shouted as they fell into the opening.

A sense of relief came over them as the cave entrance opened up into a lighted, well-maintained room. Supplies of food and blankets for warmth were stacked on shelves in the corner. The caves went deep into the mountains and could be used to hide in when invaders came looking to steal from the miners. The miners had operated and lived in the hidden rooms behind solid rock, where they could hide for extended periods of time when in danger.

Assednic had come across an old miner some time ago who was in need of some financial help and offered to sell his secrets of the caves in the mountains to him. Assednic purchased them not for the safe haven they would preciously need now, but for the possible riches they may hold. Little did he know that their true value was not the minerals but the protection they afforded them. He looked at the massive room that had been cut from solid rock and was amazed at the dedication and ingenuity needed to create it.

Monton's best mountain climbers and fighters were all ready to ascend to the caves above them and capture or kill all who were trying to escape his decree of allegiance. His scout teams with the toelions had failed, and now his full resources would be deployed against Kristella and her friends.

A command came from their leader: "Move out! Do not return until all have been taken care of. Take prisoners if they give a sign of surrender, or shoot to kill if they offer resistance. But Kristella must be taken alive." A great shout went up as the riders on toelions with grogs leading them sent rocks and clay flying in all directions as they raced up the mountains by the hundreds to destroy all who would defy them.

Kristella looked at Assednic with a worried look. "What is that great noise I hear coming up the mountain again? It's not the zells this time."

"Let's go look!" Jiltu shouted. "Soris, please stay here with the kids. Chlorise, would you stay with them for safety also?"

Kristella, Assednic, and Jiltu quickly ran outside the entrance to a ledge overlooking a valley so far away, they had to use their magnifying tubes to see what was making all the noise.

"Look!" shouted Jiltu with much fear on his face. "There are hundreds of creatures coming up the side of the mountain toward us. We have no chance of surviving this; even if we try to hide in the caves, they'll find us."

"Why do you say that?" asked Assednic. "These caves are deep with secret hiding places."

"But Monton has specially trained grogs that can track us anywhere we go, which he will send for this purpose," he sighed.

Assednic looked at Kristella and hung his head to hide his great fear. "We are doomed, unless someone has a way out of this." He sighed as he looked up. He reached out to hold Kristella and embraced her gently. Holding her tight, he could feel her heart race with fear. "Do you think that your great faith in Sifrus's ability to know when we're in trouble could help us once again?" He looked up once more as he whispered: "It's our only hope, I'm afraid!"

Kristella pulled back a little and looked into his eyes, searching for signs of belief. He'd never before thought that Sifrus could help them from so far away, wherever he was. His eyes were different now. Although scared, they were warm, compassionate. "You really believe that Sifrus can help us, don't you?"

He hesitated for a moment and then gently said, "I'm really trying."

"Okay, guys, what do we do?" cried Jiltu. "These monsters are coming at us pretty fast."

"What's that sound of wings I hear? Listen ... above us. I heard it earlier when Kristella charged at the toelions down the mountain," Jiltu said as he looked toward the sky, a little confused.

Kristella and Assednic were still holding hands, not wanting to leave the tender moment and worried that it could be their last. "I do hear something fluttering," said Assednic. "How about you, Kris?" (He'd started calling her this shorter name to make her feel closer to him.)

She listened for a short time but couldn't hear anything above the increasing noise coming up the mountain. "Let's get inside quickly and discuss our next move with the others."

"What's happening?" Chlorise cried out as they entered the cave. She was shaking and holding the children tightly to protect them, as was Soris, with her blanket over their shoulders to keep them warm.

Jiltu looked at Assednic and Kristella. He frowned and then, with great concern on his face, waved his hand toward the entrance as he said, "They're coming and will arrive soon."

Soris looked at him with fear in her eyes. "The children ... what shall we do? Can we run? Hide? Escape? Fight? What? There must be something; we can't give up."

"We're trapped," said Assednic, looking around and searching for something — anything, any way out. "I'd hoped they wouldn't come after us with this much snow on the mountaintop and just leave us in peace for the winter, but I guess that was wishful thinking."

Kristella was listening to them frantically discussing their predicament. "We can't kill them, for we don't have any weapons, and our belief in love for all won't allow for it. Could we make an avalanche somehow to scare them?"

"But how can we, and with what?" sighed Jiltu, now with his head hung down, contemplating their fate.

"Okay then," said Kristella, "we have no other options. Let's all hold hands and in our hearts cry out to King Sifrus for help. It's worked before when we were in trouble, even though you don't totally believe it, but what do we have to lose? Sifrus did say that if we really need him, he would somehow hear us and help us, no matter where he was."

They all looked at each other with puzzled faces, but they knew that Kristella had a trust in Sifrus beyond normal, and they couldn't deny some of the strange things that had been happening.

"Let's do this," they all agreed, and for the next few moments they were one, holding hands and crying out to Sifrus to help them. They didn't know how, but they hoped there were powers beyond their understanding that could get them out of their impossible situation.

Their minds drifted to different events and some fond memories of their time with Sifrus. There were beautiful memories and stories of his father, kingdoms, and strange worlds where love for others was supreme. Some of them envisioned Sifrus travelling to worlds beyond their imagination, but one thing was for real—being together as one was very comforting, and a sense of some strange power seemed to flow amongst them.

Breaking their moment of pure peace, Assednic said, "It will soon be dark; let's go have one last look while we can still see where the climbers are and determine if there's any hope for a rescue."

Except for the children, they all reluctantly went outside to look below. A beautiful starlit sky greeted them as the darkness fell on the mountaintop. They heard shouts, screams, and roars coming from their attackers, almost upon them now. They were terrified, as they knew the end was at hand.

"What shall we do?" Chlorise screamed, now almost hysterical.

Jiltu shouted, "Try pushing large chunks of snow over the edge. Maybe we can start an avalanche, even if it does seem impossible."

Pushing and throwing chunks of snow wasn't working, as several toelions were suddenly on a ledge just across from them. The riders on the toelions shouted to the other climbers: "There they are! We have them now!"

"No! No!" screamed Kristella as she looked at her friends in desperation. "Sifrus!" She screamed so loudly, it echoed throughout the mountains and the whole valley.

Everybody, including their attackers, stopped. Time stood still as the echo finished off in the far, distant mountains. Suddenly the stars disappeared, and it became very dark. Without warning, a thunderous sound of wings was heard coming over the mountaintop. A large creature with eight wings and two heads appeared, terrifying everyone who saw it. Its many eyes on both heads were like fire and were studying every creature, almost as if it could penetrate each one and sense their internal thoughts and feelings. It suddenly screamed a horrifying sound, knocking the riders off their creatures. It began moving its wings so fast, huge drifts of snow were knocked from the mountaintop, taking everything in their path as huge avalanches came from all over.

"Quick!" shouted Assednic. "Get in the cave as fast as possible!"

Running as fast as they could, falling and pulling each other from all the shaking and noise, they just made the rock cave face when all the snow behind them disappeared with a thunderous crash and blocked their entrance. Trembling and holding onto each other in a safe corner of the cave, they waited in silence.

The rumbling of snow crashing down the side of the mountain created a tremendous noise and could be heard for a long distance. They were terrified, but eventually things got eerily quiet.

Jiltu and Soris were locked together, covering the children. "Are you all right?" she asked, with a little look of hope in her eyes.

"Yes, I'm okay. How about the children?"

The children looked up from under the blankets. "We're okay too, Mommy and Daddy," came two small voices sounding very scared.

"Mom, what was all that noise?"

Soris looked at them and smiled to help them overcome their fear. "It's only snow falling down the mountain. Don't worry, we'll be safe now."

Chlorise was still shaking as she looked at Kristella and tried to speak. "What was that large, winged creature? I've never seen anything like it before."

Kristella looked at Assednic, who was holding her so tightly it was beginning to hurt her arm. He just gasped and shook his head. "Wow! What was all that?"

"Jiltu, do you know?" she asked with much bewilderment in her eyes.

"I've never ..." he hesitated then looked toward the doorway, as if to ensure the creature wasn't there. "I've never seen anything like that! It may have helped us, though. Those avalanches probably wiped our pursuers off the mountain. Those who survive, if any, won't likely try again, assuming some of them saw the creature on the mountaintop."

"Well," said Kristella, who was shaking heavily, "me neither! But that leaves the question: Did it come to help us or to destroy us? And is it going to stay here?"

Assednic pondered the question for a few moments, looking at the others intently. "We are all alive, yes. They're probably gone, and we were helped, either way you consider it. But why by a strange creature we've never seen before?"

Jiltu spoke excitedly. "Maybe it was Kristella's final, desperate scream to Sifrus. You have to admit, that was some scream she put out. And besides, she seems to have some kind of thing going on with him. Imaginary or not, strange things are surely happening around us."

The noise outside finally ended, and all was eerily silent. All of their eyes were on the entrance. Would anything try to enter? Was it all over for sure?

After several minutes, Jiltu moved and said, "Stay here, all of you, while I dig away the snow from the entrance and go outside to check out the situation. There's a small tunnel just behind you to hide in, just in case they're still there. Assednic will lead you to a safe place if anything happens to me."

"No," said Assednic. "You have the children to care for. I'll clear the entrance!" He quickly got up and moved toward it. No one tried to stop him, as it was too late and he was already digging the snow away with his hands and feet.

They all held their breath as Assednic pushed a large block of snow outward and a dull light shone in. Slowly peering out, he could see that the stars were again shining, and a beautiful, golden moon had come up, and sparkling rays of light were dancing off the beautiful, snow-capped mountain peaks all around as far as he could see. Just for moment, he saw a streak of light go across the sky, and he heard what sounded like a distant sound of wings, but he thought it was just his eyes and ears playing tricks on him.

Spectrum thought back to the incident in which the zeracks had helped save Kristella and her friends a short time ago. He had looked at Starid as he picked up a small arrow of shining light and threw it at the snow on the mountain where several toelions and riders where attacking his friends. The arrow had exploded and the snow collapsed, sending the toelions and riders down the mountain to a deep ravine below.

As the snow cleared, they could see some of the mountain zells and Kristella with her friends, safe from their attackers. Spectrum had cried, "I'm here. I'm okay! I'm okay! Can't you see me?"

"Your friends," said Taurus, "can't see or hear you."

"Why not?" asked Spectrum "I'm right here in front of them."

"Yes, you are," whispered Starid, "but when we caught you as you rolled off the ledge, you entered our phase."

"What does that mean?" Spectrum asked, unsure if he really wanted to know.

"Don't worry," smiled Starid as his wings fluttered and his face shone in beautiful splendour, "we have one more task, and then we're finished here. You'll understand soon.

"Come, follow me," waved Tarus with his wing. "You need some rest while we go for our next assignment."

He soon came to a small opening where a soft bed of down feathers awaited him.

"There's some drink for you on the stand; it will strengthen you." He moved quickly and was gone in a flash.

Spectrum took a swig of the most delicious drink he'd ever tasted and fell into the soft down, unable to move. He tried to sleep, but his mind raced with all that was happening. *How could this be?* he thought. *Why can't my friends see me? Will I see them again? What am I now? Where am I going? I wonder ... I wonder.* He dozed off for a while into a beautiful sleep.

It seemed like only a moment and he was startled awake by a very loud scream. Running to Tarus and Starid, he quickly asked what had happened. He looked all around and could see many riders on toelions and grogs coming up the mountain in hot pursuit of his friends near the caves on the mountaintop.

"There," pointed Tarus, "near the cave entrance." The great perad looked back in acknowledgement and gave a loud scream as it started moving its wings swiftly, knocking snow from the top of the mountain and causing avalanches to thunder down the mountain, taking all the creatures with them.

Running into the cave, Spectrum could see Kristella and Assednic with some others enter before the avalanche hit. "Was this your other assignment?" He looked at Starid, now signalling the great perad to break off the attack and fly upward and out of sight.

Starid pointed up to the sky. "Do you now understand that we are not from here?" We come from far, far away and came to help Sifrus's friends, wherever they may be. We are not to be seen interfering with everyday events on most planets. Our assignments are only in the case of emergencies, where the followers of *Love* are under attack. You have witnessed us rescue your friends at the request of King Sifrus and his father.

"What about me? Can I go to my friends?" he asked with pleading eyes, a little upset by what he had just witnessed.

Starid looked at Tarus with a little frown, and Tarus nodded back. "You see, you are like us now. You're different, in a different phase. Besides, we're returning with you to a much better place on our home planet of Heveris, where you will see Sifrus again."

Starid called to the great perad: "We're finished here. Fly home, my friend!"

Instantly, they streaked off through the skies, leaving only a flash of light behind.

Δ PEACEFUL WINTER

ASSEDNIC STOOD OUTSIDE THE CAVE ENTRANCE, STARING UP AT THE STARS in absolute silence. He wondered deep in his being about the many other civilizations he had never been to. Were they a lot like his? Were they loving and peaceful? Or were they filled with violence and evil? All those lights in the sky, the mystery of the universe—and Sifrus up there somewhere trying to help as many as possible believe in his teaching of *Love*. He raised his hand toward the night sky and closed his eyes for a moment.

"Thank you," he whispered with a deep sense of longing in his low voice.

He closed his eyes and focused on Sifrus. "Oh King Sifrus, I wish you never had to leave us to go to distant places while we to had to deal with an evil leader bent on destroying all your wonderful teachings of *Love*. I know you're needed by many desperate civilizations that no longer believe in your teachings and have caused much harm to their environments.

"I'm not sure if you know this, but we're being pursued up this mountain by the evil followers of Monton Repa, who has proclaimed himself absolute leader in your absence. We wouldn't follow him, and I fear he may kill us if we're captured. I hope you can return soon to help us."

"Are you okay?" Kristella's soft but concerned voice came from behind him.

Startled a little, he re-focused on where he was as her soft arms wrapped around him. "Yes, I'm okay now, thanks to you." He squeezed her close as strong emotions flooded his whole being with his love for her.

"Were you thinking about Sifrus?" She smiled.

"Yes! I wish he were here with us to strengthen and protect us from these evil pursuers. He always knew how to resolve disputes and conflict with his loving ways and teachings. I can easily see why we all wanted to make him our king."

"Yeah, I miss him very much also. He just had that beautiful way of calming us, regardless of difficult circumstances. He may be physically far away, but he's very close in our hearts. He'll find a way to help us whenever we need him." She squeezed him tightly again to reassure him.

Chlorise came out of the cave entrance, looking a little tentative, not knowing what to expect any more in a world gone mad. She looked at the two of them wrapped tightly together. "Hey, you love birds, celebrating already, are we?" She slowly looked up at the ledges above and around them to see if there were any remaining vicious animals of any kind. She began to relax a little when she realized they were safe, at least for now.

"Is it okay to bring the children out?" Jiltu looked around, his voice a little strained as he walked toward the group. He was holding the hands of two little children who were trying to hide behind him. Coming behind them with a piece of wood held tightly in her hands for protection was Soris, with a concerned look on her face. She also shifted her eyes all over the place, looking for danger.

"It seems safe enough," said Kristella as she blushed and broke away from her passionate hug with Assednic. She smiled as she bent down by the children to reassure them. "It's okay, don't be scared; here, hold my hand," she said as she held it out toward them. Some time passed before a little hand came to meet hers. As they touched gently, a strange surge of warm energy went through her hand and up her whole arm. Listy smiled and then pulled back and hid her hand in the blanket that was still wrapped around them.

What was that? How extraordinary, thought Kristella as she continued to smile at Listy. *I've felt that sensation before ... a long time ago when I was very young. King Sifrus had come to visit our home. He was a young man himself, and as he walked in, he picked me up and said he loved me, but then as his hand held mine, this warm feeling, almost like a little stinging sensation, went through my arm and radiated through my whole body, tingling and pulsating.*

Assednic was now speaking to the whole group and explaining their situation for the winter months. "It seems that this cave will be our home for the winter, unless something happens to change our present situation. At least we're all together and safe!" He hesitated as he could see a tear forming in Kristella's eyes. "Except for our dearest friend," his voice whispered off. "Spectrum." He knew that they were all hoping he had survived the fall and would catch up with them later, even though they assumed he had died.

They stayed outside enjoying each other's company and watching all the lights in the beautiful, clear night sky. At all times they stayed alert to any sound that may come from the valley below. For now, all remained eerily quiet. The avalanche had stopped and done its death roll, removing all the despicable creatures that were so bent on destroying them. They were now buried underneath mountains of snow in the valley below, where the avalanche ended its cascade.

"How sad," whispered Kristella. She peered over the rocky ledge of the mountain and looked down to the valley where the creatures were buried under the snow. "All of those creatures and followers had to die for an evil leader seeking power for his own glory. And here we are also marooned on a cold, desolate mountain with little supplies to survive, maybe to never see our homes and families again."

"What now?" asked Soris as she finally dropped the piece of wood she was carrying. She cringed as she took one more look around the mountain edges, just to be satisfied there were no more creatures coming to hurt them.

Jiltu looked around. "Well, there's not much else we can do out here, so we better get inside and start checking these tunnels to determine what supplies are available to sustain us through a long, cold winter."

"Good idea. We certainly can't go back home for a while, and besides, we need a plan for how we're going to deal with Monton Repa and his followers." A shiver went up Assednic's spine as he continued to look intently at the many lights twinkling in the clear sky above them.

Kristella seemed to be oblivious to the conversation going on around her. Suddenly, she looked at each of them, as if searching for something. "It's not us!" she quickly said with a surprised look on her face.

Assednic looked at her, confused. "It's not us what?"

She waved her hands toward the sky. "Destroy *Love*, not us."

They all looked at each other with puzzled faces, wondering if she was beginning to lose her mind.

"What are you talking about?" asked Soris, trying to concentrate on the conversation and care for the children at the same time.

"We were almost captured, or worse, just a short time ago!" exclaimed Jiltu. "And if it wasn't for the avalanches and strange creatures … you mean …"

"Exactly!" shouted Kristella excitedly. "He wants to destroy what we stand for, not necessarily us."

"Why all this effort to get us then? We've already left the city and isolated ourselves here in the mountains." Jiltu looked around at the group with great concern in his eyes.

Assednic was beginning to get the picture as he casually looked around at the group. "We are a danger to him as long as we're free to teach our message of *Love* for all. He also knows that we have access to powers he doesn't understand through our allegiance to King Sifrus."

"Yes," exclaimed Kristella, "he wants to destroy the teachings of *Love* completely, because it's a threat to his rule. He'll also try to destroy Sifrus when he returns from his travels."

Chlorise was trying to hang on to every word as she frantically studied the faces of Kristella and Assednic. "We have no help or weapons for this fight, and our ability to change our circumstances is limited. We're doomed to remain on this mountain, or die if we go back!" She was shaking, and it seemed as though she would lose control of her emotions at any moment.

Kristella was keenly aware that a fair amount of anxiety was building among their tight- knit group that needed to somehow be quieted if they were to move forward and deal with their situation. She moved quickly to try and calm everyone.

"Look to the heavens," she said as she pointed above their heads. "Sifrus is up there somewhere. He has never failed us before and will not fail us now; be strong and don't doubt him. Search your heart, and you will feel his presence for your continued journey. Feel your chest as your heart beats; its very power to beat comes from a source greater than ours, and he will provide even greater powers than we know or understand."

Soris looked up at Kristella and tried to form a smile. "We know that Sifrus loves us and will help us if he can, but we really are in an impossible situation and have to be serious about other options. We know that the power of *Love* is very strong, but Monton Repa is scared of its reality, even though he doesn't understand its true power. He has the power of his great following, and I fear that as his power grows, nothing or nobody will stop him from getting full control of our beautiful home planet."

"Ahh, I see." Kristella slowly turned away and looked across at the jagged crevasse of the Mountain ledges to see another beautiful eagle swoop across the valley with such ease, it hardly moved its huge wings. "Look at that huge bird glide so easily; nothing is impossible if we know how to use the powers that surround us. Sifrus and the teaching of *Love* are the greatest powers of the universe and will not fail us against these enemies."

She smiled as they all watched the eagle in silence. "The army will come in the spring when the snow melts. We are now their enemies, for we will be blamed for the many deaths of their followers in the avalanche. They also want us to stop spreading the message of *Love*. We must survive to stop this evil takeover of our loving civilization. We have no options!"

"But how do we do this?" cried Jiltu. "They have so many followers and so much power!" He looked around and pointed. "We have nothing!"

"No! No, that is not so. We have power, much power. We have seen many examples of it. If only we knew when and how it works," sighed Assednic as he looked intently at Kristella.

Kristella could sense them all looking at her. "It's not me," she quickly said as she pointed up at the stars. "It comes from there. It seems to come from my connection to Sifrus and his teaching of *Love* for us all. It's most prevalent when we seem to be in trouble and are most desperate for help."

"It's getting very cold out here," interrupted Soris. "Can we go inside with the children and get a warm fire going while we try to figure out what to do next?"

"Look!" shouted Assednic. "What are those strange birds coming toward us from the valley? Are they some sort of eagle?"

"No—no," gasped Jiltu. "Run—run—run to the caves. They're clicker birds! Very deadly; don't let them bite or scratch you. I'll hold them off with this piece of wood until you all get inside. Cover your heads, here they come!"

"Look out, Jiltu, there are two just above you." Assednic pulled off his coat and swung at the clicker bird just as it scratched at Jiltu's head. He brought it down under his coat and crushed its head with his knee. "Come, run this way to the entrance; all the folks are safe inside."

"Come … come," screamed Kristella, waving her hands frantically. "Behind you! Jiltu, jump down, before …"

"Oh—oh my back! It's stinging like it's on fire." Jiltu fell to the snow, unable to move a muscle.

Assednic grabbed the piece of wood and swung at the bird, hitting and breaking its leg, which was on Jiltu's back. It screamed and flew off with just one leg hanging as the other two birds got scared and flew away with it. "Jiltu! Are you hurt?"

Jiltu tried to get up but just fell back in the snow. "My back is burning and my strength is fading. I can't make it to the entrance."

"Stay awake! Don't worry, I'll drag you in. Push with your legs if you can; we're almost there. Just a few more feet. Kristella, open the entrance door, grab Jiltu's arm, and pull him in before those birds come back. Okay, we're in! Shut the door quickly," said Assednic as he fell to the floor, exhausted.

Soris came running to Jiltu. "Honey, are you okay?" She wrapped her arms around him to discover that the back of his coat was torn. "Quickly, get his coat and shirt off. Oh no," she gasped, "there's a deep scratch that's bleeding on his back. Get some dressings and any type of ointment with an antibacterial agent in it."

"Oh, it's burning like fire." Jiltu moaned in pain. He was beginning to lose consciousness, and his mind was playing tricks on him. *How did this happen?* he thought as he began to become groggy. *We were ready to go into our protected caves for a wonderful rest for the winter. Someone is calling me to come up the mountain. I can hear the voice. It sounds familiar, but it's a long way off, maybe at the crest.*

"Jiltu! Come up to where we are. You know the way; you have been here before. Remember the snow cloud. It will show you to the entrance."

His mind was racing. *The snow cloud? That was so long ago. We got lost in that cloud. How can I go there without getting lost again? But there seems to be a strong force pulling me forward*, he thought.

"I'm on my way," he said, "just keep guiding me when I get to the entrance so I won't get lost again." He moaned and tried to see from where the voice was coming.

Soris looked at Assednic with a blank stare. "What is he talking about? Jiltu, don't go to sleep; stay awake!"

"There, that's better," said Kristella as she finished covering the wound with a sterile bandage. "Let's get him over to the couch near the fire to keep him comfortable. I don't like the look of that wound; it's swelling pretty badly. These clicker birds—do we know of a cure for infections caused by their scratches?"

Assednic looked at her and tried to hide his fear. "The clicker birds were bred and genetically modified to attack wild animals that had been causing problems for farmers in the wilderness frontiers. I'm not aware of any cases in which people are injured by them, or what would be used for a cure. I fear that we're on our own to figure this one out. Let's just keep him warm and hydrated and see if he can fight this infection on his own for now."

"We'll all have to take turns watching him to ensure he doesn't take a turn for the worse." Kristella glanced tenderly at Soris, who was holding Jiltu's hand and crying softly. "The cave is nice and warm and will be our sanctuary for the cold months to come, so we must not only care for him but each other as well."

She could feel the group's anxiety as they tried to deal with the attacks, the loss of one of their friends, and now the severe injury to their most knowledgeable teammate in these formidable mountains. But as she looked around, she realized that they were at least together, they all loved

Sifrus and his teachings, and they would have a winter of opportunity to get to know each other more intimately and possibly share some of their lives and dreams with each other in safety, if only for a short time.

Assednic looked around at the cave chambers. "The second chamber seems to be the safest, for it has access to the first chamber, where we can post a guard. We can also access all the rear chambers, which will hopefully give us access to safe destinations, extra supplies, and a way of escape if we're attacked." He glanced at Kristella and nodded. "We just need to figure out the combinations or other secrets of opening the chamber doorways for the ones that are sealed."

"This is quite nice," said Chlorise as she walked around the cave chambers. "There are several bunks with petitions for privacy, a fireplace, and some dried food supplies as well as canned and bottled stuff."

"Hey, guess what I found out back near the rock wall," Assednic shouted as he hurried to get inside. "A washroom with supplies. This is truly a place of comfort now!" He chuckled as he closed the door for some privacy.

Kristella moved over to the rock wall and began to study the drawings. "What was mined here?" she asked as she touched the wall.

The washroom door opened and Assednic walked over to her, looking a little confused by her quick change of thought. He looked around and then touched the wall to find that it felt slippery and glazed. "This rock structure is a little different than most I've encountered. Do you suppose that this mountain with its strange happenings, markings, and mines has anything to do with stories of other creatures that may have come from other worlds to live here? Maybe there's an adventure story here to be discovered." He smiled at her with a sly look of mischievousness.

She smiled back at him with a little gleam of seduction in her voice. "Always looking for adventure, are we?" she said as she leaned over and gave him a passionate kiss, holding back just enough to keep him from getting too excited.

Chlorise entered carrying several packages of supplies. "Hey, you guys, stop all the mushy stuff. These food supplies don't seem to be as old as I expected them to be. How long ago were these mines abandoned?"

"There are many stories of mining activity in these mountains that have been told for a long time, but there doesn't seem to be any written records in the town archives as to when they were abandoned, by whom, or what was mined here." Assednic glanced at Chlorise. "Isn't that weird? I have a strange feeling that there are secrets this mountain has yet to show us. Look at this engraved image of what seems to be an exploding planet and many people fleeing in small vessels from the site. Maybe the miners came from a place like that, or at least witnessed such a disaster."

"Secrets or not, we have to eat. Let's get some of this food prepared before we all starve to death." Chlorise looked over at Soris and said, "Sorry, I didn't mean to be insensitive. How is he doing?" She had always admired Jiltu's strength and determination, and now to see him brought down to this level by a bird was so ironic.

Soris put her hand on his forehead as she listened to him groan with pain deep inside. "He still has a high temperature, but I'm sure he has the strength to fight this," she said, putting her hand in his for comfort. She loved Jiltu with the kind of love that needed no explanation to others. It just permeated her whole being whenever they were together. The time she had lost him for a season to the mountain had been the most difficult and challenging of all the time they'd been married.

They all enjoyed their meal and relished in the atmosphere of pure quiet as they began to relax around the fire for some fellowship and a chance to reflect on the recent events and dangers they'd encountered. All was enchanting as they watched the fire flicker and dance, leaving shades of strange creatures all over the cave walls. Nobody knew how long the winter of rest would last or what dangers the spring would unleash as the snows melted, giving access to them. But for now, at least they were safe.

"You, Kristella, are the reason we're safe," said Chlorise, quietly breaking the silence. "I've never witnessed such bravery, if not craziness, as you have shown. Charging straight at those creatures that were ready to kill you doesn't seem normal to me. Maybe you really have been chosen to help us survive this ordeal and profit from this quest we've been launched on."

"What if that were true?" Kristella continued to study the fire. "Then shouldn't we have the power to help Jiltu, who's maybe fighting for his life? I don't know how to access the powers of life and death, but I do know that there's some power available when we ask Sifrus for help. Let's hold hands and meditate on Sifrus, wherever he is in this big universe, and ask him in any manner you feel comfortable to help Jiltu recover from his injuries."

As they closed their eyes and meditated, a strange feeling moved within them as they sensed a presence that seemed to surround them with a fine glow of light. Jiltu began to stir, and his moaning stopped. Nobody dared to move or open their eyes; something beyond themselves was happening as they basked in the *Love* for each other that was filling every fibre of their bodies. The sense of peace and security had transcended them and enveloped them and Sifrus into one entity, even though he wasn't physically present.

They could almost sense what each was feeling and thinking. The intense feeling of being one entity seemed to strengthen them equally, as if they were gaining strength from each other and especially from Sifrus. They probably would have stayed in that embrace forever and lost all sense of time and need for anything else in their world. But Jiltu suddenly interrupted their time together with a loud cough.

"Hey, you guys, what's going on?" he whispered.

Eyes began to slowly open all around him as the group gradually tried to focus on the reality of where they were and the unbelievable place where they had just been. "Jiltu," shouted Soris, "you look much better. Are you okay?"

Jiltu tried to stand as he moved his hand over the back of his shoulder where he had been scratched by the clicker bird. His legs were a little weak, but the pain in his back and shoulder was definitely gone. "I think you guys have made me well. I could sense all your emotions and requests to Sifrus for me when you were holding hands in your big group hug. It seemed like a source of energy was pulsating around you, and some of it was coming into me and healing my wounds. Weird, I guess." He laughed and shook his head.

They all smiled at Jiltu and each other, knowing that a new and more powerful reality created by their love for each other and Sifrus had transcended anything they knew or understood. This new reality and a more determined sense of devotion to his teachings of *Love* would enable them to understand that the ultimate powers of the universe may not be in weapons, armies, and riches but in *Love*. They may be strong enough through their connection to a more powerful force outside themselves to actually contemplate defeating the evil and insanity going on around them.

"They're right, you know!" A strained voice from Chlorise, who had been very quiet and restrained, suddenly got their attention. "If it wasn't for you, Kristella, we may not even be here now, and definitely we wouldn't have the desire or strength to continue to stay on this difficult mountain, especially since we don't know what disasters it may bring."

"Yes, indeed," came more praise from Soris, Assednic, and even Jiltu, who was sitting up next to Soris and seemingly getting his strength back.

Kristella stared into the flickering fire, quietly trying to regain her composure and reflecting on the difficult situations they'd gotten through. She knew they were depending on her to be strong and wise as she tried to communicate with Sifrus, asking him to guide and strengthen them.

"Well," she said quietly, "you are all very brave too, just to face the harsh climate and uncertain future on this mountain. We've faced many dangers to get this far." She hesitated for a moment. "But you all know that we had help. I believe with all my heart that this help will see us through the many difficulties to come, if we just believe with our whole being."

She looked up for a moment, as if trying to see somebody. "I didn't charge those creatures back there on my own power. I could hear Sifrus's voice inside me, saying: 'Don't be afraid. I'll be with you; go straight at them!' It may sound crazy, I know, but I could feel his presence with us at that moment."

Assednic glanced at the others, trying to read by their expressions how they felt about this revelation. He was concerned that they may begin to think Kristella was losing her mind, or having delusions. "I have no doubt that you're right," he said. "We've seen many examples of power in circumstances where we couldn't have controlled the outcome as it unfolded in our midst." He slowly walked over and gave Kristella a hug to reassure her that they believed in her.

"But how does it work?" asked Soris, who was shyly looking over at Kristella with big, wide eyes. Soris was a woman of few words, but she intently studied circumstances with a keen eye to how things worked.

Kristella looked around at the inside of the cave. "Look, there are sleeping nooks, storage areas, a large central room with a fireplace, and many beautiful carvings on the shiny walls." She pointed and waved her arms at each part. "This is our safe place while here in the mountains. The miners who did all of this work knew that within this rock cavity they could survive, while outside the storms would blow and the extreme cold would kill them in a short time."

"But what does that mean?" asked Soris, looking a little confused by her answer.

"Well, our circumstances are much the same. This place keeps us safe for now, but when we leave here, we'll need protection from the many storms that face us. While the miners went into the strength and safety of the rock, we must learn to go into the strength and safety of our rock, King Sifrus, who loves us dearly."

Jiltu had been listening intently to the dialogue between the two women. "What Kristella says is true; we won't last in Monton's new world without a power much greater than our own."

"Well, this is really nice," cut in Assednic, "but we really don't know what powers there are, how much is available to us, or how to access them when needed, do we?" He frowned and shook his head.

"That's not really true!" Jiltu was now back to his old self and fully engaged in the conversation. "As you said a few moments ago, we all saw things happen that were beyond our abilities or explanation. Kristella seems to be able to access these powers through her close relationship with Sifrus."

"Interesting," whispered Chlorise as she watched with an inquisitive eye. "We are special, aren't we?"

They all looked at her with blank faces, trying to understand what she meant. It had never occurred to them that they were special. In fact, they thought that if anything, they were outcasts.

"What do you mean by special?" asked Assednic, staring at her with questioning eyes.

"Well, I was listening and thinking that here we are safe and sound because we got help from someone we can't see or touch, with a power we don't understand. Isn't that kind of special?" She looked at them with a new sparkle in her eyes.

"Yeah, I guess," mused Assednic, scratching his head.

Kristella yawned. "Why don't we all get some sleep, and tomorrow we can discuss this further with clear minds."

"Special people need special sleep," laughed Jiltu as he curled up on a cot next to Soris and the children.

"Mommy, are we special too?" asked Hasic, who was holding Listy's hand and smiling as he looked up at her.

"Yes, of course, you both are very special," she said as she hugged them tight. "Go to sleep now!"

Kristella rolled over and snuggled into Assednic, who was already sound asleep. Immediately she closed her eyes due to exhaustion from their long ordeal, as did all the others. She dreamed of flying through various worlds of strange beings of all descriptions, many she had never seen before or could even imagine in a normal state of mind, but in her dream they looked so real. She hoped they existed somewhere. She seemed to be on a large, bird-like creature travelling at extreme speeds with very little effort. A crystal-clear beam of pure white light went before them, showing the way while acting as a power source as it carried them along.

At the end of the light, a large city appeared. It was extremely bright, unlike anything she'd ever seen. Many tiny creatures were streaking out in all directions at unbelievable speeds. *What are they? Are they friendly?* She was very anxious, and her mind raced. Then one of them stopped and waved to her to come with them.

She awakened with a scream; her heart raced as she looked around, rather confused.

Assednic put his arm around her. "Are you okay?" he quietly asked as he stroked her face with his other hand.

Catching her breath, she trembled as she held his hand tight to her face. "I think so," she gasped, trying to regain her composure.

"It was just a dream; we're safe, my love," he whispered, not wanting to disturb anybody else. "Do you want to talk about your dream, if you remember some of it?"

"Sure, it's okay; I'm all right now, just a little shaken. My dream seemed so real, like I was actually there looking at a most beautiful, shining city. There were many strange looking creatures, but I think they were friendly.

I'd like to go there some day if it really exists, for it was so magnificent to behold."

"Let's try to get some sleep again, if you feel you're able. We don't have much time before the others awaken for another day." He yawned and again cuddled into her as they both drifted off into the sweet elixir of total rest.

RETURN TO HEVERIS

THE GREAT WINGED PERAD WAS NEARING THEIR HOME OF HEVERIS. IT HAD been a long distance to travel from Rimshire, but in reference to time it seemed neutral, for time doesn't exist at those speeds. The moment they left Rimshire and arrived at Heveris would be all that Spectrum would remember.

"Where are we?" Spectrum asked as he looked over at his new friends. He stood absolutely still in amazement at the spectacular sight before him.

Starid and Tarus were glowing with excitement as they got nearer to their home. "This is our wonderful home, Heveris. All of our power and love comes from here; see, we become brighter as we approach. You will love it here, our new friend. You are much like us now, and with your deep love for Sifrus, you have many unique and special powers you will learn to use here."

As they came into view, the great winged perad began to sing a melody with such high-pitched sound of intensity and feeling, it caused them all to sing with joy as their hearts were filled with praise for the glory of the place. The intense sound should have hurt their ears, but instead it filled them with an overwhelming joy of being a part of a celestial choir as many other perads, zeracks, and other unrecognizable creatures joined in.

"This sound," cried Spectrum, "it's so beautiful. What does it mean?"

Starid, who was also singing, looked at him and pointed to all the beauty before his eyes. "It's praise to the great king of all you see. Look at its incredible beauty. It can't be comprehended anywhere else, but was put in place by our great king."

Spectrum was absolutely transfixed on the picture before him as he tried to grasp the enormity of its beauty. Everything was glowing with a purity of pristine light—clear as crystal and beyond his ability to describe. He wasn't sure of anything he was seeing, as it was all different than what he was used to on Rimshire. He best described it as fields of gold, forests of silver, and rivers of jewels running through the land. Even the hills looked to be shiny bronze, with many streaks of various-coloured lights dancing above them.

A great celebration was planned for all the newcomers as well as Sifrus, who had also just arrived from his trip to Voart. Tarus and Starid couldn't hold their excitement for the coming event. They knew from past experience that when new citizens arrived in Heveris, it was the best time in the universe.

"Sifrus is here," shouted Starid to Spectrum with glee. "He's just returned with his other loyal followers in his space glider. Come, come this way with us to the beginning of the great celebration, where we will see Sifrus and his father."

The great perad touched gently down to the thunderous singing of all the inhabitants gathered around to welcome them back. He raised his giant wings and opened his back feathers to show a neat trail down his back to his tail, allowing for an easy exit for his travellers.

"Why all this celebrating for just me and a few people who came back with Sifrus?" Spectrum was wide-eyed with the amazing things going on all around him and just couldn't understand any of it.

Starid looked at him, somewhat surprised after all he had explained to him about their journey and rescue mission for him. "Don't you remember what I told you?" He smiled with the warmest glow of peace. "We always celebrate when all who are special return home with us to live forever in this wonderful place of love and peace."

Spectrum was silent for a moment as he pondered the meaning of this revelation. "What do you mean by special and live forever? I don't understand any of these things."

Tarus looked at Starid, and then both of them looked at Spectrum and said simultaneously, "You are special! Only special people can come back here once they're sent out. Don't you know that your seed came from here? We'll explain more a little later, after the celebration."

Spectrum was now totally speechless as he tried to understand. "Come back? Sent out? Special? Wow, this is certainly a strange place."

"Come now, quickly, we must get off while the ramp is in place." Starid waved for them to follow him as they moved through the path leading through the gigantic feathers that had protected them while they travelled to Heveris. The great perad looked back and hissed a sad goodbye as they departed from his back.

A group of tall, friendly creatures met them with a welcome basket of goodies as they approached the ramp. "Welcome," said the tallest one. They all had beaming smiles, and light pulsated around their bodies. "We're here to escort you to our king's Celebration Centre, but first there's time for you to get cleaned up and changed into more suitable attire for the festivities. There's also a refreshment table just over here for you to enjoy at your leisure."

Spectrum tried some of the strange looking foods and was amazed at the wonderful flavours and textures of the many foods offered by his hosts.

"Thank you very much for the wonderful snacks," Spectrum said as he looked at all the mystical creatures flying in the sky all around him. Creatures of all shapes and sizes were glowing and moving with grace, beauty, and fast speeds, yet they seemed able to maneuvre easily without obstructing each other. They all seemed to enjoy beautiful singing as they went about their business.

Occasionally, some great perads would streak away with their zerack riders heading for some distant world where their assistance was required. He'd been the one helped a short time ago, and now it would be some other lucky creature. "They are such wonderful creatures to live and serve here on Heveris, just to help others when in need."

"Yes, indeed," said his tall host. "They are very special in the way they serve without hesitation or worry for their own safety. They are specially designed, as you have seen, to travel through space and time at extreme speeds, yet never causing accidents and never getting lost in this huge universe of endless celestial bodies."

"So when they leave, are they always on a rescue mission to help somebody like me?" Spectrum shook his head in amazement.

"Usually, but not always. Occasionally a resident may need to go back to their home planet if their work wasn't finished before they were rescued. Although they love all the residents, they cannot return with the vast majority of them, because some of them chose not to love each other unconditionally as we do here on Heveris. They would therefore destroy this beautiful place with their evil desires."

"If many of my friends could see this wonderful place and all the pleasures that *Love* has created here, I'm sure they'd want to change their ways and be like you. It's so sad that most do not know the difference and may never get to enjoy this peace and tranquility. Are there creatures from many worlds allowed to come and live here?"

"Oh yes! Of course, all beings are welcome to come here, provided that they have conquered their evil desires and can accept the principals taught by the universal belief and power of *Love.* But, as you know by now, many won't accept this principle and want to continue hurting others by their selfish desire to get more for themselves at the others' expense. Only those who are honourable and pure of heart will make it here, I'm afraid."

Spectrum gasped. "How can so many be so blind to something this beautiful? I just can't fathom how the vast majority of the creatures in this universe can't want to love each other, especially when it means that all of them will have a better life."

Starid looked sad as he turned away for a moment. "We really wish there were more, but we find that as time passes, it seems that less and less are embracing the truths and goodness that the teachings of *Love* support. No matter how many good teachers we send out to proclaim this message, the desire for short term gain and power seems to delude them into thinking that loving others will only impede their selfish desire to gain what they can for themselves."

"Wow! That's really sad. How can this possibly be changed?" Spectrum was desperately hoping that he could help.

"Sadly, there may not be any hope greater than what King Sifrus can offer. He is the final good teacher to be sent. The King of Heveris has decided that his son will be the last. If he can't change the minds of the many he will encounter, then destruction will certainly come. The environmental balances of some beautiful planets will be altered by the many destructive practices carried out by the selfish, evil developers who desire to get rich at any cost."

"Rimshire … Rimshire," he shouted. "This can't happen to this beautiful home of ours." Spectrum's eyes filled with tears as he contemplated the thought of what could possibly happen. "Some are already turning from the teachings of *Love* because of their fear of Monton Repa. I know that their love for King Sifrus is greater, but he's not there, and they're scared that he won't return."

Sifrus's childhood best friend, Karmilita, had heard that he was returning home with some passengers from a small planet called Voart. She'd missed him so much since he'd become old enough to take on a leadership and teaching position on Rimshire. She couldn't wait to see him again. She ran as fast as she could to where his space vessel had landed.

Sifrus looked at Deltric, who was also spellbound by the beauty that surrounded him. "What do you think?" he asked. He smiled, knowing that Deltric's mind was probably going in many directions at once.

"How can this exist? It's beyond description. Nothing here have I ever seen before. It's like a glowing Fantasy Land that we have on our home planet for children to play in, but this whole place is fabulous." Deltric stuttered as he tried to put into words what his eyes were seeing but not necessarily believing.

Sifrus continued to smile with delight as he studied the excitement and bewilderment on his face. But then his mind had slipped elsewhere. "Karmilita is probably waiting for me! Oh, I have missed her so much while I've been away on Rimshire."

"Who is Karmilita?" Deltric slowly asked as he turned to see that Sifrus was no longer looking at him, but instead was looking off in the distance.

Suddenly, they heard a loud scream as a stunningly beautiful creature came flying straight into the arms of Sifrus, knocking him over on the ground. They rolled and held each other tightly, as if they were bonded by a force that held them together without exerting any energy. They began to rise above the ground, astonishing the onlookers. Their eyes were locked on each other in a trance that seemed to allow them to look inside their exterior being.

"You're here; I can't believe you have returned. I missed you so much," she cried as they broke contact and slowly dropped back to the ground.

"Karmilita! I've missed you so much… maybe too much. It actually hurts to be so far from you when I travel. It's wonderful to see your beautiful face again, to embrace your being and transfer my feelings through you as we did when we were together as best friends." He spoke so tenderly and continued to study her eyes with such passion, one would think they were physical mates. Time stood still. Nobody dared to speak and spoil the very tender moment for the two soul mates who were communing with each other in a way that defied any explanation

"So this is Karmilita," Deltric whispered to Creathe, as he was still in awe of the warmth and beautiful glowing light that seemed to surround them both.

Creathe slowly turned and looked at Deltric with some confusion in her expression. "But what is she?" She looked back at Karmilita, who was glowing with long, golden hair and a small horn protruding from her forehead that was surrounded by the prettiest sparkling jewels she had ever seen. Her legs were extremely long, and her arms were partially winged on the back when spread out. "I've never seen anything like her on Voart."

"You are my Sevron forever," Sifrus said in a loving voice as he finally released her from his embrace. He looked a little embarrassed when he realized that everybody had been watching their passionate re-connection, knowing that he couldn't help himself after such a long time apart. But now it didn't matter, for once one has made contact with their Sevron, all thoughts and emotions are fully focused on the bond between them. In an instant they become one, transmitting all feelings for each other in a complicated process of transfusion of energy that envelops their whole being in a connection impossible to describe or break. It is an "out of their own body experience" that can only take place in an atmosphere of pure love, where there is no contamination of one's feelings for another.

"Okay, okay, enough of this mushy stuff." A deep voice broke the silence as Trifum came through the crowd, reaching out to embrace Sifrus with an elbow lock of deep friendship. He held him tightly. "My best friend, I have also missed you very much."

He thought back fondly to the days when they travelled together to the Duram rocks, where they could ask questions of great importance about their future plans. The speaking rocks were very wise, for they had never moved and had much time to study and reflect on issues that affected the many worlds that surrounded them. People from all over would come to them for the advice and wisdom that was contained within the depths of their internal memory banks. But best of all was the peace and tranquility that surrounded the sessions in their presence. Sifrus would ask some profound question for which there didn't seem to be any answers. He would look over at him and wink his eye, as if to say, "I have fooled them this time." Only a short period of time would pass and then the rocks would begin a long, detailed explanation, with knowledge and reasoning that was usually very enlightening and sometimes impossible to understand.

They would usually laugh as they ran off after each session, pretending that they understood the profound information. They would then go into the surrounding fields to play some crazy game they'd made up, content just to be together. *Those were very good times*, he thought as a tear trickled down his cheek, unnoticed by Sifrus.

Cheers came from everywhere as the inhabitants from all over Heveris arrived to welcome them back with their new guests. A great celebration was about to begin as the skies lit up with many colours of cascading light beams going in all directions.

"There is an extra special surprise for you," smiled Trifrum as he slowly released Sifrus from his embrace. Whirldwind arrived from Rimshire just before you got here."

Sifrus looked at him, a little startled. "Rimshire? I felt some pulses of trouble this past little while as I travelled, but I couldn't quite decipher the main issue. The disturbances on Voart blocked the message somewhat. What has happened?" He knew that Whirldwind would not have gone unless there was trouble and a special rescue was needed. "I sent out my *Love* pulses to my followers, just in case they were in trouble."

Trifrum could sense the anxiety building inside Sifrus, so he said quickly: "All is well with your friends. One of your best friends, Spectrum, is here to be with us. He's resting at the moment but will be ready to see you at the celebration. I'm sure he has lots to tell you about what's happening on Rimshire in your absence."

"Spectrum," mused Sifrus. "He's one of the strongest followers of the teachings of *Love* and has been steadfast in ensuring that others know the importance of these teachings. If he has returned here with Whirldwind, that only means one thing—there is much trouble on Rimshire."

Karmilita took his hand and smiled very gently as she tried to console him, "Don't worry, things will work out. Your father is on his way back here to welcome you and Whirldwind back with the Botkins you returned with, as well as the rescuers Starid and Tarus. Come and let us get officially prepared for him." She looked straight into his eyes. "He is very proud of you."

The King of Heveris had left his Celestial Planning Centre and was on his way to the great hall to ceremonially welcome them all back with their new friends. This was always a very special occasion for him, because although he had spent an enormous amount of resources to help those living all across the galaxy, only a few would get to return and live in this peaceful and most loving place.

As the king entered the great hall, a spectacular light show exploded in all directions. Small and large creatures streaked through the expanse above them in all directions, singing as loudly as they could a beautiful, intoxicating melody that filled all corners and seemed to extend even beyond what was visible. The presence of *Love* and joy surrounded them like a soft blanket, holding them warm and secure in a wondrous feeling that seemed outside of themselves.

Deltric was with Sifrus and was absolutely mystified as he held Creathe tightly to him, as if to protect her from this strange yet stunningly beautiful place. "Are you feeling better now?" he asked as he smiled down at her, with a glow in his eyes she'd never noticed before.

She squeezed him even closer and slowly smiled back at him. "How could I be anything else in this place?"

"Come quickly," Sifrus said with excitement in his voice. "We must get ready to meet my father and his welcoming party. They'll be here shortly. Jarock and Seili, would you please bring the young ones, for he is especially fond of them. Come this way!" He pointed to a pulsating archway surrounded by beautiful, silver, nicely pruned trees. Through the archway was a quickly-moving trail covered in jewels. It changed directions constantly as many creatures stood on it to get to their individual destinations.

Seili hesitated, not sure if she should step on the trail. The children instantly jumped on, screaming with excitement as they streaked around in a fast loop back to where they started. "Come, Mom, it's fun," they screamed with delight.

"It's okay." Sifrus smiled as he held out his hand to hold her steady. Jarock followed, and instantly they were in a large hall that was filled with shiny robes of all sizes and shapes floating in rows and constantly moving to show all sides and profiles for individual taste or interest.

"How do we get one if we like it?" Seili asked with her eyes wide with excitement. "I've never seen anything like this. For a shopping experience of all time, this is it."

Sifrus studied her eyes and softly smiled. "This is pretty cool, isn't it? All you have to do is lock your eyes on the one you want and say, 'This one,' and it will instantly fit itself around you."

"Yes, this is fantastic," shouted Deltric. "Look at this shiny new robe that has attached itself to me. What do you think?" He danced and twirled with delight, as if he were a youth again showing off his first new coat in many years.

"Wow," Creathe said as she studied his new robe. "It's so beautiful and seems to make you shine sparkly all over your body. Your face is shining brighter than I've ever seen."

Deltric couldn't help but blush a little as he began to realize the truths and wonders of the place. He looked over at Sifrus, who was smiling from ear to ear, and asked him, "How does all of this work?"

Sifrus looked around and then up at the sky as he waved his hand before him to show the expanse that was stretched out in endless arrays of lights. "You see that all is different here; there is no darkness or impurity of any kind. The power of *Love*, light, purity, and goodness fill and transcend all that belongs here.

"You will learn that many of the limitations and desires you had on Voart no longer apply here. Your desires will all be met, provided that your motives are pure, much like this robe that has attached to your body. You liked that robe, so it was made available to you, as your pure thoughts created the power to have it."

"What do you mean?" Jarock, who was listening from the corner, asked. "Can we have anything we ask for without having to work for it?" He turned to look at the others with a sigh of disbelief in his tone.

Karmilita was also listening and itching to show them many wonderful things about their new home. "Of course we can," she said with a wonderful sound of glee, "but work is different here. It's not really work to us, because our time spent at it is fun. Look at something I can do," she said excitedly as she moved behind a wall of gems in the corner. "Watch me move through this wall to the other side. Here I am," came a voice instantly behind them as they stood still, looking at where she had been. They all turned in amazement to see her smiling and not hurt from her passage through the solid wall.

"But how—how did you do that?" gasped Fatemee, standing with her mouth wide open and staring in disbelief.

"Here we only have to close our eyes, focus on where we want to go, and instantly we are there, regardless of obstacles. They're not in our way, because we pass through them."

"Your world! Sifrus's powers! It's all so much to comprehend for us. We are your servants now and owe our lives to Sifrus," Fatemee mumbled with a great deal of emotion in her voice.

"No, no!" shouted Sifrus. "We're all equal here. We live in harmony to help and love every creature, regardless of colour, size, or original home planet. You will all love it here; the peace and beauty transcend your understanding as only could be dreamed or imagined on your previous planet."

"Are we really here in this beautiful place, or is this just a wonderful dream that we will soon awaken from?" Creathe asked with desperation and a pleading in her eyes for confirmation that this may just be possible.

Deltric slowly looked toward Sifrus as a little smile began to form on his face. A quick nod from Sifrus sealed it in his heart to be true. He looked back at Creathe and then approached her, placing his hands on her shoulders as he looked deep into her eyes. "We are! We are really here." He tenderly embraced her, bringing her close to his body and sending streaks of passion and a feeling of security through both of them.

"What's happening to us?" she quietly whispered to Deltric. She held him tightly and allowed the sweet elixir of intense feelings to flood their whole being beyond their natural abilities to separate, as if they had become one. They read their thoughts and love for each other, which were transferring freely between them.

Karmilita was all aglow as she watched them gradually open their eyes and slowly separate a little. "See, I told you … I told you it's much different here and that your feelings are much stronger. Your ability to love, communicate, and feel for each other is much more intense."

"Wow," Deltric shouted as he stepped back a little. He seemed rather embarrassed as he looked at the others, who were watching them.

Fris, the youngest of the children, was blushing at his mom and dad, who were now rather blushed themselves.

"Hey, you guys, stop staring already!" Creathe grabbed a beautiful robe and went into a small room to try it on the old-fashioned way rather than wrapping it around her by her thoughts. It also gave her a chance to break away from the peering eyes that had watched them during their personal emotional encounter a few moments ago.

"You look radiant!" A voice startled her, and she saw Seili, wide-eyed, looking at her from the corner. "That is the most beautiful suit, and it's glowing to match your new glow that that seems to have become part of everything around our new, pristine home."

"You know what they say: 'Those of a pure heart become part of the fabric of the robe and all that surrounds them.' This place is certainly different and wonderful beyond words."

"I don't really understand," Seili said, looking at the glowing white robe. She looked again at Creathe, who was still smiling at her to remove any doubt she may have. "This all seems so real yet so unbelievable at the same time."

Creathe gave her a thumbs up and said, "If it's a dream, it sure is a crazy good one! Let's get back to the others and see what else is in store for us to fully enjoy." She gave her a big hug and led her outside in her new, glowing robe.

Seili hesitated at the last second and glanced back once more at the reflection in the mirror. *Is it really me?* she thought and then pinched herself to check. "Ouch! It's me all right. Wow! What will this place have to offer next?"

SERVAN-HOW TO RESTORE

RICKTER LOOKED AT HIS SATELLITE SCREEN WITH A PUZZLED FROWN. "THERE!" he pointed to a small light blinking on his screen outside the area where their galaxy charts ended. "The chaser is outside our charted known worlds," he said as he glanced at the screen again in disbelief. "It's a wonder the signal is strong enough to return at that great distance. I wonder what is out there. Who is out there, so far away?"

Deman's private phone startled him as it rang, interrupting his thoughts about the many problems on his Servan.

"Rickter reporting, sir. I have the update on Sifrus, as you requested."

"Well done! Quickly, what is your report concerning his whereabouts?" Deman said excitedly, as his interest in Sifrus was becoming an obsession.

"We received a very weak signal from our chaser from the last vessel to leave our system. It probably won't be able to continue sending signals at that extreme distance. This is very strange, don't you think?"

Deman hesitated before answering as he thought it through. "Yes! Very strange indeed! You have done well, but do some more checking on all activities and contacts he may have on Rimshire, especially his closest friends and family, and give me a report as soon as possible."

"Will do. Rickter over and out for now." He whispered to himself. "This Sifrus that Deman is so interested in … it's like an obsession. He's obviously very special and seems to have advanced technology to be able to travel outside our systems. What else is there to find concerning this person?"

Deman hung up his phone, walked to his mirror, and looked at his reflection. "Well, at least my voice is returning, and I'm still alive, which gives me a slight chance of getting this planet back in order before it becomes unsuitable for life. Actually, I think I do look a bit better now that I know what I must do. I'll need wisdom to change things, but where will I get this if I can't make contact with this Sifrus of Rimshire?

"There's still time, I hope, but things are getting bad faster than we expected. Maybe there isn't time, but I have to try. Seles, Seles, I need your help to get my suit of shatel on. I can't risk another dart ripping into my body, or next time I may not …" He hesitated and then stopped as he looked at Seles.

Seles looked at him and frowned as she lifted his suit to his shoulders.

"Oh, my shoulder," he grimaced. "It still really hurts. Be careful, as it pulls on my chest area and may reopen the wound."

She gently placed the shatel over his body and snapped the locks without him even feeling her hands gently working. "There, my love, all done and covering you just right, without even being noticeable under your shirt," she said as she tried to hide her fear. "Are you sure you're up to this?" She glanced away, not sure how he would react to her question. She always knew her place with him, and that as a leader he tolerated no dissension. She looked directly into his eyes. "Be careful out there, for whoever tried to kill you may attempt it again." She kissed him tenderly.

Rickter studied the small blip on his galaxy screen on the very edge of his monitor. "I wonder," her frowned, "why does Deman need this Sifrus found so badly? He never needed advice from anybody in the past. Why now? Are we in real trouble with this dust situation, and he doesn't know how to fix it? Maybe there's a side deal going on that he's not sharing with us. His injury—who would want him dead? Maybe this is all connected somehow." He massaged the back of his neck, which was very tense.

He looked around at the spacious State Centre with all of its equipment, screens, and work centres for its ingenious employees. People were so busy with their particular projects that they didn't seem to have time to even notice what the others were doing, if they even cared. "Is our work here at the centre in jeopardy? If we find this Sifrus, will he interfere with what we do here? Our wealth that we derive from mining faldacore may have to be curtailed. I have a responsibility to my partners to ensure that this never happens, no matter what the cost!"

Rickter made his way to the vault to look at the original request for Sifrus to come to their aid. He inserted his pass code and was denied access. *That's strange*, he thought. *What's up with this?* Frustration and a little fear crept upon him as he again inserted his pass code and again was denied access. Out of frustration, he began to pull on the handle with all his might but could not move the door.

Things are sure getting strange around here, he thought as he quickly returned to his work station. *I'm going to find out what's going on here one way or another. There's always a way to get information*, he smiled.

A voice suddenly came on his communication device, requesting his reply.

"Rickter here," he said as he pushed a small button to open up a channel.

"You better get over here as soon as possible," came the voice on the other end. "We have a problem on Station 6 that I think will be of great interest to you."

"On my way! I'll have to deal with this Sifrus situation a little later, as soon as I get access to that file."

Deman moved to his secret underground door that allowed him exclusive access to his portal, which in turn gave him access to the State Centre without having to go outside and face any risks that came with being accessible to the public. He had a potential killer who may be waiting for him.

Seles opened the chamber entrance and reluctantly waved goodbye to him. He slowly and painfully climbed into his operation seat and closed the protective cover. She studied him for a moment, and then he was gone in a flash without any more goodbyes. She knew him well enough to know that when he set his mind on business, his soft, emotional side was suppressed.

He knew that things had to change before it was too late, if it wasn't too late already. "How do I do this? There has to be a way, but why do I sense that the answer rests with this King Sifrus of Rimshire. I hope by now Rickter has figured out a way to make contact with him."

Suddenly startled, he looked in shock as red lights flashed all around him, and his shuttle slowed down. There was no time to panic, as shots came at him from several directions. "This can't be—there's no access to this secret tunnel," he screamed. The safety shield was holding as he quickly pulled a cover from a secret panel marked, "Override Emergency— Pull Lever." His head lurched as he quickly streaked forward when a roar came from an extra impulse motor that sped him into the distance, safely away from his attackers.

"Wow! That was a close call! Even my secret chambers have been compromised. What now? No place seems to be safe anymore, and I have a big job to do with a tight time limit. I can only hope that the State Centre is still safe."

Rickter was waiting for him as his shuttle slowed near an exit ramp. He pushed several buttons to align several bulletproof tunnels attached to his shuttle. They surrounded his exit and sealed it to ensure his complete safety as he entered the State Centre.

"How was your ride, Commander?" Rickter asked as he stood totally still in a salute pose to recognize his superior's authority.

"At ease," he said as he cautiously looked around in all directions to ensure he was safe.

"Don't worry, sir, we checked the whole area to ensure that nobody is here who isn't dedicated to our cause. Are you feeling okay, sir? You look a little pale."

Deman cringed with pain as he reached to pull himself up from the tight seat he'd been in. "Yes, I'm fine, just a little weak from a cold bug I picked up a few days ago." *I can't let anyone know about my true condition, or they'll think I'm weak.* "Let's get to work, for we have a lot to catch up with."

Rickter led the way as they passed through several security doors that were programmed to open with their pass codes encrypted in a computer chip embedded in the right hand. Entering into their large control rooms, they could see many screens broadcasting from various parts of their planet, particularly places of strategic importance. "It looks really bad, boss," Rickter said as he pointed toward the screens.

"My goodness!" gasped Deman. "It's gotten worse since I was here a few weeks ago. What plans has our professional environmental scientist devised to correct this problem?" He kept his eyes on the screens that were showing the planet almost entirely covered with blowing dust.

Rickter stayed very quiet for a moment, knowing that this could be a defining moment in his long and distinguished career. To say they had no plans to correct the problem would show him as incompetent. If he were to provide solutions, it would cost them dearly and end their ability to remain rich and powerful. He was definitely in a difficult situation, and Deman would demand a solution. He quickly glanced at Labtan, his second in charge, who only shrugged his shoulders as he looked momentarily from the cameras and blinked his eyes. He slowly pointed to the screens to avoid direct eye contact with Deman. "Look, boss, we have a very difficult situation here, as you well know, and it will take some time to develop a solution." He knew he needed to buy some time.

Deman looked again at Rickter and then to Labtan. Pointing to the screens, he said, "Look! We don't have much time remaining to correct this toxic dust problem. You two are the best, most loyal, and brightest managers I have. You both launched this large-scale mining project and were certain that any environmental problems could be controlled. Now the dust storms are so severe, the existing vegetation is covered by toxic dust and is dying quicker than it can re-vegetate."

Rickter was becoming very uneasy and continued to look at the screens with a determined look of concern. "But, boss, this isn't our fault. We had proper legal contracts signed by the various mining companies to ensure full adherence to proper and sustainable mining practices. The contracts outlined the need for modest expansion with suitable vegetated wind breaks, buffer areas, and re-planting of all rehabilitated areas immediately after vacating a site."

Deman was now pacing the floor as he glanced occasionally at the screens. He stopped directly in front of Rickter and looked him in the eyes. "Then tell me why we have such a major problem that seems out of control."

Rickter looked down to break contact with Deman's eyes. He stuttered as he tried to retain his composure and not show weakness. "We have identified a situation that has been taking place for some time and was not reported to our district managers. We have learned from a reliable source that our inspectors on the individual mining sites have been paid off to not report additional areas that were mined beyond what had been approved in the miner's contracts. This greed for additional materials has allowed for vast areas to be stripped and not re-vegetated in time to stop the strong winds from blowing toxic dust over vast areas." He coughed into his sleeve to hide his nervousness.

"I still don't understand how that could cause the major dust problem we have in most of our regions, especially where there's no mining activity." Deman looked puzzled as he pointed again at the screens "Look at that mess."

Rickter looked slowly toward the screens as he sighed and spoke very softly and carefully so as not to provoke Deman's anger. "We've studied the situation very carefully and found that there was an extended period of drought around the same period of increased mining activity. There were also stronger than normal winds over that extended period. It may be a coincidence, but it seems that we've been hit with a perfect combination of conditions to cause much damage to our environment. To complicate matters even more, the vegetation is dying and exposing even more soil to the damaging winds, creating what we now see before us."

"And our people are dying!" Deman shouted as he slapped his hand on the desk in front of him, causing everyone in the State Centre to stop their work and look at him with fear in their eyes. "You fool! Do you think I'm so blind that I haven't seen what's really going on around here? Many of you have turned a blind eye to this problem because of the riches it has brought. You all knew the risks of excessive surface mining of this rare mineral and its toxicity if the fine particles became airborne, and now we're reaping the consequences."

Rickter was now in panic mode and wanting to get away from the situation and the coming confrontation. He knew that Deman had become wealthier than them all and had encouraged the governing bodies to approve additional mining permits for the miners. *It's very perplexing*, he thought, *that Deman has changed his mind and wants to correct these very complicated problems so quickly. Why this sudden change?*

Rickter tried to control his shaking body and again explain the situation without causing extra tension. "Well, boss, we've tried very hard to slow the rate of mining activity, but with a limited number of inspectors, and travel becoming more difficult because of the dust conditions, it's difficult to monitor all the activity."

Labtan remained completely quiet as he listened to the dialogue. His anger grew as he thought about the possibility of losing their jobs if Deman was serious about making major changes is their mining practices. *Maybe it's time to have him removed from leadership, or killed*.

A signal suddenly beeped on his galaxy screen, grabbing everyone's attention. They ran to his screen, which showed a small blip on the outside edge of his arc, indicating that it was outside their chartered territory. "This is impossible!" shouted Deman. "That's outside our known galaxy. Nobody has the capability to travel that far unless they have superior knowledge and equipment beyond ours. Are you sure that's our tracker signal?"

"Absolutely! There's a special frequency used with each individual tracker, and this one matches ours, which followed Sifrus's space glider as he exited our territory. His was the last vessel to leave, by your orders. There can't be any system of travel that could go beyond this signal location. This is very interesting. What are we dealing with?"

Deman stayed completely silent as he studied the screen intently with great curiosity. "Who are you? Where are you? How can you travel like this? I wonder!" he shouted.

WINTER LOVE—RIMSHIRE

ASSEDNIC OPENED HIS EYES AND TRIED TO FOCUS. HE TRIED TO STRETCH HIS arms but quickly realized that Kristella was lying next to him and had put her head on his chest. He looked intently at her peaceful face, so smooth and pretty. How much he wished they could marry and live in peace someday. "Good morning, princess," he said when she opened her eyes.

She smiled and felt a little uptight when she realized how close she'd been cuddled into him. "Good morning, ah—what time is it?"

Assednic lifted up his clock to allow the glow of light from the fire to illumine it so he could see the time. "It's afternoon; we've all slept for much longer than normal, but considering what we've been through, we certainly needed it."

She yawned several times as she tried to focus. "Yeah, we certainly did need that extra rest."

"I'll go out to the ledge and see if there's any activity in the valley or around the mountain edges." Assednic stood and stretched as he put on his boots. "You guys get some food ready; we'll need energy if we're going to search the many tunnels and rooms in this mountain home. I want to see if there may be any smoke from fires in any other locations around the mountain, where we could find some allies."

Soris awakened the children and began to get them dressed for the day ahead. "Come over to the fireplace and get warm while I get some porridge ready for you two," she said as she took some hot water from a steaming kettle and poured it into two bowls. "We need to make you big and strong for travelling in the tunnels when we grownups are too big and fat to get into the smaller spaces. Isn't that right, Jiltu?" She smiled at him and rubbed her fat belly.

"I guess," he said as he smacked his tubby stomach a few times and laughed. "This is all muscle; you guys should know."

The kids laughed at him uncontrollably.

"What's so funny, you little guys?" he chuckled.

"Jelly belly, jelly belly," they said between bursts of laughter.

Chlorise just watched from the corner and smiled at the fun they were all having. She thought back to when Spectrum had gone over the edge of a cliff while being chased by Monton's followers. She wondered if maybe Spectrum had somehow survived his fall, and if they were to meet again, could they possibly date and fall in love. She liked him very much but had never told him. They had always been good friends, and were also classmates for many years, which made them almost too familiar with each other. Besides, Spectrum seemed intrigued by Kristella. Whoever thought he would lose his life on the very mountain that would become their sanctuary and safe haven from Monton and his followers?

When they had all finished their meals, they gathered to plan how they would travel the tunnels in a safe manner to seek out and document the resources available to them. "Somebody will have to be with the children at all times," said Soris before any other suggestions could be made.

"Okay, all is quiet outside," said Assednic as he looked around at the others. "Do we all agree?"

"I'll go with Listy and Hasic, considering they are my responsibility, and I know a little about mountain life," said Jiltu without hesitation.

"Well, that leaves two groups of two: Kristella and me, and Soris with Chlorise."

Chlorise took Soris by the hand to show no fear as she said, "We'll be fine together; besides, we won't be very far from your groups. Let's all be careful out there, for we don't know what awaits us in these caves."

They all returned after only a short period of time to report that the tunnels didn't go very far at all, and there were no additional rooms with supplies.

"This is all very strange," said Assednic as he scratched his head. "There have always been stories told by people of the villages of many miners living in these caves for long periods of time without ever having to come to town for additional supplies. How could they only have these few rooms and tunnels?"

"There are also stories told of strange happenings and creatures travelling to and from these mountains with very strong lights that travel at extreme speeds," Jiltu said cautiously so as not to scare anybody. "Maybe someone or something brought them supplies from somewhere else."

Kristella looked around at the group and tried to smile a little to show at least a glimpse of hope. "Well, what did we find that could be used? Assednic and I found many strange markings on the rock walls that seemed to be placed at regular intervals for some reason."

Soris looked at Chlorise. "We never really got very far, because the tunnel we followed kept getting smaller the farther we went until we could go no farther. We didn't see any doorways, but we did see some strange markings on the walls of the tunnel."

"Yeah, us too," said Jiltu, who was holding the children by his side for safety, just in case something or someone showed up.

"How can this be?" asked Kristella with great confusion in her voice. "We didn't find any additional passages, so we're stuck in these several rooms with nowhere to escape to when Monton's men show up in the spring to try and capture us again."

"Okay then," spoke Assednic with a tone of desperation in his voice, "let's go sit at the fire and discuss all of our options. First, we know that we can't go down the mountain, or we'll be captured or possibly killed. We would likely face imprisonment and possible torture until we'd swear allegiance to Monton. Do we all agree on this?"

They all nodded their heads except for Kristella, who seemed oblivious to the conversation.

"Second, we have enough supplies for approximately one month in the back storage chamber. If we don't find additional food and water, we'll be forced to go out onto the ledges to seek out other caves or die in this one. Do we all agree?" He whispered as he looked over at Kristella, who was focused only on the flames as they jumped and danced in many beautiful colours and patterns. "Kristella, are you listening?"

Kristella nodded but continued to study the flames of the fire in deep thought.

Nobody said anything for some time as they just sat silently studying the fire, as if the answer somehow lay there. The silence was broken when Soris looked over at Kristella and said, "We could ask for some help."

Jiltu glanced at her with a frown on his face. "We haven't seen anybody who could help us. What do you have in mind?"

"Well, Kristella seems to believe that somehow Sifrus can help us, even when he's far away. Maybe he's been helping us all along to get this far, and maybe he can help again in this difficult situation."

Kristella looked around to see that they were all studying her reaction. "It certainly can't hurt, I guess," she quickly said. "But I must admit that I'm not really sure how or when it works. Sometimes it seems that the image of Sifrus comes to me, as if he's right there speaking to me and directing me in what to do. Maybe if we all spent some time here by the fire in silence, meditating on Sifrus and explaining our situation to him and asking for help, he may send an image to one of us, telling us what to do next." She raised her hands skyward to show that the power was up there.

"How did you get so close to Sifrus that you can contact him even when you're so far apart?" Chlorise excitedly spoke up, startling everybody from their meditation.

"Ah … hum … let me see." Kristella stumbled with her words, for she hadn't really thought about that question before. She blushed a little as she glanced toward Assednic and then back at Chlorise. "That's really a hard question to answer, because our special relationship developed over a long period of time. I just know that something special seems to happen when I think about him."

Chlorise was even more curious as she studied Kristella's blushing face. "When did he come to our planet, and where did he come from in the very beginning?" she asked.

Kristella was now transfixed on the question and was trying to sort out her memory of her first meeting with Sifrus. "Well, I was very young, maybe eight or nine years old, and I heard that we were getting a new teacher from outside our world system from a place called Heveris. He just seemed special.

"Crowds of people came to greet him, as was our custom and also because they were intrigued that he was coming from a place unknown to us. They wondered what he would look like, what kind of food he ate, how people lived where he came from, and all kinds of other stuff." She walked around in a circle, trying to concentrate on her memories of long ago.

"Let me see if I've got this correct. When he arrived all alone in his space glider and climbed down his ramp, we couldn't ask any questions. For some reason, all we could do was greet him with hugs and best wishes for his stay with us. He looked a lot like us, but there was something very different—like a glow around him, as if you were just attracted to his kindness." She shook her head. "Yes, his kindness."

"We all know how he became one of our greatest teachers ever and taught us the principle of *Love*, which we follow today as was taught to him by his father on Heveris. Eventually, because everybody loved him so much as a trusted teacher, they made him our leader and king."

"But how did you personally become so close to him?"

"Sorry, I got sidetracked, but I wanted to be sure you knew about the early days of his arrival. You would have been a little too young to greet him when he came."

Chlorise looked up from the burning fire. "I remember when the people wanted to make him king. He argued that they didn't really need a king if they were to live in love and harmony with each other, for they would all be equal in all things. I remember that there were some men who had hoped to become leader themselves and were very unhappy when they couldn't say anything because the vast majority of the people were hailing him as our king."

Kristella nodded. "I remember when he walked over to the people who were there to greet him, and he spent much time ensuring that he hugged each one. As he approached me, he stood still for a moment and then swept me up in his arms and whispered that I was chosen. I didn't know what he meant, and I still don't know to this day, but I do know that a warm, tingling sensation went through my whole body, and I always have visions of Sifrus when I'm in trouble. That sounds strange, doesn't it?

"In the beginning, when he started a new and stronger teaching on the benefits of true love and all people being equal, he encountered much resistance from several former teachers who didn't want to include this new teaching in the curriculum at our place of learning. He explained how peaceful and loving Heveris was and that we could have the same if we followed the same teachings."

Jiltu joined the conversation. "Some people thought his teachings were a joke and that he was crazy, because all people could not be equal. They said that their society was always divided by various levels of accomplishment and riches, and that made them more important than others."

"That's also true," acknowledged Kristella. "Yes, there was opposition and disbelief, but as people listened to him teach and watched him live out what he taught, more and more of them began to believe and try hard to live the same way. But there was always a small group of prominent business people who didn't like his teachings, for fear of losing some of their riches."

"It always seems to be the people with the most power and riches who oppose any teachings in which wealth is shared equally among all people." Assednic sighed as he pushed a log in the fire, sending up a blast of flames as if to highlight the statement. "It's now the same with Monton wanting to have more power and riches; he will stop at nothing to end all teachings of *Love*. A shiver went up his spine as he said, "That includes destroying us, if he can."

Kristella glanced at him and then closed her eyes, sensing his fear as she envisioned Monton's men preparing for their attack against them as soon as the conditions improved in the spring.

"Now back to our story. He easily got nominated by the people and won the vote for the leadership position. After only two years of evaluation, he was made King of all Rimshire, with only a little opposition from a few of the more prominent and influential people in the business community. He implemented his teachings of *Love* to all policy-making decisions, and quickly transformed all aspects of society for the betterment of all inhabitants.

"But all wasn't perfect, for there remained a small group who opposed him whenever they could. They were determined to get rid of him, even if it meant killing him, if they could get away with it. But this would only be a last resort, and most likely an outside assassin would have to be brought in. The vast majority of people loved him very much and did much better under his policies. Others agreed with him because they had much peace in their communities and could mingle and work in any part of Rimshire where they pleased without discrimination or suspicion. They all seemed to find a power and higher reality of living as they grew closer to him.

"He seemed to know who was taking his teachings to heart and who wasn't. He came to me one day when I was in my late teens. I was in a large crowd listening to him lecture at the front of the college. I saw him leave the lecture stand and begin walking down the centre aisle. All eyes were on him as we wondered what was happening. Then he stopped and looked directly toward me. I looked around to see if he was looking at someone else near me. When I looked back, I knew those beautiful eyes were directed at me and holding me spellbound. I couldn't look away, and I thought I might faint, but he suddenly held out his hand and said, "Come." I instantly followed without any fear at all. When I touched his hand—oh how my emotions exploded! The presence of love was overwhelming, an intense feeling beyond anything I'd ever felt before. It wasn't a physical or emotional type of love, but a universal type of love. All who were around me seemed to notice."

They were all spellbound as they listened to Kristella's story. Soris was wide-eyed as she softly asked: "What happened next?"

Kristella was shaking as she recalled this magic moment again. Her mind drifted off for a moment as she remembered the pure delight of holding his hand.

"Kristella," Assednic quietly asked, "are you all right?"

"What?" She answered as she tried to focus. "Oh yes, I'm fine—just remembering how he led me up to the lecture platform and asked me to explain the benefits of having a loving society versus one without much love for others. I didn't even have to try to remember the many points he had taught us in the past. The answers just flowed naturally from my mouth, as if Sifrus was teaching himself without making any mistakes. I wasn't even scared to be in front of all those people, even though I'd always been afraid of public speaking and was quite introverted."

"Wow! That really is quite a remarkable story of discovering where our true strengths come from," said Assednic, trying to be as sincere as he could. He'd never mentioned it to Kristella, but he secretly was quite jealous of the special place Sifrus held in her heart.

She looked around, trying to gauge their reactions to her story, but she knew that there may be some doubt, even though she knew they all loved Sifrus in their own special way. "Sifrus touches us all who believe in his teachings at a different level that is unique and personal to us alone. It all depends on how close we allow Sifrus to come to us with his awesome power of love and kindness.

"I always tried to attend as many of his teaching sessions as possible to learn from him about his way of living in peace and harmony with everything around him. Occasionally he would invite small groups to travel with him into the wilderness, where he could teach in peace without the distractions and hustle and bustle of city life. These were very special times where we could have more intimate talks with him and discuss personal as well as universal issues. On occasion he would hold my hands in his, look directly into my eyes as he first did in the lecture hall, and allow our minds to connect in a very special way, as if he were transmitting his love and knowledge to my mind and allowing for a much higher plane of thinking. When we'd finish, he'd always ask: 'Do you now understand?'

"I never had to ask: 'Understand what?' My mind was always flooded with clear understanding of whatever he taught in all those sessions. But the real bonus of being with him was the intense feelings when we touched. I just can't explain it; the feeling of love for all creatures was just out of this world." Kristella raised her hands to the heavens as she waved them back and forth with her eyes closed, whispering, "Thank you, King Sifrus."

Assednic looked a little uneasy as he got up from the front of the fire and walked silently to the back of the chamber. He was very confused by his emotions, because he loved both Kristella and Sifrus in different ways. Even though he knew it was wrong, he felt jealous of the connection Sifrus had with Kristella, as he knew he could never compete with. He again noticed the strange markings on the wall in front of him. *What do they mean, I wonder?*

Kristella felt a deep longing for Sifrus, who seemed so far away yet so close in her heart. She knew that Assednic loved her with all his heart, but she also knew that to show too much love for him would lead him to a place where she just couldn't go at this time.

Kristella slowly opened her eyes and looked at Assednic standing by the wall of rock covered with many strange markings. "How are you doing with the interpretation of those symbols?" she asked while studying his strong, shaped body. *He's very hot*, she thought.

He glanced her way and smiled a little then looked back at the markings. *I wish she wanted me more, maybe even enough to get married someday.* "These aren't similar to any I've seen or studied in the past, which makes it very strange. If these markings were made by a race of beings that may have been here in the past, then we may have to figure out patterns of communication that are foreign to us."

Kristella stood up and came close to him, sending waves of emotion through his body. She touched some of the engravings on the wall and followed their winding patterns with her finger. As she studied them, a feeling of sadness grew inside of her as pictures of creatures came clearly into vision—hurting, crying, and seeming to be reaching out for help. With a plea of panic, she pulled her finger from the wall, and all feelings and pictures disappeared. "What just happened?" she screamed.

Assednic wrapped his arms around her. "Are you okay?" he asked, sounding confused. "I didn't see anything happen. Why did you scream out?"

Kristella was very confused, as if she'd entered a new plateau of understanding and super focus. "You didn't see any creatures' faces on the wall right next to you? But they were so real, as if they were standing just to the right of you." She shook her head.

He just stared at her in silence, trying to grasp what she was talking about. Slowly opening his mouth to speak, he glanced again at the wall to ensure there was nothing there. "I'm … ah, ah … not sure what to say. Well, if you saw something, was it real or imagined?"

"You don't believe me, do you?" she hastily said and turned to walk away.

"Wait! Wait!" He shouted as her grabbed at her arm. "I don't want you to think that I doubt you; in fact, with all the strange things that have been going on around you, nothing would completely surprise me. It's just that you shocked me for a moment, and I'm worried about you."

She hesitated, not sure why she'd reacted the way she did. *It's not normal for me to get upset so easily*, she thought. "Well, if you mean that, then let's see what else will unfold with these strange messages on the walls." Slowly, Kristella approached the rock wall again. "What if something happens that I have no control over, and I get hurt or, even worse, disappear? Or maybe turn into some horrible monster with sharp fangs, and then kill you!"

Jiltu, who was watching from the side of the cave, began to laugh hysterically as he looked at the strange expression on Assednic's face. Assednic looked at Jiltu, who was now bent over on the floor with laughter, and couldn't help but start laughing too. "You a monster? No way, you couldn't if you tried! You're just too sweet," he mumbled through his laughter as he heard the others join in with them.

By now, even Kristella, who had been very anxious a moment ago, had started to laugh a little as she looked at all the others going crazy. "Okay, okay, let's get serious here, you foolish people." She spoke through her own laughter, trying to get control. "We have a big job to do!"

She slowly held out her hand, not sure whether to touch the rock or not. She noticed that everyone had stopped laughing and was focused on her hand holding just a little from its surface. *I have to do this*, she thought to herself, *but I'm scared and don't want to show that to them. I must be strong if we're to find out how to survive in these caves.*

"Kristella," came a sweet voice from across the room. "You don't have to do this if you don't want to. You're very important to us, and I'd like to take your place, just in case something happens."

Looking across the room, she focused for a moment. "Soris, that's very nice of you to offer, but I don't think the children would want you to do that. Besides, I'm not sure it will work for anybody else. The powers that select recipients to receive messages are very selective, based on belief and possible connection to the source as well as any history they may have with the particular event or persons." She hesitated for a moment. "Maybe my mind is beginning to show me some of what Sifrus sees as he travels to difficult worlds."

"Can I at least try? Then I'll know that there's hope for us to continue, if for any reason you can't." She hesitated for a moment. "I mean *if*!"

"That's okay, don't worry. I'll be with you all the way!" Kristella smiled her little sheepish smile to hide how scared she really felt inside. "Come over and touch the rock and let's see what happens."

Soris came across the room slowly, with Listy holding on to her as she approached the rock wall. Tentatively, she placed her hand where the engravings were etched. "Nothing is happening," she quietly said. "Should I do anything?"

"Let's see, what did I do?" Kristella was trying to focus on her strange encounter with the engravings. "Try closing your eyes and running your fingers slowly along the length of the engravings."

Soris slowly dragged her fingers through the winding pattern as it flowed throughout the rock wall, but nothing happened. Suddenly, Listy cried out, "Mommy, I'm scared. They're crying and reaching out."

Soris quickly pulled her hand from the wall, shocked by Listy's cry. She picked up Listy in her arms. "It's okay, sweetheart, its' okay," she said as she cuddled the crying child to her chest. Everybody stood in shock as they silently watched Soris and Listy hugging and crying in a deep embrace to comfort each other.

Kristella looked again at Listy, trying to remember the strong sensation of warmth and love she'd felt when she held her hand outside on the ledge some time ago. *I wonder if this little girl has some powers that the others don't possess! I'll have to watch for signs without alerting the others, who could scare Listy. If that happened, she may not be useful when her powers may be needed.*

"Listy, are you okay?" asked Soris quietly as she released her tight embrace and looked into her little blue eyes, which were filled with tears.

Listy kept sobbing and couldn't speak about what had happened to her. "Mommy, Mommy," was all she was able to say as she again cuddled into her mom's chest.

Assednic looked at Kristella, who was still trying to compose herself. He wondered from the strange expression on her face if she understood what may have just happened. "Kristella, are you able to continue with this, or shall we try a little later?"

All eyes shifted from Soris and Listy to Kristella, who had turned and was again studying the rock wall. *What secrets do you hold? How do I unlock something that may be dangerous, or at least very disturbing?* she asked herself, trying not to show too much fear in her eyes. "I'm feeling a little uneasy, but we can give this another try to ensure that I still can make contact with this strange message. What do you think, Jiltu? You have the most experience dealing with problems in these mountains. Are you aware of any strange happenings in the past that may have been reported to the locals but not recorded in our archives in the city?"

Jiltu studied the markings on the rock wall for a few moments and then looked toward Soris with a blank stare, as if waiting for her approval. Soris made a small nod with her head to indicate that it was okay to continue with his story. He coughed to clear his throat. "Some years ago, during a very violent snow storm, we were putting our mountain zells in the shed for cover when we heard loud screams coming from the mountaintops. We weren't the only ones to hear the screams, as many villagers were talking about it the next day as we went about our chores in our village. It was the only time in the many years we'd lived here that we'd heard such a noise." He paused for a moment and looked again for Soris's approval, as if it gave him strength to continue. "Many villagers said that it was probably the strong winds from the storm that made the sounds and dismissed them altogether."

"Did anybody go to see if the sound may have been made by people or creatures that may have been in trouble?" asked Assednic, who was now totally transfixed on the story.

Jiltu looked at Soris for more confirmation and slowly began the story again. "You see, there were two hunters in our village who knew these mountains extremely well and could survive in almost any conditions. They set out to travel to the mountaintop to check out the situation and were to report back within three days. The weather was very good for travel—light winds, sunshine, and they had sufficient food to last for five days, but they didn't return after the three days."

Kristella was hanging on to every word, wondering where the story was going and how it may affect her decision to probe the rock for more clues. "What happened to the two hunters who didn't return within the three days?" she asked with great anticipation.

Jiltu mumbled for a little bit while trying to work the words in his mind. "Well, that's the strange part. They didn't return for the whole winter, even though many large search parties looked for them whenever the weather was suitable."

Kristella looked confused as she intently studied him. "But did they return at all?"

"That's the good but very strange part. They came down the mountain in the spring after the snows had melted. They were in good shape and well nourished, just a little confused about where the snow had gone so quickly."

"But how can that be?" asked Assednic as he looked over at Soris to see if she could offer any insight.

Quietly, she raised her head from comforting Listy and nodded at Jiltu. "He was one of those hunters who did not return for the winter and was given up for dead."

Nobody dared say a word; they just stared at Jiltu with blank looks on their faces.

Several minutes passed before Kristella broke the silence with a little gasp as she moved from the rock wall. "You! You were up in the mountain all winter with no food or protection? But how?"

"We don't know. We talked to all the wise people in the village, and they couldn't understand how it could be. We thought that we'd only been gone for the three days and were returning as scheduled, except for the loss of snow. But when we arrived to the delight and shock of our village friends who had given us up for dead, we were informed that we'd been gone for three months."

"Whoa, whoa, hang on there," Assednic said, totally at a loss for words. "You don't expect us to believe this, do you? What happened for those three months while you were lost?"

Jiltu was becoming very uneasy, but he tried to keep his composure. He hadn't talked about the incident for many years, and he'd tried to forget it. He looked at Assednic with a tear in his eye and explained that many people had left their village and moved into the town because they were too scared to stay anymore. "Over time, we were the only family remaining in our little village when you found us. We tried our best to remember what had happened to try and comfort the people, but no matter how hard we tried, we had no memory of it. All we remember is that on the second day, as we approached a cave entrance, a dense shower of snow appeared, and we couldn't see where we were going. We just kept moving into what seemed like a cave in the mountain until we came out of the snow into a clearing where all the snow had melted. We realized that we were much farther down the mountain than where we had entered, and we could see the village below us.

"Three months later," cried Soris, moving over to comfort the trembling Jiltu.

Assednic pointed to the fire in the middle of the room. "Come, come, we need to rest on this. Let's get something hot to drink and re-evaluate what we've just heard and what our plans are next." He moved in close to Kristella and placed his arm around her as they sat near the fire. He noticed that she was also trembling. and he tried to get a small smile from her as she glanced into his warm eyes. "Don't be scared; I will never leave you."

Kristella moved in closer and pulled his strong arm around her for comfort. "I know," she quietly said.

They all sat quietly watching the flickers of flame dance and wave as they constantly changed in colour and intensity, keeping the audience transfixed in an envelope of warmth and security from the cold and dark outside. Listy and Hazic couldn't take the quietness for a long time and were again running around the chamber looking for excitement. Hazic ran down a long, narrow tunnel and called out to Listy to follow.

"Where are you?" called Hazic when he turned and didn't see her follow him.

Listy called out as she ran down to where she had seen Hazic go, but now she couldn't see or hear him. She went up and down the tunnel trying to find him, but when she came to the end, she turned back to tell her mom. "I can't find Hazic. Can you help me?" she said quietly without concern.

Soris looked up from the fire and said without hesitation, "Sure I will." She was used to having to help find the children when they played hide and seek and couldn't find each other. Soris smiled at Jiltu as she took Listy's hand and walked off toward the back of the chamber. "Which way did he go, sweetheart?" she asked as they neared a small tunnel entrance.

Listy pointed down toward the tunnel entrance. "There is where he ran," she said with excitement. "We'll find you now, Hazic" she called as they bent into the small entrance, which was a little low for Soris to stand up straight in.

Hazic looked around for Listy but didn't see her. "Where are you, Listy?" he called with a little tremble in his voice. Looking around, he could see that he was no longer in a tunnel but in a well lit, large room with a warm fire glowing and some nice treats placed on a small table near the fireplace. "Where am I?" He cried as he called out to his mom. "Mommy, Mommy, where are you?" He went over to the table. He wanted to eat because he was hungry, but as he sat in the chair, a small, furry creature came into the room from behind what seemed to be a rock wall. He jumped down and started to run because he was so scared, but there was nowhere to run to, so he sat down near the far wall and began to cry.

The furry creature stood still, studying the little boy with a puzzled look on his small, curled up mouth. After a while, he decided that the little boy wasn't dangerous, so he slowly moved toward him.

Hazic glanced toward the little creature approaching him, peeking through a hole between his arms, which were covering his face for protection. As he continued to look at him, his fear began to dissipate. Eventually, he ventured to show a little smile. "Are you real?" he asked.

The little creature stopped, looked a little puzzled at the question, and then smiled back. "I am real, and my name is Toran. I live here at this station when I'm needed. Who are you?"

"I'm Hazic, and I'm here with my family, trying to escape danger from the bad men in the city below the mountain. But I kind of got lost when I came down this tunnel when I was playing with my sister. I think she might be looking for me, because we always stay together."

Listy and Soris were becoming a little tired as they looked up and down the tunnel with no sign of Hazic. They shouted out to him many times with no reply. They decided that he must have found a good place to hide, so they returned to the others to get help with this game of hide and seek.

Jiltu looked up from his gaze on the fire as they entered the chamber. "Where is Hazic?" he asked with a wisp of concern in his voice.

Soris looked at Listy with a little smile. "Well, he sure is good at hiding, because we couldn't find him, could we, sweetheart?" The others began to listen in. "I guess you'll all have to come and help us find him before he thinks that nobody is coming to look for him."

Assednic looked at Jiltu and could read the concern on his face. Although he tried to hide his feelings as much as possible, the memories of his disappearance story came immediately to his mind. Quickly he jumped up as he said, "Come, let's find this little hiding genius! Let's meet back here in twenty minutes to report on what we've found and to ensure nobody else gets lost. Stay together or within shouting distance of each other."

They all went searching through the tunnel where they figured he should be, but to no avail. Calling his name and banging on the wall to see if there may be some secret, small entrances that were not visible didn't produce any signs of him. As they regrouped at the main chamber, they knew that they may now have a problem of a missing child to deal with. Soris began to cry, and Listy soon joined in as they tried to console her.

Kristella looked at Soris, who was crying and very distraught as she held Listy tightly. She seemed to be very scared and wasn't going to allow her daughter any opportunity to get lost also. Kristella tried to convince them that all would be well if only they believed that Sifrus could help them, as he had done many times in the past.

Soris looked up and tried to control her weeping so as not to upset Listy. "Kristella, that's really nice to say, but with Sifrus so far away and dealing with so many problems in this universe, I don't think he can deal with a misplaced little boy."

Kristella paused to think about what Soris said and to reflect on the things that had already happened to them to keep them safe so far on their journey. Her mind raced back to the sinking holes they had crossed, the deep snows, the toelions and riders, the grogs, the zells, the large flying creature, and especially the avalanche that had wiped out most of Monton's army. "But we have to keep believing that he's with us and protecting us. If we don't, then we have no way to survive this ordeal. We may be the last few to keep to the teachings of *Love* given to us by Sifrus. This may be the only way for our homeland to survive in the future in peace and hope for each other."

"What is this place we've come to for safety?" asked Soris as she continued to weep. "We have nowhere else to go, and now even this mountain seems to have turned against us!"

What can I say to make her feel better? thought Kristella, trying to look confident but sympathetic at the same time. She hesitated for a moment, looking for the right words. "I'm not sure," she thoughtfully said, "but there seems to be a sense of safety coming from this mountain, even if we have had some difficult times occasionally. But we're still alive and free, and even more importantly, we're together. We will find Hasic, don't worry. I just know somehow Sifrus will help us."

Toran continued to look at Hasic with a strange expression as he asked, "How many of you are in this group?"

Hasic started to think. "Well … there's me and my sister, my mom and dad. Then there's Miss Kristella, Miss Chlorise, and Assednic, and we also left some zells down the mountain where we lost Spectrum, who fell over the mountain."

"He fell over the mountain!" gasped Toran. "How did he manage to do that?"

"He got chased by an ugly creature with a rider on his back, and he was going too fast on the edge of the rocks and went over. We haven't seen him since then, but we hope to again somewhere, if he can find us. And the nice, friendly, furry zell went over the edge with him." Hasic trailed off with a little tear forming in his eyes. "I hope he's okay … and survived the fall."

A little lump formed in Toran's throat as he looked at Hasic and thought about what he had said. "Ah …ah … I see," was all he could say. He turned to go back to where he'd come from, but a little voice called out to him. "Don't leave me here alone! Please."

He turned around to see Hasic coming toward him with outstretched arms.

"Okay, come this way. I'll show you my living space in the next chamber." He came to the wall, which seemed solid, and then reached out his furry, little fingers and moved them in a circular fashion as he traced some strange markings until a small opening appeared for them to walk through.

Hasic looked surprised to see a clear opening where there was solid rock just a few moments earlier. "Cool!" he shouted as they walked through the opening. As they passed through, it immediately filled in again behind them as it was before. "How did you do that?" he asked with great excitement.

"Watch this!" Toran said with a little smile. He reached back and again made a circular motion on some markings on the wall, and again an opening formed behind them. "For you to be here in this room, you must have made the same motions as you ran your finger on the markings on the outside wall. Were you playing with the markings out there before you got lost and couldn't find your sister anymore?"

"Ah—ah, I'm not sure what I was doing, but I know that my mom and Miss Kristella were trying to do something with the markings but got scared when something strange happened to them."

"Well, that is interesting," said Toran as he rubbed his little chin. "I'm here to show all visitors how this mountain works, but I'll need to meet with your group to find out the purposes of your trip to this mountain. They must be very worried about you by now, so we better get you back before they get too upset."

Hasic smiled as he ran to hug the little, furry creature. "Thanks … thanks," he said with a little shout of glee. "But will they be scared of you?"

"We'll have to deal with that when the time comes, but let's just get you back there. Come over to this far wall. Now watch what I do and concentrate on the wall opening as you run your fingers in a circular fashion to the right." Instantly, an opening materialized in the rock wall for them to travel through. "We can spend more time together once your mom is comfortable with me being around you. For now, you tell them about me so that they can get used to the idea before we meet. Now run down that tunnel and you'll find them in the main chamber discussing what to do about finding you."

"Mom! Mom," Hasic called as he ran down the tunnel, excited to see his family again. He couldn't wait to tell them about what seemed like a weird dream in which he met a strange, little, furry creature inside the rock chambers.

"Hasic … Hasic, is that you?" His mom cried out when she heard his voice. Running into the chamber at full speed, he jumped into her arms, knocking them both over as they hugged and kissed. The others were all excited as they watched them and gathered around to hug him.

She released him just a little and looked at him with tears in her eyes, "How? Where? Why did you disappear? Hasic, I love you so much; I was so scared for you."

"Oh Mom, you didn't need to be scared; the little furry creature took care of me."

All went silent as they looked at each other and studied Soris and Hasic to see what would happen next. Soris gasped a little and then asked: "What little furry creature?"

Hasic didn't hesitate to answer. "Down there, in behind the rock wall, there are rooms where he was. He was nice! I was a little scared at first, but something about him made me not afraid, and he wants to meet you all."

Soris glanced around and saw that all eyes were fixed on them. She needed to be careful with her answer so as not to scare Listy or lead anyone to think that Hasic was lying or having hallucinations. "But Hasic," she quietly spoke, "we haven't seen any signs of anyone here. How did you get in through solid rock?"

"He showed me how it works, like Miss Kristella was trying to do with the markings on the wall, except you have to make circles as you concentrate on opening it."

"Could you show us?" asked Kristella, who was listening intently to every word. She looked quickly at Soris to see if she was okay with this, and she could tell by the widening of her eyes that she was concerned.

Hasic looked to his mom, who slowly moved her head from side to side. "I'm sorry, Miss Kristella, but my mom doesn't want me to do this, and I'm a little afraid that I might disappear somewhere else and not find my way back."

"That's okay," smiled Kristella. "You don't have to do it if you don't want to. Maybe if you just explain to me how to do it, then it might work for me. I know that you all have some concerns about this, but we need to figure out how to get through these chambers, or ..." She hesitated for a moment and then said, "Remember, I told you that Sifrus is always with us if we truly believe."

Assednic looked very concerned as he approached Kristella and gently touched her hand. "We know that you're correct, but we need you so much here to strengthen us. What if those sounds and images you saw are trying to hurt us in some way?"

"We can't put this off. I have to try, or we just may have to give up and travel down the mountain and be captured, killed, or imprisoned." Kristella looked around sternly at them all, as if to say, "I have made my decision." She approached the wall and slowly put her hand on the markings. She gradually began to make circling motions as she followed their pattern. She closed her eyes and concentrated on the wall opening. Suddenly, she had the sensation of floating and being very light. Then she heard a scream. When she opened her eyes, she was no longer with her friends.

They all gasped in horror. "Where did she go?" asked Soris, who was holding her children tightly.

Assednic quickly grabbed at the wall and pounded on it with his fists until they were sore. "Where are you? Where are you?" He called out several times to no avail. "It's no use trying to talk to her, is it?" he said as he sank to the floor, frustrated and tired.

PLANNING ATTACK
ON THE MOUNTAIN-RIMSHIRE

MONTON PACED THE FLOOR OF HIS HEADQUARTERS. HIS GENERAL HAD returned from collecting as many bodies as they could find of those who had been killed by the mountain avalanche. The snow was beginning to melt at the base of the mountain as spring began to get a little warmer. The avalanche had wiped out most of his army as they had pursued Kristella and her group up the mountain just before winter.

"How many bodies did you recover?" he shouted sternly as soon as his general entered into his presence.

The general choked as a lump seemed to form in his throat. "Well, Sir Monton, there was much snow … actually much more than you would expect from an avalanche in this zone. We worked very hard to dig through as much snow as possible, even though much has melted, and we managed to find 105 soldiers, 40 toelions and 17 grogs."

Monton looked at his general in bewilderment as he scratched his head. "How did we lose so many? These mountains aren't known for that much snow, or avalanches that could kill so many. I will never let those followers of Sifrus get away. They will pay with their lives for these deaths. We will go after them again very soon, and this time we will not fail. General, gather our best fighters and especially trackers for mountain conditions."

"Yes, sir! I will get them ready immediately, and we will not fail for your honour." He bowed and then turned to exit through the door.

Monton continued to pace the floor with his head bowed in deep concentration. He was angry. "How did we lose so many fighters to such a simple group of Sifrus followers? They are very dangerous because of their beliefs in the principles of absolute *Love* for all. They must have some secret power and must be destroyed. Their message is so simple but very profound for those who believe in it. I can't let them destroy my plans for total control of Rimshire." He shouted and slammed his fist down on a small table, smashing it to pieces. The many workers stopped what they were doing, startled, and looked toward him with fear in their eyes. They could see his angry mood and shaking hands.

The general arrived at the barracks where most of their best fighting soldiers were training. He decided to study their training from a distance so as not to distract them and allow them to train without knowing they were being evaluated. "If I could harness the strengths of the very best fighters, we'd be undefeatable. Monton would surely keep me in this important position, and my future would be secure. But how can I motivate them to be the best?"

He specifically studied a medium-sized fighter in a cage surrounded by several rocky ledges and training with two large grogs. The speed and accuracy with which they ran, jumped, and climbed while destroying mock creatures as they appeared from hidden locations was astonishing to see. But even more amazing was the speed and agility of the trainer as he moved between the ferocious creatures, directing them to the next attack site while keeping them under his control.

The grogs had large, sharp teeth with four outside canines turned upward, which were used to rip open their prey with one swift, upward jab. They would then use their long, straight front teeth to tear through the carcass as the long, curved claws held it in position with a deadly lock. They were the ultimate killing machines and had been intentionally bred for this purpose.

The trainer of these vicious animals must be the bravest of all and must be part of our attack team, he thought as he smiled confidently.

He moved quickly to another training pen where a toelion was standing motionless while watching a nearby hummock of flowers swaying gently in the breeze. After a short time, he began to move slowly toward the flowers. Suddenly, several small, fast-flying creatures came bursting out in all directions. The toelion moved in all directions at once, grabbing all the creatures with its sharp beak within seconds.

Wow, these are also very good, he thought as a rider came into view on the back of a larger toelion. They began to circle the cage at a good speed for such an awkward running style. The toelion tried every possible maneuvre to dislodge its rider, but to no avail. He could not be removed. Even jumping and spinning only seemed to make the rider more determined. He clearly enjoyed the challenge.

"I need this guy also," he noted in his electronic pad. *How could we ever fail with such fighters?* he thought as he raised his fist skyward.

He next went to the sleeping quarters to study the sleeping patterns of his best fighters. Most of the fighters were chatting as he entered. They all stood and saluted when they realized that he'd entered. He announced that they should get extra sleep, for they would be leaving in the morning for combat duty.

Some of them looked a little uneasy, which puzzled him, considering the rough looking bunch of fighters standing before him. "Is there anything wrong?' he asked with a look of concern on his brow.

Many of them looked at each other awkwardly but were very reluctant to show any weakness. From the middle of the group came a very rough voice. "Well—ah—ah, we were talking between ourselves, and—well, what happened at the mountain the last time we were there was unexplainable. Some of the guards who were stationed at the base camp say they saw a strange creature, unlike anything they'd ever seen before, and it scared some of them."

"What do you mean? I wasn't made aware of anything being seen, or of any other cause for the deaths except the avalanche. Speak of what you know!"

The guard looked around and began to sweat as he saw all his fighters watching him. "It is said that a blue streak of light came up behind the mountain and … well, this may sound weird, but they say a very large bird-like creature with two heads and many eyes blew a blast of wind at the mountain, causing the avalanche."

All went silent for a short while as they studied the general to see what he would say about this disturbing revelation. He watched them as he paced a little to allow some time to construct a good answer. "What shall I say? They're tough, no doubt, but they're concerned, and I don't want to weaken their resolve. We just can't fail this time, or Monton will have my head. How do I motivate them?" he whispered to himself.

He stood straight and looked directly at them and asked: "What if this was true, and you were the strongest and bravest fighters we have? How could we defeat such a creature?"

They all stood speechless, for they thought that he would have called the whole idea silly, an excuse to whimper out of having to go back to the mountain. Suddenly, a loud shout came from the back of the group. "We can defeat any foe! Let us go up against this creature and all of Sifrus's followers. We can destroy them all."

The whole group followed in chorus, shouting and banging their chests to the delight of the general. He allowed them to express their excitement for several minutes before he again gained their attention.

"That's more like the brave fighters I know you to be, and I have no doubt in your abilities, nor does your leader, Monton. I can work with this." He shouted his agreement with them. "Okay then, it's very late, and you'll need a good night's rest. Lights out!"

Morning came very quickly as the general shouted for them to wake up. "Get yourselves ready, for today we will begin our march to victory. We must destroy these followers of Sifrus—every last one!"

"Today, sir?" Some confused voices were heard throughout the group as they were getting out of their bunks. "We're not ready yet," one man whispered to himself.

"Yes, today. Now. Present time," the general shouted as he slammed his heavy boot on the floor, making a loud sound. "We couldn't release our plans to ensure secrecy for a surprise attack on the mountain."

"But we're not ready," a soldier in the back stuttered with fear in his voice.

The general marched straight to the soldier as all eyes from the group followed him. He stopped only a few inches from his face and looked straight in his eyes. The soldier trembled inside but tried not to show it. He hesitated for a few moments and then suddenly smiled. "You are correct. You are not ready!"

He walked back to the front of the group, leaving them totally confused as they looked at each other, trying to figure out what this meant.

"You are the best!" he shouted. "Those who feel they are not ready will not be needed. I have watched you all train for weeks now, and you are correct that some are not ready. There are, however, some of the toelions, grogs, and riders who are super ready. We do not need a large group this time, just the best.

"A large army trying to ascend the mountain passes would destroy any surprise we may have. A small, fast group this early in the spring would give us a huge element of surprise. All riders who feel they are ready and have no fear must proceed to the arena at sunrise. Have I made myself clear?"

He turned and exited the building as voices were heard mumbling "Yes, sir" in their confusion. He knew only the bravest would show up, which was exactly what he needed. As he looked toward the mountains in the far distance, they seemed to be ominously closer than they should be. He raised his fist skyward and shouted, "You will not defeat me this time."

"Let's get ready to ride!" General Zilti screamed as he returned to the training area.

The guard rang a large bell to get their attention as he hastened to get behind his protective cage. "They will assemble here as practised, sir, in a few moments. If you don't mind me saying, I believe they are the best trained and most vicious I have ever seen."

Within a few minutes, creatures with riders began to appear. Growls, snarls, roaring, and gnashing of sharp teeth were heard as they approached the assembled group. The riders had strapped their belts tight and struggled to keep the vicious animals under control, to the amazement of the group.

One very large, ugly toelion was snarling loudly and trying to dig a hole under the cage with its large claws. It suddenly snapped at the cage, breaking the bolt as it sank its curved beak into the guard's leg. Blood squirted everywhere as it tried to rip his leg off. The guard screamed with pain and horror as he tried to kick the beast with his other foot, but to no avail.

The rider of the toelion quickly drew his lightning stick and pushed it into the base of the brain, administering such a jolt of magolight that the beast went instantly to the ground, unconscious. The guard's leg was removed gently by the medics from the mouth of the toelion, as the guard by now had passed out from the ordeal. Moments later, he awakened and screamed as he saw the damage to his leg. "My leg! My leg! It's ripped to shreds. Why didn't you control him? I'll never be able to walk again."

The rider looked around indifferently at the guard and the others watching him. "You should have ensured those cages were strong enough to protect yourself and others from the strength and viciousness of these creatures." He paused and looked at Captain Zilti, not showing any emotion for his actions. Grabbing the toelion by the back legs, he hooked it up to a drag cart that had arrived to assist, and it pulled the creature back to the stables to recover.

Magnificent, thought Captain Zilti as he watched them both disappear behind the stable doors. *This is just the type of warrior I need to ensure success when we go up the mountain to pursue our enemies.* "Take care of this injured guard," he shouted to the medical team as they tried to get him on a stretcher. "He had his leg pulverized by a toelion and is very lucky it wasn't a grog, or he wouldn't be alive to get a second chance."

"Yes, sir! That would be true for sure if it had been the grog that attacked him. As it is, we may not be able to save his leg with so much muscle damage."

"Oh, what a mess!" cried one of the medics as he saw the patient come into the emergency room. "We'll need to work on this immediately if we have any hope of saving his leg." One of the staff members turned white and became sick as she saw the severe damage done by the toelion.

Captain Zilti was moving cautiously toward the grog portion of the arena, where two guards were watching the creature with their lightning sticks held close for immediate action if necessary. He had seen what the toelion could do with a little freedom, and he also knew how vicious and fast the grogs were said to be.

"Do you hear that awful screaming sound?" one of the guards asked the other.

"It sounds like some kind of animal is making that awful screaming sound coming from inside the arena." They looked at each other in bewilderment, trying to figure out the source of the sound.

Captain Zilti knocked on the secure, large steel door and ordered the keeper to open it as he displayed his clearance badge. As the door opened, the scream came again even louder than before, startling him. "What is that?" he shouted to the keeper as he looked in the direction of the sound.

The keeper excitedly explained that they had captured two of the rare mountain zells that may have assisted Sifrus's followers to escape on the mountain peaks. "We're using them to train the grogs to track and bring down these creatures as fast as possible. The screams are from the slash of the grogs' long claws as they cut into the legs of the zells. They're being trained to injure them, not kill them, in the hope that they may lead us to our enemies in the mountains."

"Excellent! Excellent!" Captain Zilti looked off to the mountains in the distance. *Not this time*, he silently murmured as he raised his fist to the sky. "Show me some of this training before I check out the other centres."

"Come this way." He pointed as he led him through several sets of locked steel doors that slammed behind them as they passed through, startling him.

"Don't be alarmed; this is necessary to ensure that the grogs don't escape into the barracks and kill some of our own soldiers."

"Are they really so vicious that all of the guards have to carry their lightning sticks?"

"Yes! They've been known to try to chew through steel rods. Luckily their teeth aren't quite as hard as steel, or we'd all be in big trouble."

When they entered the arena, they went into a caged viewing area far above the field. They could see a beautiful, white, furry creature standing in the middle of a field, feeding peacefully. "That's one of the mountain zells we captured. They're quite beautiful, as you can see," said the keeper.

"What will it do when it's attacked?" Captain Zilti asked as he intently watched the beautiful creature. He had a little sense of caring for its wellbeing pulling unexpectedly at his heart strings.

"We have duplicated its natural environment as much as possible by putting in some small hills with snow on top and vegetation at the base to provide hiding places for them. When they see danger approaching, they use their speed to get to the top of the hills and use their wide paws in the snow to their advantage to outrun their pursuer. Look at their large foot pads," said the keeper as he studied the captain's eyes to see his reaction.

"The grogs are the most vicious creatures we have at this training centre. Why do they only slash the zells' legs and not kill them outright?"

"Well, they will kill their prey when they're ready, but they like to play with their prey first, and the best way to prolong the excitement is to slow them down without causing critical injuries. They know that a slash across the legs will accomplish exactly what they need."

"That sounds extremely cruel and is just what we need for this assignment." Captain Zilti smiled at the trainer as he patted him on the back.

"We've trained them to outsmart the zells, which are faster than the grogs, by showing them shortcuts rather than depending on a pure chase, which they'll eventually lose. Just watch as the next session begins."

Suddenly, the grog with a rider came racing across the field from a hidden hummock. As the zell saw them, it sped away toward the snow-capped hill, with them in hot pursuit.

"Watch closely between the hills to see what the grog does at this stage of the chase."

"I can hardly see what's happening at such great speeds and with dust clouding my vision. Do you have any magnifying glasses?"

"Here, take these spotter glasses; they'll help you see better," said the trainer as he passed the captain the glasses.

The two guards on duty joined them to watch the action. "Wow," said one of the guards, "those zells are so fast!"

Several minutes passed as the zell continued to outrun the grog. The grog growled loudly, growing frustrated with the chase. Suddenly, the grog cut across the small pass between the two small hills, to the surprise of the zell, who instantly screamed as sharp claws cut through its tough leg skin, bringing it to a screeching halt as the grog pounced on it. The zell struggled to breathe with the weight of the grog and rider sitting on its hind quarter. The rider was holding his lightning stick in the stun mode setting to restrain the grog from hurting the zell any further.

"Excellent! Excellent! These are fabulous creatures. How many of these do we have trained and ready to ride?" Captain Zilti asked with great excitement.

"Let's see, there are thirteen riders who've been given positions because of their strength and ability to survive the tremendous pounding encountered while riding on these creatures. We lost three riders who were thrown and eaten by the grogs. That leaves us with ten riders and grogs that could be ready immediately. They could survive this dangerous trip provided that …" He hesitated to look toward the mountains. "… nothing strange happens up there again—I hope!"

He knew they were still struggling with the unknown situation that caused so many of their fellow soldiers to be killed by an avalanche that seemed to have come from nowhere. They were very tough and dedicated to their cause, but they were only as strong as circumstances permitted. If there really was some strange creature up there assisting Sifrus's followers that was capable of moving large quantities of snow with ease, then the fearless behaviour shown down below may quickly evaporate when confronted with this creature. A backup plan would definitely be needed. He sighed as though he was beginning to believe this crazy story.

"What will happen to the mountain zells you have in captivity?" he asked with a curious smile.

"They will be destroyed to ensure that they can't help our enemies anymore, I guess," said the trainer, looking at the arena as the mountain zells came back into view, limping and covered with blood on their back legs.

"Hmm," mused Captain Zilti, "maybe I have a better idea. What if we were to fix up their injuries and then release them at the base of the mountains' forested area? They're known to always seek their pack and previous owners with cunning and determination. We could follow them and hopefully be led straight to our enemies without having to expend too much time and energy searching for them in snowy passes and caves at the top."

The two guards looked at each other, pondering the idea. The trainer, who was listening to the conversation, nodded to the captain and said, "That's a brilliant idea."

They motioned the rider to come over to hear his feelings on the matter, as he knew the grogs and zells better than any of them.

"What do you think the zells would do if we released them near the mountain base?" they asked.

Without hesitation, the rider said, "They'll seek out their pack, if they have the strength to climb up the mountain. They're weak from training and the injuries they've sustained."

"We can bandage and medically treat their injuries," the captain offered, "and in a few days release them, if all are in favour." The captain could have made the decision himself but felt that keeping them all in the decision-making process would create harmony. "Okay then, let's get them healed and rested for our plan." He smiled as he again looked cautiously toward the high mountains in the distance.

The rider again spoke up. "We've trained the grogs to detect the scent specifically of the zells' blood at great distances, and I have no doubt they can follow them anywhere and in any conditions. We can extract extra blood samples from these two zells before we bring them to the release site, to ensure the grogs always have fresh scent to familiarize themselves with."

Captain Zilti raised his laser stick as he shouted a confident victory shout. "You will all be well rewarded for your dedication and hard work once we have these rebellious enemies in our hands. We will not fail this time!"

PEACE AT LAST—HEVERIS

SPECTRUM COULDN'T CONTAIN HIS EXCITEMENT ANY LONGER. HE FELL TO the ground on his knees and looked utterly amazed at the fascinating happenings all around him. He closed his eyes. "This must be a wonderful dream from which I will soon awaken," he whispered. "The beautiful singing and music from instruments—I've never heard anything like it on Rimshire. It vibrates and seems to fill one's whole body with intense emotions of love and peace."

He stayed on his knees, oblivious to anybody for a long time as he tried to absorb as much of this new feeling as he could. He wanted to stay in the moment for as long as he lived … or whatever his existence was now. For a moment he remembered the mountain zell, and the ledge he hit. "What am I now? I feel more alive than ever before—but I think I died! How can this be?"

A gentle hand touched him on the shoulder. He opened his eyes to see what looked like a man looking down at him with eyes that sparkled. "Spectrum," said the familiar voice. "It is me, my friend."

"I know that voice!" He thought for a moment. "No! It can't be. King Sifrus, is that really you?"

Sifrus smiled as he put his hand on Spectrum's face. "My dearest friend, Spectrum," he cried. He lifted him up and hugged him with such intensity, he thought he'd break a bone.

"How did you get here so quickly?" Spectrum looked deeply into his warm eyes full of love for him.

"It doesn't matter for now. I'll explain it all to you later after the great celebration for all newcomers. Come now, we must all get some rest and prepare for the greatest celebration you'll ever attend." Sifrus smiled and hugged him once more.

"For us? What have we done to deserve a great celebration?" Confusion swept over him as he looked around at all the activity and creatures going and coming in all directions.

Sifrus again smiled at him. "You have won the battle of life. Don't worry, this is a most beautiful and peaceful place. You will love it here. This is Heveris, my home where I lived before coming to Rimshire."

Starid came running over to Sifrus, with Tarus in quick pursuit. "Wait for me," a sweet little voice cried out.

Sifrus turned toward the voices just in time to see a shiny little creature come flying into his arms, while another wrapped his arms around his legs.

"Sifrus! Sifrus! You're really here!"

"Hi, you guys." Sifrus took them both in his arms and hugged them tenderly. "Gosh, I've missed you both so much." He glanced toward Spectrum. "I see you've brought back my very special friend from Rimshire."

Starid was so excited, he continued to hug Sifrus. "You know we always bring back your loyal followers—we never fail on our missions for you. We've also missed you so much since you went to Rimshire. But you're here now, and we'll celebrate with you. It will be the greatest celebration ever!"

"Come! Come now, we must get to the great hall. Look up there!" Sifrus pointed to the sky as it suddenly filled with a panorama of beautiful flying beings of all shapes and colours. They were bright and shiny and left streaks of all colours trailing behind them as they raced across the sky. Their audience below was delighted with the graceful display of shimmering pictorials created as they flew in various patterns to fill the sky with their beautiful designs of unimaginable beauty. The songs and music filled every corner of existence as their beauty left them spellbound with the intensity and message of love and peace.

"This is incredible!" Spectrum said as he glanced one more time upward at all the wondrous sights and sounds. "It must be a dream; no place can be this beautiful!"

"Come inside," Sifrus said as he waved his arm for them to follow. "I have some special Botkins who came back with me from Voart who I'd like you to meet."

As they entered the great hall, it seemed that again they had entered a fantasy land of immense beauty. They slowly walked through an archway made of all sorts of jewels and precious stones that shimmered and sparkled with streaks of bright light emanating in all directions. Spectrum reached out to touch some of them. "Are they real?" he turned and whispered to Tarus.

Tarus looked back at him, a little surprised. "After all you've come through with us thus far, do you still doubt your senses? You have seen only a small sampling of what Heveris has to offer. This place has endless wonders to enjoy, to grow, and love as you become a different kind of special person that you were meant to be."

They stepped onto a large platform that overlooked a huge assembly area that seemed to have no distinct end point. The open roof allowed a clear view of all the displays in the heavens above as they had seen them outside when they arrived.

"Isn't this place great?" Starid cried as he fluttered all about with great excitement. "I just love all of this!"

"What is this place?" Spectrum gasped, unable to speak another word as he stood in complete awe.

Sifrus looked directly at him as he spun around on his heels and pointed in all directions with his hands. "This is my home! My secret, blissful place of rest and pure delight, where all dreams come true for those who love."

"Hold tight!" Starid shouted. "We're taking newcomers to enjoy the ride of their lives."

Suddenly, the platform they were standing on began to move, gliding gently without any propulsion system toward the centre, where most of the residents were gathering. As they travelled, they passed over unbelievable scenes of streets covered with rainbow-coloured crystals.

Along the streets were many types of plants covered with beautiful fruit of all colours and shapes to delight their eyes. They were glowing as if covered with some type of sparkle dust.

"Hey, look!" Sifrus pointed at a platform coming straight toward them. "It's my friends that came back with me from Voart. Look how excited they are as they smile and wave at the masses with their hands in the air with great delight."

Within seconds, the sky above them filled with little flying creatures that came straight toward them. "Hey, duck!" Spectrum shouted as he dove down to the platform floor for safety. Time passed and all was quiet as he looked up to see Sifrus smiling down at him with many shining zeracks fluttering above him.

"Come up," he said as he stretched out his hand. "Don't worry, these are my friends. They've come to welcome and escort us into the reception arena. Get ready to meet our new friends from Voart. They are very nice Botkins and will love to share their stories with you."

"Hey, Sifrus, here we are, as you requested." Tarus smiled at Starid to acknowledge that they were always where they were needed. "We're so happy to see you again, Mr. Spectrum. Who are your new friends approaching your platform?"

"I see you all got your new robes for the great celebration! They look great on you." Sifrus waved his arms and smiled most pleasantly at them. "These are my new friends who travelled back with me from Voart." Sifrus pointed to his zeracks as he introduced them to his new friends. "This is Tarus and Starid, my very special rescuers, who just returned from Rimshire with one of my best friends on that planet, Spectrum."

Tarus smiled at Starid as he spoke. "We are very pleased to meet you all. Any friend of Sifrus is a friend of ours."

Deltric pointed to his group and replied that they were all indebted to Sifrus, because he had rescued them all from Voart before it was destroyed. "This is my wife, Creathe, and our children, Fatemee and Fris. Next to them is my cousin, Jarock, his wife, Seili, and their children, Phatima and Selda."

"Congratulations!" Sifrus clapped his hands and smiled at each of them individually. "You have all been chosen and have succeeded in your mission, and now you will receive your just reward."

"Chosen for what mission?" Jarock glanced around at his friends and then back at Sifrus with a look of confusion.

"You have all tried your best to always follow the teachings of *Love* and put others before yourselves. Besides trying to share with others this most powerful and essential teaching, you never doubted your teachers who came before you. In essence, you have always believed in a higher power where *Love* comes from and is now at the centre of *Love* itself. You will understand all of this very soon as you become more enlightened here on Heveris." Sifrus raised his hands above his head. "Thank you, Father," he said quietly.

"Now that we're all together, we can proceed to the presentation of your gifts, and you can be declared with great honour as citizens of Heveris. I am very proud of you, as are my father and all the inhabitants of Heveris. Many would love to be in your place, but regrettably, few will make it here."

"Gifts!" Deltric looked at Sifrus. "Why do we get gifts?" He still seemed very confused by all that was going on. "We were rescued by you, Sifrus, and the zeracks. Shouldn't you be the ones getting the gifts and recognition?"

Sifrus waved his hand and smiled. "Look around you at all this beauty. We already have all the gifts one could ever dream of, but you had to struggle for a very long time under difficult and evil opposition to keep and spread the teachings of *Love*. These teachings came from the King of Heveris, and all who hold to them deserve gifts from him."

The platform began to move toward a beautiful, radiant light in the centre of the great hall. Thousands of zeracks began to flutter their wings as they sang a victory song of such beauty, it filled the whole place and resonated in their hearts for what they'd finally accomplished.

"Who is the large, glowing figure standing on the jewel-covered stand?" Spectrum whispered to Sifrus with a great sense of awe in his voice.

"Here, put some of this cream on your eyes to protect them until they adjust to the bright light, or you may become blind. The beautiful, large figure you see is the King of Heveris—my father."

"Your father!" he gasped. He went completely silent, not sure what to say next. Spectrum's mouth hung open in astonishment.

"Your father is king of all of this?" stammered Jarock, looking as if he would faint.

As they neared the king, they saw streaks of rainbow colours flashing in all directions. The singing intensified to a pitch that was so beautiful and intoxicating, it seemed to totally captivate every creature in the whole place.

The group suddenly began to realize whose presence they were in, and they became very anxious. Fear showed in their eyes as they were faced with their insignificance compared to the powers all around them.

Sifrus sensed their anxiety and moved quickly to calm them. "Do not be afraid, my friends. My father loves you, and I do too, beyond description. All you see around you is now yours to enjoy, and every being will love you as their very own family. They will teach you all the loving ways of this place. Relax now and learn to enjoy everything your heart desires, for you deserve this and more."

"What shall we do to show our gratitude for all of this?" Spectrum leaned in and gently touched Sifrus's shoulder as he pleaded with his eyes.

"Just be you," Starid shouted as he excitedly fluttered his wings. All will be fine, and you'll get your special honour, as all who live here did when they were made citizens."

The platform again moved, and this time no more discussion was necessary, as glorious praise for their king was coming from everywhere. Suddenly, all went completely silent as the king raised his hand to indicate he was about to speak.

Sifrus quietly sensed a calling from Rimshire for help. "Kristella? Kristella, where are you? Please give us a signal that you're okay? "Wait … is Assednic calling out to Kristella?" He thought about what he was sensing for a moment.

He glanced off into space for a few seconds then quickly glanced at Spectrum. "How much trouble are they in?"

Spectrum looked a little confused. "Who?" he quietly asked.

"Our friends on Rimshire! I feel they are in trouble. How much trouble are they in?"

"Very bad trouble, I fear. They have defied Monton Repa and are on the run from his followers, who want to kill them. I fought with them against our enemies until I fell over a ledge and … well, came to be here with you."

"Okay, my dear friend, try to relax and enjoy the celebration. I will return to help rescue our friends on Rimshire as soon as I am able."

"Citizens of Heveris!" sounded the very clear and powerful voice of the king. "We have come together once again to celebrate the return of my son, Sifrus, from the small planet of Voart. He has rescued some very special Botkins who have proven themselves worthy for honour and to become citizens of Heveris. While on their home planet, they worked tirelessly to maintain and spread the teachings of *Love* passed on to them by their loyal teachers and predecessors.

"We also welcome back our rescue team of Starid and Tarus along with their great perad, who went to Rimshire to help our dear friend, Spectrum. He also is worthy of honour and citizenship because of his loyalty to the teachings of *Love* given to him by our own special teacher, Sifrus."

Applause went up in a thunderous triumph as horns began to sound.

Following several minutes of applause, the king again raised his hand to signal for silence as he again began to speak. "My friends, come forward into my presence."

They looked at each other apprehensively and then looked at Sifrus for affirmation. He nodded and waved his hand toward his father to signal that they were coming.

As they slowly moved forward, they could feel small specks of what looked like silver dust falling and sticking to their already-radiant robes. The ever-brightening glow of the king seemed even more dominating and beautiful than they could have imagined in their wildest dreams. Standing in his presence, they could only bow their heads in humble respect for such an awesome king. The fear and apprehension they'd felt only moments ago was quickly evaporating and being replaced with a deep feeling of love filling every fibre of their being to overflowing.

The voice now seemed quite gentle as he looked into each of their faces as they raised their heads. Spectrum looked up, and the instant their eyes met, he knew he was changed forever. The feeling of love for all creation was beyond description. His whole body glowed with the essence of love and understanding for his fellow beings. The king's eyes glowed so intensely and brightly, he couldn't even describe with his great intelligence what they were like.

"You are all very special!" The king spoke directly to them so they would know it was real. "You have proven yourselves worthy to live here on

Heveris." He glanced around and waved his hand in all directions to show the expanse of Heveris and its endless borders. He gave them a vision of endless beauty as they looked and followed the direction of his hands.

"Love and delight in this place permeates every aspect of life. We protect our home from any evil-doers who would destroy our peaceful and loving way of life. Your tremendous effort to retain and live in a loving manner under hostile and difficult conditions on your home planet is very honourable. You suffered under the threat of torture and possible death without giving in to their evil ways. He smiled as he placed his hand on his chest.

"You are all therefore declared worthy to receive these citizenship badges to place over your hearts to forever protect you from any evil influence that may come against you, wherever you may be in this universe now and in the future."

As the king placed the badges on them, they instantly began to glow. They bowed before him in respect for his authority and power. The whole place again erupted into the most beautiful singing of praise to their king and acceptance of the new members of Heveris.

"Thank you, Father," Sifrus said as he placed his hand gently on each of his friends' shoulders to reassure them. He then told them to rise and wave to their excited audience.

"You have done well, my son. Go now with your new friends and enjoy the celebration feast set before you, and we will talk together a little later."

"Come, my friends. Look, the feast has begun, with you as our honoured guests for all to meet. Your special seats are placed just above the crowd, so all can see and acknowledge your new position among us."

Rows of all sorts of strange but delicious foods were presented to them, floating on trays for them to try as they desired. At first, they didn't know what to try, because it looked very strange to them. As they began to eat, though, the most beautiful flavours exploded in their mouths, beyond anything they had ever tasted before in their whole lives.

"Yum ... yum ... yum," Spectrum tried to speak with his mouth half full. "What are these most wonderful foods?" All of his friends were doing the same as they tried as many types as possible without looking greedy.

Jarock looked over at Spectrum and tried to speak with his mouth also full. "I don't know what these are, but they are by far the most delicious foods I've ever tasted. I think this will be the most desirable place for us to live."

They were all laughing after shaking off some of their fear. "I think you're right," Spectrum said as he glanced at all the food and then at Sifrus, who had moved toward a secluded corner and seemed to be speaking to someone he couldn't see. *That's strange*, he thought.

He noticed that the king had also disappeared, even though the celebration had only just begun. "I'm sure there must be a good reason, especially considering that he seems to have Heveris and the entire universe to care for," he whispered to himself. "Hey, Jarock," he said, "do you think we'll ever want to go to any other place after being here for a while?" He laughed and pointed to the sky, where several explosions of star dust shimmered with many colours as it floated and spread in all directions.

Jarock looked away into the sky and remained silent for a long while.

"Are you okay, my friend?"

Jarock looked back at Spectrum and seemed confused. "I'm sorry, but I just remembered that we don't have a home to go back to. It was destroyed right before our eyes as we were leaving."

Spectrum stopped eating. "Oh man—I'm really sorry for you guys. I didn't know!"

They continued with their feast for many hours, enjoying the company of their new friends. Spectrum could see that although Sifrus was very happy to be back with his family and friends, his mind was elsewhere.

Sifrus arose and explained that he must leave and go meet his father at the Celestial Planning Centre, and that they should retire and get some rest. "You, my friends, have done very well to adjust to all that is happening to you. You must be very tired, and I'm sure you'll need some time alone to reflect on all these events. I have summoned our greeters to come and bring you to your new homes. I will come and see you in a few days, after I've finished my business at the planning centre. Go now, rest well, and enjoy your new homes."

"We get new homes!" Seili screamed as she smiled at Jarock.

Within seconds, the greeters were standing in front of them with a device for selecting a home that was most suited to each family or individual. It could read their desires and particular needs for their lifestyle, work, leisure, and even fantasies.

"We're here to show you to your new homes," one of them, named Farlong, said. "We'll only need to do this the first time, as soon you'll learn the secrets of instant passport through mind control. First, we need to get your personal preferences into our destination device for generation of you perfect choice. Come, place your hands on this device and let's see what wonderful things happen."

"Spectrum, you have selected a beautiful farm-type home with sufficient space to grow things and enjoy nature full of plants and animal-like creatures. I guess on Rimshire you were probably an outdoorsman and didn't enjoy crowded spaces or too much technology interfering with your peaceful and quiet lifestyle. Here's a mind picture of your home."

Spectrum smiled from ear to ear. "That's exactly what I've always dreamed of but could never afford to build on Rimshire. It's like you took the image straight from my mind. Thank you so much."

Farlong laughed. "Well, actually you did, as you focused on your greatest desires. A mental picture was transferred to the destination machine for verification."

"That's great!" Spectrum cried. "We always get exactly what we desire if our heart is pure."

"Not quite!" Crylit looked a little worried as he spoke. "I spoke with Deltric and explained to him that the machine also detects memories of past experiences that could negatively impact your best situation. It instantly plays through many models to get the best possible situation, considering all the aspects of the inputs generated. It may not always match what you wish for, but it will always be the best for you."

"So it picks through my brain to generate all negative and positive experiences to get the best model for my future. That's pretty cool!" Spectrum shook his head. "Great job! I love the picture I see of my new home."

"Deltric and family, your information is combined to generate a best-case scenario for all of you. Okay, let's see what comes out of all this data."

Farlong could see the excitement building in Creathe's eyes. Within seconds, the machine produced a mind picture with detailed information of their new home.

"This is very interesting!" Farlong said as he sent Deltric the mind picture while Creathe and the girls gathered around him. "Oh my," gasped Creathe, "we don't deserve this." The girls started dancing around with glee because of the beautiful playground that was shown in their minds. Deltric was breathless as he hugged Creathe. "It's exactly what we always dreamed of, and even more spectacular."

"So your desires are much different than Spectrum's, for you chose a location near other families with many children around. This will allow for many friendships to develop and activities for you all to be involved in with your many friends to come. That's just wonderful," Farlong said with a big smile.

"Sparkling jewels surround our new home, and the trail seems like gold. How can we deserve all of this?" Creathe shook her head, trying hard to believe that the picture of their new home was real.

"Well," Farlong smiled as he tried to explain, "to you, all of this seems impossible and very expensive to create, but here on Heveris, we all have the wishes of our hearts fulfilled—not because we deserve it, but as a reward for the faithfulness shown and the sufferings endured for the sake of *Love* at all costs. Our king delights in rewards beyond our comprehension, and he doesn't consider it much at all by his standards. Just try to believe in this place, and the joys will flood your mind forever.

"Okay, only one more family to sort out. Come, Jarock, let's see what your deepest desires will give us for your new home."

Jarock looked at Seili, who was holding tightly to Phatima's and Selda's tiny hands. He seemed to be waiting for confirmation from them before they could continue. Seili was whispering something to the children and then looked back to Jarock and nodded her approval.

"Sorry for the delay," he said cautiously, "but we were hoping to live close to cousin Deltric and his family, if that's possible." He bowed his head and continued. "We mean no disrespect, and know that you have to do your job and must accept whatever choice the destination device picks, but we would really appreciate any consideration you could give."

Farlong waved to Crylit to come and join him. "Please give us a few moments to discuss you request, Mr. Jarock. We both know that the prime objective of the destination device is based on happiness," said Farlong as he glanced back to see both families cuddled together and talking and laughing.

Crylit also looked and could see the closeness of these two families who had been through so much distress. "Well, if this request is what makes them all most happy, then we've met the prime objective. The program in the destination device does allow for a bypass code in special circumstances like this situation. Input the same data from Deltric's sensors and select the nearest home available, and we should get the best possible match."

They both walked back to the anxious families awaiting their decision. Farlong produced a picture taken from the device and sent it to their minds with a great smile.

"Oh my," Seili screamed. "This is like a dream home! It's so beautiful, but ..." She hesitated. "Is it near our friends?"

"Yes," Crylit grinned as he glanced at Farlong. "Because of your love for each other, we were permitted to input a bypass code and got you the nearest home, only a few minutes apart. But always remember that all residents of Heveris are friends and family here. When you are trained, you will be able to travel instantly anywhere you wish to meet anyone you want within seconds."

"Are you all ready to go to your new homes?" Farlong asked as he pointed to a moving trail made of a shiny, golden substance. "These trails you see moving very quickly are used to transport residents to any destination they desire by just concentrating on where they need to go. They're usually used for short travels or for those who are having trouble with the more advanced mind control techniques required for long distance travel."

"Yes, please ... please." Creathe cried as she grabbed the little hands of Fateme and Fris and began to walk toward the trail.

"Okay, okay," Crylit gasped with excitement. "You're going to so love this ride. Now when we stand on the trail side rail, you just say "home." The home sorter device has previously provided your personal information to the travel system of Heveris and will instantly recognize your voice and locate your home destination. I'll go with Deltric's and Jarock's families, while Farlong will accompany Spectrum to ensure you all get settled into your beautiful new homes properly." Crylit just couldn't contain his excitement.

Creathe squeezed her arm to ensure everything was real. She looked across at each member of their group and felt a little concerned about getting separated along the way. "How will we communicate when we're separated?"

"Oh don't worry, you'll all have the ability to talk privately in your minds by just focusing on the person's image and calling their name. A mind link is made directly to the person you wish to speak with without any worry of interference from any other contact. It will take a little getting used to, but like everything new to you in this place, it's wonderful. Once you get good at communicating, you'll be able to speak with more than one individual at the same time." Crylit smiled at them all. "Don't worry, this is the most beautiful, loving, and special place ever, with endless possibilities for those who want to try anything they may have dreamed of."

Sifrus's father had asked him to come to the Celestial Planning Centre as soon as he could free himself from the wonderful celebration. As he entered the large room, he saw display screens showing environmental activities on each inhabited planet. His father met him and placed his hand on his shoulder.

"I'm glad you could come so quickly. I wouldn't have called you until after the celebration, but we seem to have an emergency developing on Rimshire." He sighed as he pointed toward the screens. "Have a look and let me know what you see."

Sifrus studied the many screens that were constantly changing as operators zoomed in and out, analyzing every activity. He was somewhat bewildered by the many situations playing out before his eyes. Some planets showed many dark areas and storms, while others were pristine and clean. One small planet seemed to be spinning out of control and was moving dangerously toward its sun. "Which planet is that one?" He pointed toward the screen where he knew it would soon show a planet burn up.

His father closed his eyes for a moment. "I am very sorry, son, but that is Voart from which you just returned with your new friends. It was damaged too much by that super laser blast and extreme gas explosion for us to correct its natural orbit.

Sifrus wiped a tear from his eyes. "That's just so sad to look at." He scanned the others to get his mind of Voart. "That clean, pristine one," he pointed to the screen. "Is that one Rimshire?"

His father smiled. "Yes, it is, son. You did a very good job as King of Rimshire and have kept the environment clean through your good policies and practices."

"Then there's no emergency there at this time, is there?" He looked at his father with great delight.

"Well, the environment is okay for now, but we've been informed of a major problem developing with the residents. You see, there's an ambitious and evil resident named Monton Repa who, in your absence, has declared himself as leader and now king." He cringed and sat down as he continued to study the screens.

Sifrus was stunned—not that it had happened, but that it had evolved so soon. "Father, we can't let this happen. My friends and followers won't accept this and will be in real danger. Spectrum is here with us as a testimony to what will happen to them if they defy him. I must return to help them." He was shaking and his voice had risen, attracting the looks of many of the operators.

His father remained silent for a few moments, still studying the screens. "I understand how you feel, and I agree that we can't have an evil, illegitimate leader destroy our beautiful Rimshire. But before you return, you will require some additional training and must study the dangers of dealing with evil adversaries." He stood and looked directly into his eyes. "We have a dangerous situation here."

Sifrus looked a little confused. "But I thought I was trained to handle all situations as they arose."

"Yes, you can in most situations on well-managed planets. This is not a usual situation. This guy is a ruthless dictator who won't tolerate any opposition to his rule. We will need to train you on how to deal with unthinkable things, like warfare, torture, murder, and other horrors. I have tried to protect you from these types of evil as much as possible, but it seems that its influences on many of our inhabited worlds is growing." He pointed again to the screens. "I will do everything in my power to stop this evil."

Sifrus hung his head as he whispered. "Hang on, my friends. 'till I come."

DON'T MISS
RETURN TO RIMSHIRE,
COMING IN SPRING 2021!

BOOK

RETURN TO RIMSHIRE

DEMAN WALKED SLOWLY UP TO HIS MULTI-VIEWER SCREENS, ONLY TO SEE that the dust storms were now impacting every district. He slammed his fist on the desk, sending broken pieces of wood in all directions. "What am I going to do? What can we all do?" He shouted angrily at the workers who were surrounding him.

"Sir! Sir!" A low female voice came from behind him. "What do you mean?"

He glanced toward the voice and saw a young woman whom he did not recognize. She was rather pretty, with blonde hair, a medium build, and beautiful blue eyes. There was something uniquely different about her countenance—a peace seemed to emit from her, making her even more attractive than she already was. Struggling with his words, which was very unusual for him, he finally cleared his throat and asked, "Who are you? I haven't seen you here before. You need special security clearance to be in this room."

She shyly opened her mouth to speak, but before she could, Rickter cut in with an explanation for her. "This is Crystal, our new long-range communications specialist sent up from our high security communication centre, Safe COM.3. She has Level 10, maximum security clearance, as per our management code for this location."

"That is very impressive indeed!" Deman announced as he continued to study Crystal, rather intrigued by her. "And you, Miss Crystal, what is your objective here at our State Centre?"

She hesitated for a moment and tried to gather her thoughts. She glanced at Rickter, who nodded to reassure her that it was okay to present herself. Looking back toward Deman, she quietly spoke directly to the situation. "We have a situation that requires some special tracking technology, which I have been specially trained for. Your space chaser has gone beyond any distance that our present technology and our mapped systems allow us to track."

"Wait!" Deman spoke with impatience as he looked toward Rickter then back at Crystal and scratched his head. "You're here to explain that we don't have the technology for this project, but you can fix this situation for us, even though we've gone beyond our limits. Is that correct?"

She looked down for a moment to hide her fear and then pointed toward the galaxy screen as she began to move toward it. "May I?" She looked directly at Deman with all of the confidence she could muster.

He nodded his approval.

"We are here." She pointed at the screen. The last weak signal we received from our space chaser tracking device came onto our screen at the edge of the known galaxy. With our existing technology, we can't send or receive signals beyond this location."

"Okay, okay." Deman sounded a little annoyed. "We know this; please get to the point."

"Well, Sir, there's a possibility that with a new technology I have recently developed, we may be able to extend our range and make contact with other communication devices beyond our known worlds. The new equipment has the capacity to increase our output four times greater than at present, and who knows who could intercept our signal? Even if we can't receive regular signals for normal communication, we may be able to pinpoint where it's located and where we could find Sifrus."

Deman glanced toward the galaxy screen without saying a word. Everybody was watching him to see what he would say next. Suddenly he shouted: "Where are you? What is out there?"

Crystal jumped a little and looked toward Rickter, who just smiled back at her as if to say, "All is okay."

A short time passed as he continued to study the screen. "Crystal, you must try to make this work, for our future survival may depend on you making contact with Sifrus, wherever he is. I fully believe that this man Sifrus has answers for our problems. We must contact him, or we may not survive."

All of Deman's staff that were in his State Centre were in shock as they looked back and forth at each other in disbelief.

"Not survive! Aren't you taking this situation a little bit too seriously?" Rickter said with much fear in his shaky voice.

Crystal was now studying Rickter's face as he began to sweat heavily and turn red. "Are you guys serious?" she asked, turning again to study the galaxy screen, which had been refocused on the area from where the tracker signal had come.

Deman's voice was loud and serious and carried a sense of urgency in it as he spun around and looked directly at her. "Look at the pictures from our outside cameras in the various mining areas. Those toxic dust storms you see are bringing our whole planet to a standstill. Do you all know what that means?" He looked quietly at each one of them, studying their reaction to see how much fear they would exhibit.

"We can't function normally anymore, so we can't produce food for our population. Water supplies are contaminated. Our air is becoming toxic at an alarming rate, and people can't go outside without a breathing mask. People are dying, and many will blame us for not controlling this problem. How much longer do you think we can go on like this?" He looked across the group at their shocked eyes, seeking an answer from somebody—but none came.

"Shoot!" Crystal shouted as her eyes met Deman's. "You are serious, aren't you? I think we better get to work immediately and use all of our resources to find this Sifrus, King of Rimshire, before it's too late."